SHROUDED HEARTS

AN UNEXPECTED ROMANCE - BOOK TWO

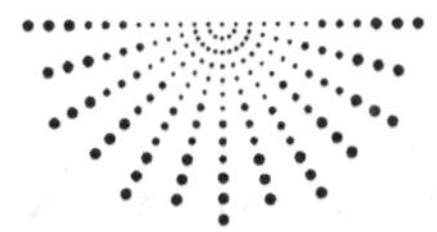

ROSIE CHAPEL

ULFIRE PTY. LTD.

First printing: 2024
ISBN: 978-1-7635407-3-6 (eBook)
ISBN: 978-1-7635407-4-3 (Paperback)

Ulfire Pty. Ltd.
P.O. Box 1481
South Perth
WA 6951
Australia

www.rosiechapel.com

Cover: Erin Dameron-Hill of EDH Graphics

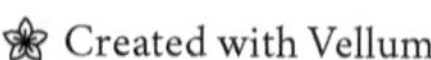 Created with Vellum

ACKNOWLEDGMENTS

Thank you, from the bottom of my heart to…

My husband… for everything.

Mum, Melanie, Paola, Brian, and Jackie for their amazing support.

Graham from Fading Street Publishing Services for his awesome editing.

Erin Dameron-Hill for this gorgeous cover.

My wonderful readers for your loyalty.

Trust your heart

Shrouded HEARTS

An Unexpected Romance - Book Two

ROSIE CHAPEL

PROLOGUE

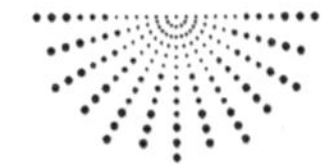

The Lodge, London
August 1817

Madeline Galleron was dreaming. It was a wonderful fantasy featuring a noble knight who was coming to the rescue of a dark-haired damsel, locked in a tall tower.

There was every chance her dream was a combination of her favourite _contes de fées_, not to mention Greek legends and medieval folk tales, but that made it all the more captivating.

It was the same every night. The minute slumber took her, Madeline entered an imaginary world where handsome heroes battled sorcerers, or mythical creatures, or pirates, to claim her hand before the clock struck midnight, or the sun rose, or the moon waned.

Madeline's dreams were an escape. A place where illusion eclipsed reality, a place of romance and happily every afters, and a place where she became the focus of attention... however fleetingly.

The antithesis of her life, in fact.

. . .

At nineteen, Madeline — an honest young lady — could not say she was miserable, *per se*. Neither could she say she was content; her mood hovered somewhere in between.

Her marriage to an earl, sixth months previously, might sound auspicious to the disinterested observer, but the nuptials were arranged in order that her widowed suitor might begat an heir. Raymond Galleron, 8th Earl of Parham and twenty-five years her senior, bore little resemblance to Madeline's idea of an adoring husband.

Raymond, a friend of her father's, had no interest in Madeline as a person, nor did he care how adversely she was affected by this union. Her dowry was the attraction, as it was substantial and had settled his gambling debts with coin to spare. The agreement was drawn up with blank indifference to Madeline's feelings, and she was informed of her obligations a week before the ceremony.

Madeline did not argue with her parents. It would have been a waste of breath. She had long known her only value to them was as a means to increase their status. She settled into The Lodge, a spacious residence just off Grosvenor Square, and assumed the role of countess and wife with well-schooled proficiency.

Her husband summoned Madeline to his chamber when he saw fit to bed her, but not once did he set foot in her private abode, for which she was grateful. While his ministrations were... to his wife's innocent mind... considerate, there was no shared passion, or any sense they were connecting emotionally.

It was nothing more than a business deal.

She had merely exchanged one gilded cage for another.

Madeline's sadness that she would never experience true love was mitigated only in her dreams.

.   .   .

Her noble knight took her hand and led her to the sun-drenched glade. Slowly, he peeled off her clothes, scattering kisses across her skin, as his fingers wove their magic.

He lowered her gently onto a bed of flowers, then removed his armour, and lay alongside her.

Balanced on one elbow, he traced her shape from the curve of her thigh, over her hip to the dip of her waist and upwards to cup her breast.

She heard herself whimper, arching into him, desperate for him to slake her hunger.

A voice interrupted, but her hero's lips were on her neck.

It was not he who spoke.

Confused, she frowned and glanced around in search of the interloper who dared intrude.

The scene fractured; the dream faded, her romantic interlude morphing into the grim decor of the master bedchamber in the Parhams' city residence.

She blinked, her eyes adjusting to the gloom. She did not recall being summoned. To her right, a single candelabra flickered. To her left, her husband, sitting in a chair watching her, an odd expression on his face.

She tried to turn, but found, she could not.

Her arms were stretched above her head, and something bound her wrists, something silky. She gave a tug, to discover she was tied fast. Panic prickled when she realised her ankles were secured in a similar fashion.

Worse… she was completely naked.

The languor of sleep fled.

.   .   .

"Husband, what is the meaning of this? A new game perhaps?" She peered at him, trying to gauge his temper. His eyes glittered. *Was he drunk?*

Raymond Galleron's penchant for less traditional methods of coupling was nothing new to Madeline, although the bindings were unexpected. Seemingly, the nubile body of his bride was not enough to arouse his ardour, he required… accessories.

Madeline tugged again, then smothered a shriek when a shadowed face loomed over her.

A finger was pressed against her lips.

"Hush, my pretty, let me test the goods."

It was the voice from her dream.

"Test the goods? Unhand me, you brute." The words were out before she could curb her tongue.

Cruel fingers gripped her cheeks, and the face came so close there was scarcely an eyelash between them.

"I said, hush," he snarled, then canted his head away from her. "I thought you said she was biddable."

"She is usually meek as a church mouse." Madeline heard her husband reply.

Her thoughts churned. *What the dickens is going on? What are they talking about. Never mind that, who **is** he? Why is he touching me? Since when have I ever been meek?* She might comport herself as the wife of an earl ought, but meek? Hardly.

An intelligent woman, Madeline's heart urged her to fight, to tear off the restraints and run, as fast and as far as she could, quashed when her inner-self reminded, *you have nowhere to go.* Another scream bubbled up.

"Galleron. Raymond," she appealed. "What are you doing, why?"

There was a lengthy silence.

Even as her brain registered what was in store, Madeline

felt a wild giggle clamouring for release; her mind conjuring up a picture of this bizarre tableau from above. She, naked and spread-eagled on the bed, displaying her… assets… to the voracious gaze of a stranger, while her husband observed proceedings from the sidelines, as though this was perfectly normal.

The gravelly voiced man cleared his throat, to be interrupted by Raymond.

"I have debts."

"I thought you had paid them off with my dowry."

If Raymond was surprised his wife knew of this, he hid it well. "It is gone."

"What of the silver, or the paintings? Sell something," Madeline could not help the thread of fear lacing her question. The reality of her situation sinking in.

The face reappeared, the quirk of the thin lips was nothing short of triumphant.

"He already has."

Before it flew over her lips, her scream was stopped by the same hand that had gripped her face.

And so, it began.

CHAPTER ONE

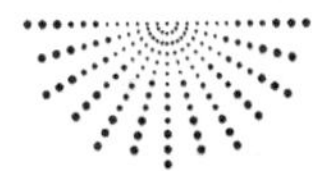

The next two years were a nightmare.

Madeline was traded like a commodity among those of her husband's friends to whom, he explained, he owed money.

She had no recourse — she was as much a possession as the silver she had begged him to sell — and who would believe her anyway? Her husband was well-respected, sat on important parliamentary committees, and did good deeds. They would laugh in her face.

One, a rather shy viscount, wanted nothing more insidious than a conversation. His hesitant questions focussed on how to please a woman, which — under any other circumstance — Madeline would have found amusing.

That was the only time he visited.

Sardonically, Madeline presumed her answers had assisted his endeavours.

. . .

Another *slaked his thirst* once, and never returned... to her relief.

Three developed a habit of calling at The Lodge without warning, expecting her to attend to their needs, immediately, whether or not Raymond was at home. This was a line, Madeline determined none would cross and, refusing to be cowed by her husband's ire, denied them entry. It was a small victory, but a victory, nonetheless.

Of the three, one was kind, which perplexed her. One was always in a rush — likely embarrassed by his behaviour but unwilling to curtail it — and each treated her like their pet whore.

All, save the sheepish nobleman, were married. This betrayal of their wives was almost as abhorrent to Madeline as the deed itself. She had demanded of one man, why her? Why not take a mistress or visit a brothel?

"This is easier." Was his wholly inadequate response.

"*Easier?* Oh, do please elaborate," she had scoffed.

"No one questions my presence here, especially as Parham and I are on several committees together. To use a brothel leaves one open to blackmail, and taking a mistress is a shocking expense. One my wife would not countenance."

"Do you love your wife?" Madeline had asked curiously.

"With all my heart."

Expecting him to say his marriage was unhappy, his avowal floored Madeline.

"How can you claim to love her yet use me this way?" she had pressed, stunned.

"My wife finds this," he waved his hand between them, "distasteful. She has given me two sons and deems the... act, unnecessary. I have needs like any other man, but do not wish my beloved to bear the brunt of malicious gossips, should a dalliance be exposed. Parham's arrangement offers the perfect solution."

That Lord Peter Masham, Earl of Swinbourne did not see the irony of his remarks, left Madeline speechless, but discovered it was a sentiment echoed, to a greater or less extent, by his fellow *callers*.

To her utter mortification — exacerbated, if that was remotely possible, because her husband liked to watch — two of the men, she was expected to accommodate, could, despite her resolve to remain unmoved, induce heady surges of pleasure, make her cry out, bring her to the peak with galling frequency.

The only one to use restraints was he who had sparked this degrading sequence... the Duke of Alberforce. In her head, Madeline had dubbed him the Odious Knave.

The passion she once dreamt about, had become a twisted reality.

As the months ticked by, Madeline gained a morsel of satisfaction by committing salient details about each man to memory. Such information might prove valuable one day.

Her humiliation was concealed behind a veneer of cordiality and, to an outsider, the newly wed Countess of Parham appeared to be the epitome of contentment.

As expected of a lady in her position, Madeline threw dinner parties, held musical evenings, and hosted picnics.

Everyone who was anyone prayed for an invite. Had the guests cared to look more closely, they might have noticed the young countess never addressed her husband directly, neither did she make eye contact with him or, indeed, made any effort to be at his side.

· · ·

She considered running away. Once, she even packed her valise, but where could she go? Her family would send her back with dispatch. Her friends, such as they were, would never believe her claim, nor would they wish to be associated with the ensuing scandal. Neither could she survive on her own — she had no idea how.

This did not prevent her threatening her husband, whose response was dismissive, "As you like, my dear, but remember whose coin keeps you alive and well-clothed. You would not last five minutes on the streets."

That he was correct drew an exasperated growl from his wife who stamped her foot, impotently, and marched out of his study, his contemptuous laughter following her.

Accepting she was basically Galleron's slave, did not stop Madeline from asserting herself when the occasion necessitated.

Aside from the risk of contracting some unmentionable affliction... a fear not unwarranted... Madeline's greatest dread was falling pregnant. To this end, she had seized the bull by the horns, so to speak, and negotiated a deal with her husband. She would submit to the iniquity of these *visits* without complaint, on the condition the *visitors* used a barrier device.

"To be sold off like a brood mare is reprehensible, and you ought to be ashamed of yourself. You have robbed me of my innocence, my self-esteem, and my reputation. I hope your first wife is turning in her grave." Madeline had taken her husband to task one evening, shortly after that first night.

"However unpalatable the situation, I concede you have the right to do with me as you please but, mark my words, if you do not consent to my request, I will make your life more of a living hell than you have made mine."

To her surprise, Raymond had agreed, and Madeline kept her part of the bargain.

A silence that lasted two long years.

November 1819 - The Lodge

The Odious Knave gratified himself, once, twice, three times. Madeline, bound and passive, closed her mind to his exertions, her ears to his grunts, and tried to distract herself by compiling a mental list of medieval torture devices and in which order she would use them.

Ensconced in his favourite chair, his tongue running over his lips, Raymond played spectator to his wife servicing his friend.

Madeline was past caring; he might as well invite the whole of the bloody *ton* to witness her ignominy.

To save her sanity, she had withdrawn into herself, becoming reserved and solitary, her innate vivacity, buried, her heart shrouded.

Once the gossip surrounding her marriage to the Earl of Parham began to dwindle, Madeline sought to reduce the number of gatherings so adroitly, her husband — preoccupied by horse racing and the tables — did not notice.

She seldom attended balls or soirees; it was too difficult maintaining the illusion that naught was amiss, especially given the inevitability of coming face to face with her callers... *and* their wives.

. . .

An odd sound caught her attention. She angled her head to look at her husband. His colour seemed peculiar and his breathing, hoarse. He was clawing at his cravat as though it was too tight.

"Alberforce," she hissed at the man balanced above her. Either he did not hear or chose to ignore her. She never spoke to him during their sessions.

"Alberforce," she repeated more loudly.

"What?" He glanced down at her, his countenance hostile in the weak light thrown by the candles.

"Galleron. He is ill. Ring for Blake."

"You are addled, woman, I am not summoning the damn butler for a touch of indigestion. Parham will be fine."

Madeline bucked her hips, dislodging the duke, who retaliated with a slap to her jaw.

"Get off me, you slimy oaf," she snarled, jerking her limbs in an effort to loosen the bonds, a flash of her old spirit rekindling. "Untie me."

A ghastly gurgle interrupted.

Raymond grabbed his portly chest and gasped for air; his features warping into a tortured mask.

"Help him," Madeline begged, for no other reason than seeing a fellow human being writhe in agony was terrifying.

"Shut up, wench," Alberforce bit out. He eased off the bed, pulled on his breeches and slid his feet into his black Hessians.

Raymond was gagging, his face turning purple. Before the duke could render any aid, a violent convulsion wracked the earl, who slithered off the chair and lay motionless.

"The fool is dead," Alberforce declared indifferently. "His debt is paid."

Sobbing from shock more than sorrow, Madeleine cried, "Release me."

"I was never here," Alberforce spoke close to her ear, a cold hand curving around her throat.

"Get out of my house, you cad," she wheezed.

"You would be well-advised not to make an enemy of me." His grip tightened,

"An enemy of you? Pah. Do not flatter yourself. If Parham is dead, I am free and my revenge will be more egregious than you can possibly imagine," Madeline vowed.

Their eyes met, forbidding blue on hostile green.

"Do you believe me?" she challenged with a lift of her chin.

"How many times do I have to tell you to shut your yapping, bitch? You are nothing more than a slattern, and no threat to me." He trailed a gloved finger down her body, administering a series of bruising nips, chuckling when she tried to avoid his remorseless fingers. "You cannot escape me, my dear, remember that," he warned, his caution steeped in menace.

"That works both ways," Madeline countered, determined not to be cowed.

"Is that so?" He increased the pressure on her throat until spots danced before her eyes.

"I swear, you will rue the day you used me for your own ends," she spat, suffering another slap for her pains.

The last she heard was the door closing on his soft laughter.

Gathering her scattered senses, Madeline took stock.

She was naked, tied to the bed, while her husband lay unconscious or, and more probably, dead on the floor beside her.

Her screams were ripped from a throat already sore.

She continued until her voice was reduced to a hoarse croak.

No one came.

Parham's suite of rooms occupied a wing of The Lodge at the opposite end of the residence from the domestic quarters. It was this very seclusion which had allowed him, so he thought, to maintain the subterfuge — unaware his staff knew everything.

Two years previously, Mr Blake had discovered the countess huddled on the floor, sobbing wretchedly. He took control, summoning a bevy of maids to care for their distraught mistress. Following a soothing bath and a tisane known for its calming properties, Madeline was bundled into bed, watched over by Mrs Watson, the housekeeper.

She never divulged the cause of her distress, assuming the staff was in collusion with her husband. Neither was it appropriate to discuss private matters with any in the domestic sphere.

Her transformation from blithe young bride to detached wife, troubled them. Their diligent — if, by necessity, furtive — investigation uncovered the truth, and they strove to gain Madeline's trust.

It took weeks. Madeline, status notwithstanding, was not disposed to disclose the source of her misery. Eventually, Lottie, her personal maid, could stand it no more, and confessed that the staff in their entirety was well acquainted with their master's *arrangements*. Whenever possible, Mr Blake foiled attempts by certain noblemen to gain access, informing them, in implacable tones, the countess was not at home.

"I promise we will do everything in our power to protect you," Lottie had said, her sincerity a balm to Madeline's aching soul.

"Thank you, my dear. I appreciate your solicitude, but please do not risk your positions here on my behalf. Regrettably, we all know, I wield less authority than the kitchen cat." She had patted Lottie's hand and changed the subject but was heartened by the maid's words.

Dawn had long since broken when Lottie, perplexed by her mistress' notable absence, began a systematic search of the house. Usually, she avoided this suite of rooms because Lord Parham had made it very clear, no one was to enter without express invitation. This morning, she had no choice. Lady Parham was nowhere to be found, and Mr Blake was confident, she had not left the house.

Opening the double doors into Lord Parham's private sitting room, Lottie heard a rasping sob. She darted across the carpeted floor, dodging around the ponderous furniture, and burst into the bedroom, horrified by the sight which met her eyes.

"Oh, my lady," she cried, clamping her hand over her mouth to stifle the shocked exclamations threatening to spill over. Averting her eyes from the prone figure of her master, she hurried to the bed and untied Madeline who, by now, was blue with cold, her teeth chattering.

Madeline's arms, secured for hours above her head, were locked in place and the slightest movement was agony. Gently, Lottie moved the aching limbs into a more natural position, covered her mistress with a thick coverlet, and rang for Mr Blake.

"We need to get you warmed up, my lady, or you'll catch your death."

"Not the worst thing," Madeline quipped cynically.

Wanting to get Madeline away from the scene, Lottie did not wait for the butler, and helped the exhausted woman to her bedchamber through the silent house.

Mr Blake appeared, and Lottie paused long enough to apprise him of the situation, speaking in undertones so as not to upset Madeline further.

"Pray do not whisper on my account," Madeline interjected. "'Tis not as though I am grief stricken. I daresay there are formalities which will require my attention, but before I do anything else, I should like a bath to be drawn." She shuddered. "I must rid myself of the taint." She had no need to clarify, both Lottie and the butler knew to what she alluded.

"I shall organise that immediately, my lady." Mr Blake bowed and retraced his steps.

Within minutes, the quiet house buzzed with activity. Buckets of hot water were carried up to Madeline's dressing room, slowly filling the bath to which Lottie added a few drops of perfume. The light fragrance soothed Madeline's overwrought senses and she slid under the surface, immersing herself completely.

While Madeline scrubbed her skin red to eliminate every last vestige of *his* touch, wishing it would also obliterate her memories, Mr Blake sent a footman for Doctor Smythe with strict instructions to be discreet.

While Lady Parham was helped into a morning gown, and her hair towelled dry, the doctor pronounced Lord Parham dead, probable cause... a heart attack. The earl was known for his love of rich foods; his corpulent frame and florid complexion, prior to death, attesting to an over-indulgent lifestyle.

Mr Blake had taken pains to remove any trace of the night's activities and, to anyone unaware of the earl's proclivities, the diagnosis was the only logical conclusion.

"I am more surprised he has survived this long." Doctor Smythe shook his head lugubriously. "I warned him on countless occasions, but would he listen?" He gestured towards the body, his question, patently, rhetorical. "Now 'tis too late. I hope the good Lord is ticking him off.

Mr Blake kept a straight face, thinking the good Lord would have no desire to speak to Raymond Galleron, Earl of Parham. Far more likely that the devil himself was welcoming his newest guest.

CHAPTER TWO

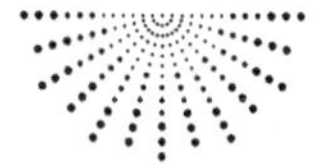

December 1819

adeline wandered the quiet halls of The Lodge. The funeral was — according to those who attended — a dignified ceremony at odds with the manner of her husband's demise. The wake, a rather more rowdy affair had lasted well into the evening, the last guests only departing when Madeline feigned distress.

A slight smile played around her mouth, she had fulfilled all the obligations expected of a grieving widow, and the relief was almost palpable. During the previous fortnight, her features, schooled into solemnity for each onerous duty, had fooled all bar her own household.

Her husband's friends, family, and colleagues believed her devastated by Parham's death, a pretence she was happy to perpetuate… for the time being. Mourning could be used to one's advantage.

Assuming she was not about to be tossed out on her ear, the next task was to rid this house of anything which reminded her of the late earl, including everything in the master suite.

A huge bonfire would be a pleasant method of destruction, but it was not the done thing in this genteel corner of the city, moreover, Madeline knew of a refuge which might be glad of the furnishings. She intended to turn that side of the house into a guest wing, hopefully the change might quash some of the bad memories.

To that end, Madeline decided to begin her catharsis with Galleron's private study, a place she rarely ventured. As with his suite, he had made it plain it was out of bounds unless he demanded her presence. She was happy to avoid it. A dismal room at the best of times, today it was dark, cold, and slightly damp from disuse.

Suppressing a shiver, she hugged her heavy shawl around her shoulders. Ringing for Mr Blake, she asked him to light the fire, while she fetched a candelabra from the library. Setting it on the vast oak desk, she walked around to the ugly chair, trailing her fingers over the ornate inlay, seeing her reflection in the polished surface.

Dawson, one of the footmen, entered carrying the tinder box. Madeline sank onto the seat and watched him complete the painstaking ritual of striking the steel until one of the sparks caught and held.

Crouching in front of the hearth, Dawson blew softly on the tinder until it was alight, then used a sulphur match to ignite a taper, which he slid under the kindling in the grate. Wielding the bellows, he encouraged the little flame until certain the wood was smouldering.

. . .

"Would you like some refreshment, my lady?" Dawson straightened up and replaced the damper in the tinderbox, ready for the next time.

"Coffee would be lovely, thank you, Dawson." Madeline smiled.

Dawson hesitated.

"Was there something else?"

"No, only 'tis very cold, my lady. Would you prefer I serve coffee in the library until this room heats through?" His concern was obvious.

"I appreciate your consideration, but here is fine. See..." she nodded at the fireplace where the logs were beginning to crackle. "...it will be warm in no time."

Bowing, Dawson backed out, a faint frown marring his brow. He made a mental note to ask Lottie to check on on their mistress throughout the day, whether summoned or not, conscious Lady Parham had a tendency to become engrossed in whatever she was doing to her own detriment.

Hardly aware of his exit, Madeline's gaze was fixed on the hypnotic cadence of the blaze. Her vivid imagination creating pictures which formed and dispersed in the dancing flames as they wove around the great hunks of timber; tendrils of aromatic smoke coiling up the chimney. Such a restful pastime.

With effort, she dragged her eyes from the hearth, to focus on the desk and what it might contain. She anticipated finding papers associated with the various Galleron houses and estates, the administration of which she must assume.

An intelligent woman, a fact she had concealed from her husband, Madeline, cognisant of the laws pertaining to inheritance, had made it her business to learn all about estate management during two long summers spent alone at

Chaldhaven — the earl's seat in Surrey. The stewards, while mildly perturbed at their mistress' unorthodox request, saw no reason to refuse, and discovered they enjoyed the exercise.

A quick study, Madeline did not take long to grasp the intricacies associated with running the different properties, how to balance the accounts, how to recognise inconsistencies, and how to distinguish between the authentic and the fake. The hours she had devoted to her endeavour were about to bear fruit.

Methodically, she opened and examined every drawer in the desk. All except one contained little of importance. A few outstanding accounts… easily settled. A neat stack of blank paper. Quills, blotting sand, three seals and sealing wax… the customary accoutrements.

The shallow drawer in the middle of the desk was locked. Madeline scrabbled about through the other drawers, eventually finding a tiny key, tucked away in a corner. It worked and, as the narrow wooden casing slid out, she stared at the single item therein.

A slender, leather-bound notebook lay in the centre on the drawer. Outwardly, an innocuous thing, yet it seemed to bear great significance, not least because of its concealment.

At that moment, Dawson reappeared carrying a platter on which stood a steaming pot of coffee, a cup, and a plate of tiny cakes. "Biddy thought you might appreciate a little light sustenance," he said, and placed the tray on the desk.

"Please thank her for me, and thank you, Dawson. No need to pour, I can manage." Madeline smiled her dismissal, and the footman withdrew.

All was quiet save the fizzle of the flames devouring the logs, the room becoming more comfortable. Sipping her coffee, Madeline retrieved the notebook and studied it. It was quite old; she could see the edges of the paper were yellowed, and it creaked when she opened it.

The first thing to catch her eye was her own name. Her brow creased, and a prickle of unease ran down her spine.

"What do we have here, Galleron?" she murmured and turned the page.

Flicking through, the notebook appeared to be nothing more sinister than a tabulation of accounts. Madeline presumed it concerned his properties, perplexed as to why her name was penned at the front.

"Why is this separate from your ledgers?" she mused out loud. "What are you hiding, and why is my name attached to it?" Topping up her coffee, she carried it and the book over to the fire where she settled into one of the aged, wing-backed chairs. Taking her time, she read the notebook from cover to cover, but was none the wiser.

"There has to be a reason it was locked away. What am I missing?" she asked the empty room which, of course, remained mute.

She tapped the book against her palm, mulling over the contents. Raymond was not a man for frivolities, everything he did was calculated. She ran her mind over his business ventures, coming to an abrupt halt when she remembered he owned racehorses.

Did the numbers correspond to wagers?

She opened the book at a random page. At the top, two letters. Initials perhaps? Underneath, a list of dates, opposite each, an amount. She turned the page, same basic list, except the letters, dates, and amounts differed.

"It must be a list of people who owed him money," Madeline surmised. "Which still begs the question as to why he wrote my name at the beginning. Was it in hope that anyone who came across it, inadvertently, might think it related to the household expenditure."

It seemed feasible, but Madeline was not convinced by her own argument. Something didn't sit right. Rising, she returned to the desk and picked up a cake, nibbling it absently. She ate a second then a third, barely registering the fact. She was mulling over the racehorse angle when, suddenly, everything fell into place, and she knew.

Nausea threatened, and she had to swallow several times to palliate a recalcitrant stomach intent on expelling every last crumb of the treats she had just enjoyed.

Madeline sank onto the floor, heedless of her gown. "You, vile wretch," she hissed. "Was not my nightly humiliation enough? You had to *record* each one. How could you?" She battered the rug with angry fists, wishing it was Raymond's head. "I hope you suffer an eternity in purgatory. Hell is too good for you."

The need to vent her fury had her upright and pacing the floor, cursing her dead husband to Michaelmas and beyond, while the hunger to exact revenge consumed her.

Slowly, her outrage receded, supplanted by the merest scintilla of an idea.

Interesting.

Uncaring that it was not yet midday, she crossed to the drinks cabinet and splashed a large measure of brandy into a glass. She swirled the amber liquid before tossing it back in one gulp. The fiery spirit seared a path down her throat, triggering a bout of coughing, but it cleared her head.

"How to use this to my advantage." Madeline resumed her seat by the fire and perused the notebook, applying her shrewd brain to the task.

· · ·

True to his word, Dawson mentioned his concerns to Lottie who checked on the countess at various times throughout the day, coaxing her into some luncheon and, later on, afternoon tea.

Madeline was aware of Lottie's presence enough to thank her, but the minute the maid stepped away, she was forgotten.

While a protracted and painful death sounded rewarding in theory, the practicalities of eliminating sundry members of the *ton* — not to mention, she would face the noose if caught — compelled Madeline to revise her plan. She *did* permit herself a few moments fantasising about what could not be, then dismissed the whim completely.

The curs did not deserve the tributes they would receive at their funerals.

By the time dinner was served, Madeline believed she had the basis of a scheme which should serve a dual purpose. A form of retribution whereby each of her visitors had the choice to pay or be exposed, but one which also benefitted those who, after suffering similar abuse, had found themselves reliant on charity to survive.

That night, cosy and warm in her bed, Madeline pondered the day. One of mixed and extreme emotions, but one which she believed may well have sparked the beginning of her healing process.

The next morning, she sent a note to her solicitor.

"Mr de Wilton," Blake intoned, as he ushered a tall gentleman, clad in sober greys, his cravat in turquoise paisley silk, the only hint of a nature ordinarily cheerful.

Madeline stood to greet her guest. "Mr de Wilton, thank you for coming at such short notice. I appreciate you taking the time."

"I am at your service, Lady Parham." Emory de Wilton bowed over Madeline's hand before making himself comfortable in the indicated seat. "I have brought the documents as requested."

"Excellent. Mr Blake." She turned to her butler. "Please will you organise some coffee and a slice or three of Biddy's delicious cake, if she has any going spare."

"I am certain she has." Mr Blake nodded and withdrew, knowing Biddy always had a freshly baked cake ready, on the off chance their mistress could be tempted into a morsel. He tsked to himself. Lady Parham didn't eat enough to keep a bird alive.

Madeline found herself unable to settle. She circled the elegantly appointed drawing room, wringing her hands nervously. The contents of the will might stymie her plan.

It would not surprise her to learn that Galleron had left her destitute; her future dependent on the goodwill Of others. A parsimonious man in every aspect of his life, Raymond, while ensuring Madeline was attired in the manner expected of a countess, had mandated she be frugal with the household accounts, requiring her to justify even the smallest expense.

"Please sit, my lady," Emory entreated. "Your husband's last will and testament makes for interesting reading and, permit me to put your mind at rest. You have been provided for with generous consideration."

"That is always assuming he did not gamble it away," Madeline muttered, relief edging out agitation.

"True, true, but let us deal with things one at a time. I shall read the will and then we can discuss the next step.

CHAPTER THREE

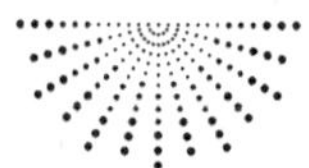

An hour later, Madeline's brain reeled with the numbers she was attempting to process.

"Pray, let me get this straight. At no time during the past two years was Parham suffering from financial distress? He did not owe his racing cronies astronomical sums?" Madeline tried to staunch her rising anger, tired of battling her fury over her dead husband's litany of transgressions.

It was bad enough when she believed he had no choice, because he was destitute but, to discover he had — for want of a better word — sold her for his own entertainment beggared belief. If there was no debt, why had Alberforce stated it was paid, the night Galleron died?

"Not a bit of it. If my calculations are correct, and I have triple checked them, his estates are flourishing, and he has no monetary debts, other than the usual business accounts due this month."

"The scoundrel," she hissed." I wish I could bring him back from the dead, in order to make him endure an agony worse than being flayed alive."

Not wholly unaware of Madeline's history, Emory held his tongue.

Lady Parham was one of Emory's first clients, and the person she had approached to explain the complexities of primogeniture, entails, and estates, long before she raised the latter with Parham's stewards.

One afternoon, while discussing Chaldhaven, Madeline had, unwittingly, let something slip.

To anyone else, the remark would seem innocuous, but Emory was more perceptive than most. His older sister, Kitty, had suffered at the hands of her now, and thankfully, dead husband. Something about Madeline's comment and her demeanour reminded him of Kitty. The similarities could not be ignored.

Emory was concerned enough that he had dared, with the utmost tact and diplomacy, to pry. He did not expect Madeline to confide in him but, being an astute fellow, was quite able to read between the lines, and the countess' determination to maintain a very British stiff upper lip, won his loyalty from that day onwards.

Messrs Dunstan, Dunstan, and Fitch: Solicitors, had acted for the Parham family for decades and, in her turn, Madeline was impressed that a son of an earl, rather than aspiring to be a barrister — an occupation usually associated with the gentry — had chosen to remain a lowly solicitor.

Madeline had persuaded her husband to request that Mr Dunstan make Mr de Wilton responsible for their business. Given the partners supervised their junior staff, Raymond had no objection.

Mr Dunstan, knowing Emory to be a conscientious

fellow, was agreeable, and Lord Parham had never regretted assenting to Madeline's proposal. Young, he might be, but Emory had proven himself discreet, dedicated, trustworthy, and proficient. Traits lacking in many who practiced law — money or, and more likely, status, trumping ethics.

Lady Parham's visceral reaction to his statement, merely affirmed that his nebulous suspicions were correct.

"Beg pardon, my lady. I had no mind to cause upset. I presumed this would come as a relief rather than a shock."

"If you had the slightest inkling." Madeline stopped abruptly. There were moments, like this one, when the urge to unburden herself was almost irresistible, but fear of how her revelation would be received always held her back.

"No matter, what was done was done and cannot be undone. Now, have I inherited anything from among the sundry assets, or has everything fallen to the trustees? That I might be living here," she waved her hand to indicate the house, "on borrowed time, so to speak, unsettles me."

Emory was quick to allay her concerns. "There are no entails attached to this house. Lord Parham purchased it a decade or so prior to your marriage and it is listed as a separate item in its own right. The will states that, in the event of the earl predeceasing his wife, this particular property transfers, lock, stock and barrel to her; neither is there an accompanying stipulation. The remainder of his estate will pass to Lord Walter Parham, your husband's cousin, as closest male relative."

Madeline shuddered. Walter Parham was a sanctimonious nitwit whose thrift made Galleron's miserliness look like reckless philanthropy.

"What do you mean, no accompanying stipulation?" she asked, unable to recall hearing that phrase during their manifold discussions.

"It means if you decide to remarry, the house does not revert to Lord Walter."

"So, it is mine for life?"

"Yours and your descendants to do with as you please. He set aside ample provision for its upkeep, along with a personal allowance in the amount of three-thousand pounds per annum."

At this, Madeline gawked… she could not help it. "Please could you repeat that?" she croaked, struggling to comprehend her husband could leave her so well provided for, bearing in mind, his callous indifference to every other aspect of her life.

Emory did so, adding delicately, "Hopefully this annuity will help you begin a new life."

Madeline's sharp green eyes bore into him, but he held her gaze. "I shall pretend you did not just exceed your position," she observed, her tone colder than the winter's afternoon.

Emory did not flinch, nor did he apologise. "Lady Parham, you really ought to meet my sister. It would do both of you a world of good to know neither of you are the only ones to have suffered at the hands of your respective spouses."

Madeline's composure slipped. "B-beg pardon," she stammered.

"I may not be cognisant of the details but, much like a doctor, my job is to recognise the subtle nuances which determine a person's veracity, rather like a gambler's 'tell'. I see in you the same distress which afflicted Kitty. Her husband also died before the damage he inflicted was irreversible, but it was a close thing. Sometimes Fate intervenes before it is too late." He smiled gently.

Madeline opened her mouth to brush off his justification, but his words struck a chord. Perhaps he was correct. She nodded slowly. "Evidently, I am not as accomplished at disguising my emotions as I believed. I confess, my marriage was," she cast about for a polite term to describe her ordeal, choosing, "irksome," as the least offensive.

Emory dipped his head. "Fret not, my lady. Your skill at concealing your pain is masterful. 'Tis only because I have witnessed the same in another that I am able to discern it. With your permission, I will ask Kitty to call on you. Her presence ought not set the tongues wagging, and I have an inkling, the pair of you will find solace in an honest exchange of experiences.

"Now," his tone became brisk, "let us talk no longer of harrowing memories. Today is one for celebration, not sorrow. Hope is renewed."

By the time Emory departed, Madeline felt that her life had, indeed, turned a corner — the outlook, not so grim.

That is not to say, she had shelved her plan.

Teasdale House, London
Home of Adam and Kitty Marchmain
30th December 1819

Fortuitously for Emory, Lady Kitty Marchmain, Marchioness of Teasdale was in Town for the winter season — not that she would be attending too many balls.

Despite Kitty's argument that the midwife near their country estate was eminently capable, she had been persuaded by her, inclined to worry, husband to stay in London until after the birth of her second child, due sometime in March.

In the middle of a conversation over tea, five days after Christmas, Emory managed to slip in a vague reference to Lady Parham, just enough to pique his sister's interest. Within ten minutes, Kitty had decided it was imperative, she meet the young widow.

"Perhaps it will not raise too many eyebrows if I invite her here for an afternoon," she suggested. "Adam might have something to say if I start gallivanting around London." She shot a sly glance at her husband, waiting for him to rise to the bait.

Which he did.

"He might at that," Adam interjected drily. "You are supposed to be resting, not dancing attendance on Emory's lost causes."

Emory chuckled at Kitty's comical eye roll. "Forgive me, I had no mind to cause upset. 'Tis only..." he expanded somewhat on the reason behind his request, concluding with, "you see why I think it would be beneficial, for both of you?"

About to point out this subject was one which had already been discussed to its death and did *not* need revisiting, Kitty looked at Adam who was close enough to catch her gaze. He reached for her hand, interlaced their fingers, and pre-empted her reply.

"I know we have talked about what happened but, although I ache for what you suffered, I can only sympathise and offer my love and support. I cannot and will never be able to comprehend to what he subjected you, for I did not endure it personally.

"If I understand Emory correctly, this Lady Parham could

be the one person who *does* understand, who has surmounted a comparable anguish. If you could be of benefit to each other, where is the harm? If nothing else, you are reaching out to a lady who sounds unbearably lonely, and your brother would never place you in an untenable situation."

Kitty pondered the truth of his words and nodded slowly. "I cannot contest your logic, my dearest."

With Kitty to think was to act. She walked across to the escritoire and penned an invitation to Madeline, choosing a date after the hubbub of the season had subsided. "There, 'tis done. I suspect this could turn out to be most interesting."

Emory permitted himself an optimistic smile.

The Lodge
New Year's Eve, 1819

Madeline descended the stairs, musing over a year she hoped to consign to the dustbin.

Unusually, she had slept late and felt the day half-wasted, despite the clock telling her it was not yet ten. Spotting the short stack of mail on the platter at the bottom of the stairs, she picked it up.

Not expecting anything interesting — she would not be expected to attend any of the customary revelry — her eye was caught by a letter bearing her name in flamboyant penmanship. Intrigued, she slid it out of the pile.

Turning it over, the name on the back prompted her to break the seal with haste.

Dear Lady Parham,

I am aware you are in deep mourning but imagine you might welcome a change of scene. I should be delighted if you would join me for afternoon tea, two weeks hence, Wednesday 12th January. Please come at two, that will give us plenty of time for a proper chat.

Yours sincerely,
Kitty Marchmain

Madeline was surprised and warmed to see the marchioness had signed the note with her given name rather than her title. Before her brain talked her out of it, she accepted with pleasure, and asked Mr Blake to ensure it was sent at the earliest opportunity.

Tucking the invitation behind the clock on the mantel, Madeline's attention turned to the rest of her day.

After Emory's recent visit, a fortnight previously, she had whiled away a pleasant hour or so planning the refurbishment of The Lodge.

To be assured the house was hers in perpetuity had come as a relief, but it was also a responsibility, one she did not take lightly. It was one thing to administer the domestic sphere and leave her husband to settle the associated bills, quite another to manage the accounts herself, thankful she had retained Emory as her man of business.

Today seemed as good a day as any to begin. Preparing to leave behind the old and welcome in the new. Inspired, she found a pencil and ascribed the name of a room which required redecorating to a piece of paper.

The number of sheets necessary was a trifle extravagant,

but preferable to getting things mixed up and, at least, she was not being wasteful by leaving the reverse blank. Gathering them into a neat sheaf, she began a systematic inventory of the house.

Madeline focussed on her task, which turned out to be both invigorating and exhausting. By dusk, three days hence, every nook and cranny of The Lodge had been inspected and, in consultation with Mr Blake and Mrs Watson, she knew what she wanted to do.

It would take time, and probably cost the earth, but it would be worth every penny.

On the periphery of her consciousness the other plan skulked. Sitting at Galleron's desk in the study, Madeline doodled absently on a spare sheet of paper, the caricatures she was sketching becoming text as a verse formed in her head.

She played with it, changing the phrasing, swapping the lines, and trying different words, until she was satisfied with her efforts.

She wrote it out in full and read it several times.

For the sin committed
And the pain endured,
For the respect omitted
And the silence secured,
For the dignity stolen
And happiness lost,
For promises broken
You must now pay the cost.

She envisioned the card she would write it on. Something funereal, perhaps with a black edge. She glanced out of the window onto the little courtyard garden, her gaze falling on the rose bushes, dormant in the frosty weather.

A dead rose… oh yes, that was perfect… a dead rose.

An avid reader, Madeline was fascinated by Greek and Roman mythology and knew the rose was linked to Aphrodite, the Greek Goddess of Love, and her Roman equivalent, Venus. While unlikely the recipients had the intelligence to recognise the significance of a *dead* rose, the inclusion was certainly… poetic.

She smiled grimly, envisaging the confusion of each sorry individual when presented with a verse, accompanied by a dead rose, and a polite suggestion as to how much and to where he should 'pay'.

She pulled open drawers to see whether Raymond had any appropriate notepaper, finding nothing suitable.

A visit to the stationers was in order.

If she was going to do this, she was going to do it properly.

CHAPTER FOUR

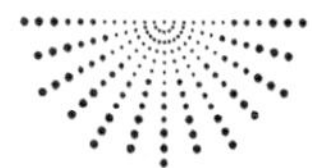

The next morning, Madeline spent a productive hour viewing samples of stationery. She wanted something the size of an invitation or an announcement, but edged in black, like mourning notepaper for her special project, as well as to replenish her dwindling supply of standard paper.

After a detailed discussion, Mr Appleton, the helpful proprietor, suggested his client order a duchess cut in a slightly higher quality finish for the invitations, along with two quires of conventional writing paper.

"That gives you forty-eight sheets, Lady Parham. An adequate sufficiency for even the most inveterate scribe." He beamed at her across the large table over which the samples were spread. "Would you like me to arrange for any printing?"

"Thank you, no. I prefer the personal touch," she replied, "but, I would appreciate a watermark on one quire."

"Certainly, my lady. The Parham crest perhaps?"

"A dead rose."

Only his long years dealing with the foibles of the

nobility prevented Mr Appleton's jaw from dropping. "Interesting, if a trifle morbid," he managed to sound unperturbed. "I am sure the printers will have something suitable. Leave it with me, I shall organise everything and arrange to have your stationery delivered to The Lodge, by…" he peered at a ledger, "…next week's end."

"Excellent, you are a treasure, Mr Appleton." She smiled, and the affable gentleman bowed his acknowledgement.

"Always a delight to be of assistance, my lady."

They chatted a moment longer, then Madeline took her leave.

It was a lovely morning. Cloudless blue skies with enough heat in the winter sun to keep the chill at bay. She was not too far from The Lodge, and a walk would be invigorating after the last few weeks. To the well-concealed surprise of her groom, she sent the carriage home, and struck out briskly along quiet paths swept clear of snow.

Too early in the day, and far too frigid, for any self-respecting member of Society to be abroad, Madeline slowed her pace, relishing the solitude. Save the occasional rattle of a coach, or trundle of a trader's cart, there was not another soul to be seen. It was long since she had felt so… free… if ever — her life a series of instructions, rules, and expectations.

In fact, now she pondered it, Madeline could not recall a single occasion, until recently, when she had not been controlled, either by her parents or her husband.

In that moment, she made a decision.
This new-found liberty would not be relinquished lightly.
Madeline Galleron was not for sale… no matter the bidder.

An unfamiliar *joie de vivre* settled over her.

Madeline had a fondness for winter. Something about the austere landscape, a world slumbering beneath a grey and white blanket resonated with her. Trees, bereft of foliage, shed contorted motifs across the snowy ground.

Here and there, the misty blue of conifers, along with the dense green of magnolia and laurel could be seen peeking out from under their white shawls. All sound was muted, even the quacking of the ducks was muffled.

Snug in her warm winter coat, Madeline strolled along the Serpentine, letting her mind wander.

Half-way around she came upon a surprisingly snow-free and dry, wrought-iron bench.

She could not resist the impulse to pause for a moment and, sinking onto the seat, watched the waterfowl foraging among the frosty reeds. Their antics on the icy edge of the water bringing a smile to her lips.

To Madeline, London had never looked more beautiful and, for reasons she could not fathom, the scene evoked her long-forgotten dream. The one featuring the gallant knight who could transport her to the heavens — an indulgence she surrendered to… for once.

The tranquillity of her surroundings soothed and, for a time, all other cares slipped away with the morning.

An icy draught jolted her back to reality with a shiver. "Get your head out of the clouds, my girl," she chastised and, shaking her head to dispel the illusion, rose to her feet.

Lost in thought, Madeline did not hear the crunch of gravel under booted feet, neither did she pause to check whether the path was clear and walked slap bang into a solid object. She stumbled backwards, apologies bubbling over her lips, aware of a steadying hand curving around her elbow.

"The fault lies with me, my lady, I was not concentrating." A deep voice, laced with suppressed amusement, assured. "Please forgive my inattention." He released her arm.

"Y-you are too kind," Madeline stammered, brushing her skirts to hide her discomfiture.

"Are you hurt?"

"Only my pride," she replied dryly.

"Fear not, my lady, no one witnessed our… err… collision."

The heat receding from her cheeks, Madeline faced the speaker. Silhouetted against the sun, his features were shaded, but his height was imposing and, she surmised, his hair was a rich, dark brown.

"Thank you… my lord." Although unfamiliar, a glance at his attire suggested he was, at the very least, a wealthy merchant, thus formal address seemed appropriate.

He inclined his head. "Not at all. One never knows whom one might… run into, in the park." He smiled suddenly, and Madeline found herself reciprocating.

"Lord Carnforth at your service." He removed his topper and bowed.

She did not recognise his title but, she socialised so infrequently, that was no surprise. "Lady Parham. A pleasure to make your acquaintance, however incongruous the circumstances." Madeline inclined her head.

Another man approached from a different path. "If you will excuse me, my colleague." He tipped his hat and strode away. Madeline observed the two greet each other with a handshake, falling into conversation as they hastened towards the gate, scuffing up traces of snow with each step.

While the viscount exuded confidence and authority, this

did not appear contrived and, if she was not mistaken, were traits also found in his associate.

Watching them disappear into the distance, Madeline registered that she had not flinched at his touch. Although practised at masking her revulsion when prepared, she usually could not help but recoil if the contact was unanticipated. Neither had she felt uneasy in his company — however brief — in fact, and curiously, had experienced quite the opposite, something she didn't think possible.

Perhaps the trauma of the previous two years *was* beginning to dissipate. To shed that oppressive weight would be most welcome.

Her stomach rumbled, informing her she was late for luncheon. Ruminating over this unexpected development, she turned for home.

Wednesday 12*th* January 1820

Madeline was gripped by mild panic. A raft of questions raced through her head. *What was I thinking accepting an invitation from a stranger? Why on earth had she listened to Emory de Wilton? What good could come from meeting the marchioness? I have acted heedlessly.*

She was sorely tempted to cancel.

"Oh, no my lady." Lottie, helping Madeline to dress, patted the countess' hand in a motherly fashion, making Madeline bite her lip to prevent a chuckle. "Her ladyship is lovely. My cousin, Sally, you know — the one as works for the Marquis of Clarence — well her grandmama is Mrs Milward who is the Teasdales' cook…" Lottie launched into a convoluted family connection to the Marchmains, the upshot being that they were an honourable family who treated their staff with the utmost kindness and respect.

Madeline tuned Lottie out, aware her maid had a tendency to prattle on about her relations most of whom, seemed to have found gainful employment in the houses of the *ton*. She studied herself in the pier glass.

Not a hypocrite, Madeline had refused to plunge the whole of her household into a state of mourning, permitting the bare minimum of bereavement rituals.

The only room draped in black was the one where Raymond had been laid out. She eschewed the use of the black tea-service — which last saw the light of day when Edith, Raymond's first wife, died — neither did she organise for mirrors or portraits to be shrouded, although she *did* agree to the black linen on the door — it kept uninvited 'well-wishers' at bay.

In her eyes, the pall which had descended on the day of her wedding was finally lifting and she had no intention of imposing its return.

Madeline could not countenance the severe black of mourning, given she was not in the slightest upset at her husband's demise, but the leaden-grey gown, she had chosen for today's visit did nothing to enhance a complexion already pale.

Her rebellious streak impelled her to alleviate the drab garment with one of her less... sober shawls. Rummaging through her chest of drawers, she withdrew one in a dark, blood red. Suitable enough to mollify even the strictest adherent to convention but, at the same time, lifted her spirits.

At two o'clock precisely, Madeline dismissed her driver, assuring him she wanted to walk home, and climbed the steps to Teasdale House, her stomach in knots.

Before she had a chance to knock, the door opened to reveal a butler, so like Mr Blake that Madeline blinked and checked the name on the plaque, momentarily questioning whether her carriage had merely driven her in a circle and brought her back to her own home.

"Lady Parham?" he greeted with a welcoming smile and a bow. "Please do come in. Lady Teasdale asked me to take you straight through." He took her cloak, then ushered her across an airy hall and into a beautifully appointed library.

"Lady Parham," he announced.

A swish of silks and a friendly, "Lady Parham, I have been looking forward to this afternoon immensely. Come in, come in and take a seat," met Madeline who, with no small amount of trepidation, did as she was bidden.

"Thank you, Pembroke. Hot chocolate I think…" She raised a brow at Madeline, who nodded with a shy smile, "… and some of Milly's delectable cake."

"Certainly, Lady Teasdale." Pembroke bowed and backed out of the room.

Madeline waited until the door had closed, and the two within were seated. "Thank you for your generous invitation, Lady Teasdale. I trust you do not think I coerced Mr de Wilton into arranging something you would rather he had not. What I mean is, I hope you did not feel under obligation."

. . .

Kitty Marchmain noticed Madeline twisting her hands together in her lap, a sure sign of disquiet. She corralled her thoughts. Emory was correct, her guest was discomposed, and she meant to get to the bottom of it.

"Fret not, Lady Parham, I never do anything I do not want to. Emory said you might benefit from a sympathetic ear and, while I have no mind to exacerbate your discomfort, your demeanour tells me, you are in dire need of a shoulder to cry on." Kitty reached over to press her hand on Madeline's. "I posit you will feel better if you trust me and unburden yourself."

Madeline gulped, swallowed hard, and gulped again.

Her hostess' kind voice, obvious concern, and gentle touch undid her long-held resolve. "'Tis a tawdry tale, my lady, and not one for such refined surroundings."

"Tawdry used to be my shadow but, by the grace of God, along with the love of my family and my husband, I have learnt how to banish the darkness. While I confess, it took time and a lot of patience, to shed that which encumbers you, is a blessing worth fighting for."

A quiet knock interrupted their conversation, and a footman appeared, bearing a large tray. "Hot chocolate, my lady, and Mrs Milward says to warn you the ginger biscuits are just out of the oven, so they might be hot."

"Thank you, Johnson, and please thank Milly." Kitty smiled.

"My lady." The footman withdrew.

The aroma of freshly baked biscuits was irresistible.

"I know 'tis early for afternoon tea, but I have discovered, of late, little and often is better for me." She bit into a biscuit. "Oh, Milly is a sublime cook, I am surprised I am not the size of an elephant. Regrettably, I cannot use the excuse I am eating for two forever."

Kitty's mischievous grin broke the faint tension, and Madeline, for the first time in longer than she could recall, laughed.

"There. That's better. Laughter is such a healthy reaction, do you not agree?" Without giving Madeline chance to reply, Kitty handed her a plate on which she had piled an assortment of dainty morsels. "Enjoy," she entreated.

A comfortable hush descended on the room as the two women partook of Mrs Milward's mouth-watering cakes. Without seeming to, Kitty encouraged Madeline to talk about her childhood and her family, steering clear of weightier topics while they ate.

A pleasant half hour or so passed then, after refilling their cups, Kitty leant forward and took Madeline's hand.

"Now, my dear. 'Tis time to divest yourself of the strain you carry. Perhaps once you know a little about what I endured, you will understand why Emory wanted us to meet."

CHAPTER FIVE

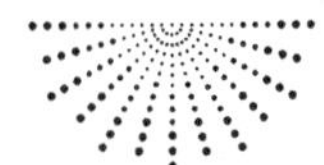

*M*adeline listened with growing horror, as Kitty's story unfolded. Married to a man whom she presumed had loved her, only to discover he wanted to control each aspect of her life, and sought to disparage and humiliate her at every opportunity.

"His abuse, while not physical, left scars as deeply as though he had cut me. In order to avert his bouts of rage, it was necessary for me to become a different person. I was so successful, even my family scarcely recognised me," Kitty said in a flat voice.

"His death came as a relief but, even then, I could not escape his grip, because I harboured guilt that my freedom came at his demise…" she looked Madeline in the eye. "… because I wished him dead more times than I care to count."

Madeline winced and the fine china cup clinked in its saucer as her hand trembled. Carefully, she placed it on the little side table between them. "My lady…"

"Do please call me Kitty," the young marchioness beseeched. "The confidences we are disclosing would be incomprehensible to most, yet they have transformed our lives and are now an important element in our bond. Oh yes," Kitty elaborated when Madeline's brow furrowed in bemusement, "we are going to be great friends, and friends do not need to stand on ceremony. Moreover, Madeline is a beautiful name." She smiled winningly and Madeline felt her reserve melting… just a little.

"Kitty," she dipped her head in acquiescence, and started to speak, only to find the words wouldn't come. It was too stark, too raw. "Forgive my stuttering, like an inebriated hen, might I beg your indulgence momentarily. I suspect my coherence will improve if I start at the beginning rather than the end."

"Take all the time you need. I am not going anywhere and, as you are supposed to be in deep mourning, I do not suppose you are either." Kitty winked and, abruptly, the last of Madeline's misgivings as to the wisdom of this meeting, fell away.

"Thank you. Do you mind if I stand?" Madeline asked. "I think better on my feet."

Kitty chuckled. "I am the same. To pace around a room is as though I am oiling the cogs of my brain. Adam despairs, tells me I look blurry, and it makes him dizzier than the tops our children spin. Adam has very limited eyesight, from the war, you know," she added by way of explanation.

"That is it exactly." Madeline circled the furniture, soothed by the elegant ambience of the room and an uncustomary sense of equanimity.

"I have long known I am little more than a commodity. As the third child and second daughter of an earl, my value was measured by how favourable a match, my parents could arrange. While I was growing up, they were neither kind nor unkind, in fact, I scarcely saw them. Indifferent is probably the best description.

"In all honesty, I do not think they realised; they were

simply treating us the same way they were treated. As long as we were clothed appropriately, spoke when addressed, and mastered the assorted accomplishments expected of our status, they had no complaints, but woe betide us, if they judged our efforts inadequate.

"My knuckles smarted for a sixth month when I learned to play the piano, and my ears rang with the number of times they were boxed while I practiced walking with five books balanced on my head." Madeline flexed her hands, studying the backs of her fingers. "I still hate the piano." She scowled.

"Please understand I am not bewailing my childhood. Doubtless it was the same for most of my peers. I am fortunate to be born into luxury not poverty and thank the Lord every day for that boon. I am merely setting the scene." She paused at one of the bay windows, her eye caught by the bright red of holly berries a cheerful display of colour against the dark evergreens dotted about the garden.

"I was brought up to accept my parents' decisions without question, so when they informed me I was to be married to Lord Parham, I did not argue. My dreams of being rescued by a knight in shining armour were and still are, just that… dreams." Madeline stopped pacing and resumed her seat, staring into the flames leaping in the hearth, welcoming the warmth.

She bent her head.

"Raymond Galleron, Eighth Earl of Parham, was a loathsome individual, who hid his true nature until we had been married for several months…"

…and like a river bursting through a dam, her tale spilled over. Words tumbled out in a veritable torrent, clawing for release as though, once heard, they would cascade down a waterfall, into a tranquil pool and evaporate, diminishing the nightmare.

Not yet.

. . .

Madeline came to a shuddering halt, a legion of conflicting emotions fighting for dominance. Rage, pain, betrayal, humiliation, degradation, and self-loathing, all eclipsed by a piercing sense of grief in the knowledge she had been forever ruined, by the one man who had vowed to protect her.

An odd hush descended.

Madeline could hear the crackle of the fire and the ticking of the clock. Comforting sounds.

"Forgive me," she husked. "My mouth ran away with me."

Thankful Emory had alluded to the extent of Madeline's suffering, Kitty said, her voice warm with sympathy, "There is naught for which to apologise. It needed to be said. Burying the torment does not eradicate the trauma, it merely loiters in your subconscious. An insidious blight, festering until, before you realise, it has consumed you."

"I do not know how to erase that chapter of my life. Their faces haunt me, the memory of their touch makes me nauseous, and as for *him*… what I would give to be a man and call him out. That said, death is too good for him, I…" she stopped abruptly. Appraising Kitty of her plan when they hardly knew each other was imprudent. While the marchioness might understand her guest's craving for revenge, in all likelihood, she would deem it essential to talk her out of it.

Aware Madeline was about to say more, Kitty felt it wise not to push, saying instead, "The only way to conquer that which plagues you and, thus, weaken the grip they have over you, is to talk about it. Talk about it until you are tired of talking about it, but can do so without wanting to vomit, or scream, or throw a tantrum. Keeping it inside is what gives it power," she paused. "That and imagining how much you would enjoy filleting them with a blunt knife."

Kitty's contemplative tone in contrast with her last remark, and accompanied by a truly hideous grimace, wrested a stifled gurgle from Madeline. The two women looked at one another for a few seconds then burst into gales of laughter.

Their mirth cemented an already burgeoning friendship.

Although they did spend some time consoling each other on their respective pasts, the conversation moved — deliberately orchestrated by Kitty — to lighter topics.

"Goodness, I have monopolised your afternoon." Madeline heard the clock on the mantel chime five and rose to her feet. "How inconsiderate of me."

Kitty shook her head. "Not at all. I have enjoyed every minute of it, even the disquieting parts."

Madeline questioned whether the butler possessed the gift of second sight because there came a quiet knock and, at Kitty's invitation the door opened to reveal Mr Pembroke carrying Madeline's cloak.

"Thank you, Pembroke. Lady Parham is ready to leave. Is her carriage there?"

"It will be momentarily. Mrs Millward pressed her ladyship's driver into a spot of tea."

"Well, how odd, I told Grantley I would walk home." Madeline frowned her confusion.

"Aye, he said as much, but reckoned the weather might be taking a turn for the worse and didn't want you getting caught in a blizzard. I confess 'tis looking rather grim outside," Mr Pembroke explained, as he helped Madeline into her cloak.

"Most thoughtful." Madeline smiled. Her staff was without doubt, more caring than anyone she knew... except, perhaps, Kitty Marchmain.

Goodbyes exchanged and promises of another visit made, Madeline took her leave, waving at Kitty who, ignoring Pembroke's exhortations to stay in the warm library, insisted on coming to the door.

Amusement played around Madeline's mouth as she settled into the cosy travel rugs. Lady Kitty Teasdale was a force of nature… in the nicest possible way.

Friday morning, as promised, Madeline's stationary order was delivered.

She ran her hand over the three beautifully wrapped bundles and plucked out the printer's card from under the string binding. On the back was penned…

Dear Lady Parham,

Our greatest wish is that you are delighted with this product. If you are in any way dissatisfied, please do not hesitate to inform us, and we shall make haste to rectify the problem.

Yours faithfully,
Messrs. Appleton, Richmond, and Forster.
Stationers and Printers.

Smiling at the wording, Madeline set aside the note, untied the string on the smallest packet, and removed the brown paper. There sat a neat pile of white cards edged in black with the merest hint of a curl in the middle at the bottom — as though the person wielding the brush creating the fine border had been jarred. A touch of whimsy, Madeline had asked Mr Appleton to include.

The result was exactly what she wanted.

The second package proved to be the plain quire, which Madeline slid into the bottom drawer of the desk, then turned to the final package. As she tore off the paper, she felt a frisson of excitement. *Had they been successful with the watermark?*

She slid out the top sheet and held it up. The weak January sun glinting through the window, highlighted the design ghosted onto the paper. The drooping head of a rose with a crushed leaf at the base of the stalk.

An exultant grin spread across Madeline's face, and she clasped the paper to her chest. Oh, this was better than she could have anticipated.

Ever polite, Madeline scribbled a brief 'thank you' to Mr Appleton and his colleagues, then mulled over how best to implement her plan.

She wanted to hand-deliver the letters. Not because she did not trust the mail service but because she needed to be certain each one was received intact, meaning the dead rose had not somehow become detached in transit or tossed away by the post-boy.

To ensure her intended target was at home when she delivered her 'request', Madeline realised a little surveillance was necessary. A thrill ran down her spine... *was this how spies reacted when tasked with a clandestine assignment?*

January was probably *not* the best time to launch her mission. The days were short, the weather execrable. Bearing in mind, even the hardiest tradesman did not dawdle at this time of the year, to loiter outside the house of a nobleman would attract attention.

Frustrating though it was, Madeline conceded that to

wait until Spring was the more sensible course of action, and it was not as though she was in a hurry.

Which meant, she had plenty of time to get everything prepared.

The bright light during the dark months of winter was Madeline's budding friendship with Kitty Marchmain.

Kitty encouraged Madeline to talk about her ordeal and believed the latter was making some progress but, mostly, the pair simply enjoyed each other's company.

Prior to meeting Kitty, Madeline's friends could be listed on the fingers of one hand. Her parents had discouraged fraternisation, limiting her social circle to those people they deemed suitable — none were her own age.

Lady Helena Drummond, then Trevallier and whose father was the Earl of Winchester, had been about the only one of whom they approved.

Madeline had seized every opportunity to escape to the relaxed atmosphere of Winchester House but, upon her marriage, unable to face Helena's penetrating gaze, Madeline had allowed even that friendship to lapse. Another bond she hoped to repair.

January slid into February and, suddenly, it was March.

In between her afternoons with Kitty, and rather than twiddle her thumbs awaiting a suitable time to begin her scheme, Madeline used the quiet weeks of winter to commence the herculean task of refurbishing The Lodge.

While her staff polished and, where necessary, cleaned windows and chandeliers, wall sconces and candelabra, floors and balustrades, a veritable orchestra of artisans and craftsmen tackled the rest.

The luxurious rugs, richly patterned carpets, and hard-wearing hall runners, scattered throughout the house had been well cared for, as had the beautiful rosewood and mahogany furniture, negating the need for replacements. An expense which would exceed the renovation of everything else in the house combined.

Furnishings, Madeline judged old, dingy, or just plain ugly were either — if beyond hope — burnt or placed in storage to be donated.

Apart from Galleron's hated suite, which she had instructed be locked until she felt able to deal with the contents, there was only one other part of the house she did not enter. The rooms belonging to her husband's first wife, Edith who had died four years previously. Galleron never talked about her, except to declare these rooms off limits. They were to be kept clean and tidy, but to remain as she had left them.

Eventually, she would deal with both chambers, but they could wait.

Slowly, the hated drab and dreary palate of The Lodge made way for a blend of subtle pastels and warm tones; the delicate colours embellished by vibrant splashes of colour in the cushions and curtains. Aged and worn chairs were revived using a variety of materials chosen for comfort rather than show, a bright counterpoint to the dark wood of the furniture.

As winter yielded to spring, the grim and sombre house was transformed into a restful and welcoming home.

CHAPTER SIX

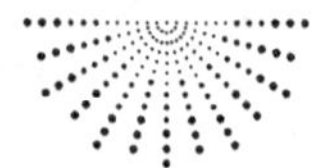

April 1820

After a few false starts, when the longed-for change of season was delayed by a series of late and somewhat severe snowstorms, spring finally prevailed.

Days of uninterrupted blue skies and sunshine lifted subdued spirits. Trees, once bare, sprouted leaves in shades of green so bright, it was almost painful after the leaden hues of winter.

Blossoms came into bud and a profusion of flowers carpeted the parks; their fragrance heady. Birds, singing lustily, dashed about in search of the perfect piece of nesting material. Along quiet streets, window boxes offered bursts of gentle colour.

An air of optimism pervaded the city.

Meticulous to a fault, Madeline arranged to call upon Lady Helena Drummond. Sister of the current Earl of Winchester and married to a shipping magnate, Lady Helena, although quite reserved in nature, was well regarded.

An enthusiastic supporter of Sanctuary House in both word and deed, Lady Helena persuaded members of the *ton* to donate all manner of items from coin to clothes to unused buildings with naught but a smile.

What began as a single residence had, a month previously, expanded to three, each with a specific function.

The main house continued as before, offering temporary accommodation and the opportunity to learn an array of skills. The second and third buildings were a dedicated clinic and a school, respectively, established to answer an increasing demand.

Recently, and with reluctance, Helena had taken a step back following the birth of her daughter but refused to relinquish her involvement completely.

Until Madeline's marriage, Helena and she were quite close. While their once frequent afternoons spent gossiping had dwindled of late, the countess did not believe their affection was lost.

Helena's delighted response when Madeline sent a note asking whether she might call, attested to the latter's conviction.

Helena greeted Madeline as though it was two days since they had seen each other rather than almost two years. As discerning as Kitty Marchmain, Helena was not fooled by Madeline's explanation that she wanted to discuss a donation to the refuge. With a perception and sensitivity born of experience, Helena extracted the truth.

"You surely do not think I am indifferent to your plight?" she said half-way through Madeline's diffident excuse for her protracted seclusion. "My dear, you are too thin, hollow-eyed, and pale. None of which, I suspect, is because you are grieving for your dead husband.

"Come, Maddie, how about you stop prevaricating and tell me what is really going on. I guarantee, your story will not shock me. Remember where I work." Helena's use of the diminutive and her quick squeeze of Madeline's hand had the desired effect.

It proved to be a most enlightening afternoon. A friendship was revived, and another plan initiated.

Perched on an aged, but well-loved — if the high sheen and beautiful cushion was anything to go by — Queen Anne chair, in a sizeable office in Sanctuary House, Madeline sipped fragrant tea. A note from Lady Helena lay open on the desk between Madeline and the two ladies seated opposite, currently staring at her agog.

"Mrs Parry, Mrs Forester, forgive my bluntness, I had no mind to offend your sensibilities," Madeline apologised, blushing, "but I see no point in beating about the bush. These men will be asked to atone for their behaviour in a manner which benefits others desperate to escape similar circumstances. Lady Helena assures me of your understanding."

Mrs Parry gathered her senses first. "Lady Parham, distressing stories are nothing new to us. In all honesty, while saddened you suffered thus, your tale is benign compared with most. No, my reaction relates to the fact that you, a countess, are courageous enough not only to divulge your trauma, but also is prepared to exact revenge in so… inventive a fashion.

"I have heard many of our regulars mutter dire threats against the men who brutalised them but, given their lack of autonomy, that's all they can ever do… threaten. Prudence, nay common-sense dictates, I try to persuade you to abandon your endeavours or, at the very least, encourage you to speak to Major Withers, the epitome of tact, who might offer an alternative form of retribution but, I surmise such an entreaty will fall on deaf ears." She offered a wry smile.

Madeline responded in kind and, aware of Major Withers' reputation, countered, "I fear Major Withers would be obliged to act as the voice of reason, bearing in mind my intention borders on the unlawful, and I am not feeling particularly reasonable.

"I have long been privy to Lady Helena waxing lyrical about Sanctuary House and what you have accomplished. This place is more than just a haven. It is where lives are salvaged, dignity regained, and hope renewed. To assist your endeavours, even superficially, means something good can come from something egregious.

"The donation *must* be anonymous, and all I ask is that you advise me of receipt. Included in my behest will be a pledge, affirming, once each man has paid the requested amount, his… for want of a better word… debt will be discharged."

"Lady Parha—" Mrs Forester began.

"Please, call me Madeline. Few people do, and I tire of being addressed by a title which serves as nothing more than a reminder of what I wish to forget."

"Madeline," Mrs Forester acceded with a compassionate

smile. "Unorthodox your methods may be but, I confess, possess a devilish appeal. An oblique hoist with their own petard so to speak. Rarely do the abusers get a taste of their own medicine and, while I imagine this will not assuage your distress entirely, hopefully by engineering even so minimal a retribution will help mitigate it."

The ensuing conversation was concluded to the satisfaction and, it cannot be denied, fiendish glee of all three ladies.

Early the next morning, Madeline ventured into the little garden nestled between the study and the dining room. Here, a handful of hardy roses had withstood the ravages of winter, undoubtedly protected in the sheltered courtyard.

Madeline knew it was unlikely the remaining blooms clinging doggedly to the gnarly stalks would survive until needed, hoping, by then, she could purloin a rose or two from the new growth.

Avoiding vicious thorns, she snipped one of the wilting roses, its petals the livid charcoal of a fresh bruise.

A parallel not lost on her.

Dodds, the gardener, perplexed when Madeline asked him not to trim the roses in February as was his habit, was mollified when she explained her request only pertained to this garden, not those bushes in the formal flower beds at the rear of The Lodge.

Carefully, Madeline carried the rose into the study and laid it on a swatch of linen she had cut from an old chemise. She studied the flower, struck again by the sheer eloquence of her scheme.

Settling into the leather chair behind the desk, Madeline

plucked the stack of black-edged cards and one sheet of the watermarked paper from the drawer.

Ensuring the inkwell was full, she sifted through the wooden box sitting alongside to find the quill she wanted. After checking it was trimmed, she fished out a partially used sheet, dipped the nib into the ink and wrote the first line of the verse to ensure the quill was smooth.

Just right.

Retrieving the notebook, Madeline flicked through the catalogue of her humiliation, as though the details were not already indelibly imprinted in her brain.

The first few pages were dedicated to Lord Douglas Gould, the Duke of Alberforce, known to Madeline as the Odious Knave, and the catalyst for what followed.

She stroked her chin with the end of the feather, calculating the number of times he had visited — a galling thirty-seven. Her nose crinkled in distaste. He could be left until last. He deserved nothing less.

Scanning the book, she came across the name, Lord Audley Richmond.

A mocking smile curved her mouth in recollection. He was the shy, nervous Viscount Saville who just talked, and who was gratifyingly appalled upon realising the woman Lord Parham had sent him to was actually the latter's wife *not* his mistress or a high-class prostitute.

A somewhat unworldly young man, his sole purpose was to learn how to please his betrothed, a lady for whom, it was obvious, he cared deeply. Sickened by his supposed friend's deceit, Lord Richmond had made to leave, shame-faced, apologies spilling over his lips.

Recognising genuine remorse, Madeline had taken pity on him and invited him stay for a cup of tea, whereupon she offered him some suggestions — which bore no resemblance to her own sham of a marriage.

She knew he was recently wed and hoped her advice had proved... fruitful. The viscount was as much a victim of Raymond's chicanery as she, and he did not warrant a reminder. Her smile widened; compassion was not an emotion she expected to feel. Maybe she was going soft.

The following page recorded Lord Grenville Bennet, the Baron Merryfield. Raymond had documented five dates, all during the first year, each with a monetary amount.

Bile rose in Madeline's throat, and she had to swallow repeatedly to quell the nausea. *Would this gut-wrenching sense of betrayal ever subside? Am I prolonging the agony by setting my plan in motion?*

Her resolve wavered, then memories intruded, and she stiffened her spine.

They had never shown her an ounce of humanity. It would be churlish not to return the favour.

She continued her perusal.

The next notation was the one Madeline was looking for. Lord Hubert Multon, the Earl of Holles, had only visited once and never returned.

She sneered at the modest sum alongside his name. *Is that all I am worth?* Her expression hardened. This was where her knowledge of each man came to the fore, recalling Lord Hubert had amassed a considerable sum of money by investing in merchant shipping. His *gift* would not be quite so paltry.

Picking up the quill, Madeline copied the verse onto one of the blank cards, taking care to centralise the lines.

Finished, she left it to air-dry, rather than use the blotting sand, and began the accompanying letter.

19th April

Dear Lord Holles,

The death of your facilitator does not eradi-cate your guilt. The offence was not committed against him.

You are fortunate, I am of a magnanimous nature, and will consider your sin expunged if you make an <u>anonymous</u> donation to Sanctuary House in the amount of ten pounds. The reason I chose this charity should be self-explanatory.

Like the gentleman you purport to be, it would behove you to honour my request. While I care little for my reputation, you, however...

Madeline left that dangling... an unspoken warning was far more unnerving — not to mention less illicit — than an overt threat.

I expect the donation to be made no later than one week from the date of this letter. Rest assured, I shall be informed immediately 'tis paid, at which point, I give you my word, any reference to you will be obliterated from the list I hold.

Oh, and before you act rashly, should anything, anything at all, untoward happen to me,

I have given instructions for your indiscretions to be broadcast.

M

Placing the quill in its stand, Madeline leant back in the chair, letting the contents roll around her head for a few moments.

She rather liked the mysterious M, which she had penned with a flourish. It would not take a genius to recognise the sender, but she doubted her identity would be revealed.

Yes, that should do nicely.

Taking advantage of every break in the weather during the previous two months, Madeline had ascertained the London addresses of her quarry.

Most lived within a one mile radius of The Lodge... not unexpected but galling all the same. That, blessedly oblivious, she had passed their residences with frequency, left a bitter taste in her mouth.

She imagined they never gave her a moment's thought, continuing with their lives as though debauching someone else's wife was nothing untoward.

If, by chance, they met at a Society event, each man treated her with the aloof politeness they reserved for distant acquaintances or unwelcome relatives. She was nothing to them — their servants held more significance in their respective lives.

An indifference they were about to regret.

· · ·

Folding the letter around the card, she tied them with a length of black ribbon, sliding one of the dead blooms into the bow securely.

Madeline rang for Mr Blake and asked him to have her coach brought around to the front.

It was time.

CHAPTER SEVEN

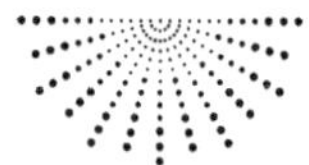

earing a dark, forest-green medieval-style cloak, deliberately chosen to conceal her identity — its capacious hood covering her dark locks, Madeline rapped on the door of Multon House.

The door opened to reveal a portly butler who bowed and smiled a greeting. "Good morning, my lady, how may I be of service?"

"Might you be so good as to present this to Lord Holles?" She handed over the neatly bound package, which the butler accepted, narrowly disguising his puzzlement. His long years of service and innate professionalism coming to the fore, he pretended it was not at *all* peculiar that a beautifully attired lady with a smart carriage would be delivering mail.

"The contents are confidential, and for his eyes only. I assume you are to be trusted?" Madeline held the butler's gaze until he inclined his head. "Thank you."

"Your name, my lady?" he risked a rebuff.

"I have no doubt Lord Holles will recognise the sender," she hedged, and bestowing upon him a bright smile, hurried down the steps.

. . .

The butler watched her climb into the carriage. The driver's livery was immaculate, but there was no visible coat of arms to assist in identifying the visitor.

He studied the package, which proved no more enlightening. A black ribbon, tied around a withering rose and a letter, without a seal seemed somewhat funereal yet, as far as he was aware, no one known to the earl had died recently.

He cast his mind back over the last few months, concerned he had missed something, but came up blank. The woman was unfamiliar, leading him to discount her as one of Lady Holles' friends.

"A conundrum indeed," he declared to the quiet street and, shrugging his shoulders, closed the door and sought his master.

Mimicking his butler, Lord Hubert Holles eyed the letter with a healthy degree of caution, particularly as Mr Thorne could tell him nothing about the woman who delivered it. Hesitant to open it, curiosity got the better of him.

Curling his lip, he tossed the rose in the bin, the petals exploding in a cloud of desiccated decay. The cloying scent tickled his nostrils, making him sneeze. Balefully, he glared at the letter as he untied the ribbon and unfolded the sheet.

Lord Holles scanned the words, then shook his head in disbelief. *What the deuce?* He squinted at the M... *who was M?* Blackmail whispered on the fringes of his mind, but to his recall, he had done nothing to instigate so sordid a threat. *Have I?* Ten pounds. It was not so much the sum — that was inconsequential — no, it was the demand.

He read it again.

For the sin committed... *what sin?* He wracked his brain but failed to find an answer.

And the pain endured... *pain... what was this nonsense?*

For the respect omitted... his brows furrowed. Was this from a man, a business colleague, an associate in the racing fraternity? No one came to mind — he thought he was on good terms with everyone. Clearly not.

He scanned the remaining lines, utterly at a loss. They meant nothing, yet the tone of the letter indicated he ought to be fully cognisant of its meaning. *Do I ignore it? Do I pay? Ought I to inform the authorities?*

Tapping the edge of the card on his desk, the earl ruminated over the contents. Surely verse was not the typical bailiwick of a blackmailer. He suspected those who employed such methods of extortion were barely literate. Neither did it seem likely to have been penned by a man.

In Lord Holles' opinion, poetry was favoured by simpering females, not swindlers — not that he had any experience of the latter...

His thoughts screeched to a grinding halt. *Simpering females*. Nausea lurked as that which he had striven to erase, lurched to the forefront of his mind. Now, the initial at the end of the letter made sense.

Madeline.

His execrable behaviour taunted him. He shook his head to expel the image, but it refused to be dislodged. What a fool. Seduced by Galleron's assurances that Madeline was a willing, nay enthusiastic participant, the sheer lascivious thrill the invitation engendered had blinded him.

His own marriage was neither good nor bad, more it ticked along in a state of serene indifference. There was no rancour — that would suggest a mutual affection — and they lived relatively separate lives. The only time they showed any emotion was when it came to their three children, one son and two daughters, who were the apples of their doting parents' eyes.

While familiar with the Earl of Parham's predilections, his tantalising invitation had overridden Holles' common-sense. One visit, one glance at Madeline's despairing counte-nance, was all it took for wisdom to prevail.

It was a trifling matter to take a mistress — most every man of his acquaintance had done so — quite another to take advantage of the fact, wives were considered property to be exploited as their husbands saw fit.

He never returned to the Lodge. He never spoke to Galleron again.

Hindsight was a wonderful, if frustratingly belated, thing.

Unbidden, the thought that any individual, more specifically, a man, he believed to be trustworthy, might treat his own daughters thus, formed an ugly picture.

He bowed his head. He was a monster.

When viewed from that perspective — ten pounds was a small price to pay.

Three days later, a politely worded message arrived to inform Madeline, Sanctuary House had received the sum of twenty pounds from an anonymous benefactor. She was at once astounded and baffled that the amount donated was double her stipulation. Perhaps Lord Holles *did* possess a granule of compassion. There was hope for him yet.

She tore the page bearing his name from the notebook, and burnt it, toying with the idea of affirming this with the earl in question. About to discount it — she was not the one who needed assuaging of guilt — Madeline had a change of heart, and scribbled a terse note…

Your generosity implies a contrition unexpected. Your debt is erased.

…then dropped it on the platter for mailing.

One down. Four to go.

4th May 1820

Peter Masham, the Earl of Swinbourne glared at the card bearing the peculiar verse. Someone thought they could swindle him, did they? *Pah*, they were dealing with the wrong man. Outraged that some snivelling blackguard had the temerity to intimidate him, the earl called for his coach.

Shortly thereafter, he was wearing a hole in the aged rug covering the floor of a quiet office on the first floor of a nondescript building on Bow Street, venting his spleen and waving the slender package in his hand. His erratic gesticulations flinging dead rose petals in all directions.

Perched on the edge of his desk, Major Lucas Withers appeared riveted; in truth, he had stopped listening at the third rendition of the earl's tale. Lord Swinbourne seemed an odd target for blackmail. As far as Lucas knew, and he knew far more than most gave him credit for, the man's life to date seemed to be unblemished. He behaved in a manner expected of his status, was a retired naval officer, served on the usual parliamentary committees, and was well respected by his peers.

"Please, let me read the letter," Lucas asked, masking his rapidly evaporating patience.

Swinbourne all but threw the sheet at Lucas. "Get to the bottom of this, Withers," he snapped. "Darned cheek."

Lucas unfolded the sheet and scanned the words, noting it was dated the previous day. "You cannot think of anyone who would send you such an… unusual missive? An unpaid debt, perhaps? The amount is oddly specific. Forty-six pounds. A disgruntled business partner, or someone you may have slighted, however inadvertently?"

"Preposterous notion," the earl blustered. "Unpaid debt. Disgruntled busin—" his reply choked off in his ire.

"Well, you must have upset someone," Lucas contended mildly. "Otherwise, why would anyone send you so cryptic a letter? It is evident this has been penned so the recipient and only the recipient, in this case you, will recognise the alluded to sin. Have you been party to anything less than honest?"

"Do not be ridiculous, man. How dare you accuse me of scurrilous behaviour?" His chest heaved with righteous indignation. "I am not donating a single penny to this, where is it again?"

"Sanctuary House," Lucas supplied.

"Is that the one the esteemed Lady Drummond blathers on about?" He saw Lucas nod. "Pah, could be her, tired of begging for handouts. Reprehensible, reprehensible."

Lucas fought to maintain his impassive demeanour. "Please do not tell me you are suggesting Lady Helena Drummond would resort to blackmail?" An edge to his tone.

The earl had the grace to blush. "No, no, beg pardon, that was uncalled for."

Lucas inclined his head. "Lord Swinbourne. Might you leave this with me to investigate? It is probably a prank. Naught for you to worry about."

Lord Swinbourne studied the man in front of him. A fellow veteran — although their paths did not cross during the wars — Lucas Withers was known for his discretion, as were the men who worked for him. "Don't make me regret this," he growled.

"I make no promises." Lucas held the man's gaze. "You understand, while whatever we find is treated with the strictest confidence, my enquiries may unearth information you prefer remains buried?"

"Can I trust you?"

"Unequivocally."

"Then get on with it. I have nothing to fear." Lord Swinbourne strode from the office, slamming the door, papers scattering in his wake.

"The earl doth protest too much, methinks," a contemplative voice paraphrased from the far corner of the room.

"What do you make of him?" Lucas walked across to where the speaker was sitting. "Do you think he's hiding something?"

"Aren't they all? If they come to us, they have a skeleton hidden somewhere. Our task is to discover whether the skeleton needs to be unveiled."

Lucas passed the letter to the younger man. "Read this and tell me what you think."

Wolfstan Colleville, the Viscount Carnforth, took the proffered paper and read it three times. He felt a grin twitch at his lips. "A clever verse indeed. Someone is deeply vexed with Peter Masham. I posit this is no prank."

"I concur. A conclusion I had no wish to share with the earl... yet." Lucas sank into the adjacent chair. "What's your take?"

Wolfstan looked at the sheet, scrutinising the writing style, the choice of words, the black edged card, the dead rose, and accompanying letter signed with the flamboyant *M*.

Lucas did not rush his employee. One of his newer recruits, the viscount — adept at deductive reasoning — was proving a valuable member of the team.

"There is nothing random about this. Each element was included deliberately. The cost of the cards alone, particularly given the black edging, indicates an individual of means. Why bother with a dead rose?" Wolfstan foraged through his brain.

"Wait… in Greek myth, the red rose was a symbol of love until death. The Romans associated roses with beauty and love, and it is not confined to antiquity, other cultures and creeds have similar philosophies. Throughout history, roses have been synonymous with love and romance. In which case, a dead one represents the antithesis. A love or a heart destroyed. Goodness, this has Greek tragedy written all over it." Wolfstan tried to lighten a mood becoming sombre.

"I agree 'tis macabre. Let me have another look."

As Wolfstan passed the paper to his superior, the afternoon sun through the window highlighted the watermark.

"Definitely not a prank." Lucas lifted the sheet. "Do you see that?"

Wolfstan whistled. He started to speak, then stopped. Something clicked in his brain.

"What?" Lucas prodded.

"I think 'tis a woman."

Lucas stared and was about to refute the likelihood when the verse caught his eye. Wolfstan was correct. The words were not those of a man. They were skilfully chosen, delicate but direct, and the poem had taken time to compose, not dashed off in a moment of pique.

Then there was the letter. A man would not insist redress be made by donating to Sanctuary House… a haven for abused women. That made no sense.

Their perpetrator was a lady.

. . .

The pounding of boots on the stairs told the pair their colleagues were returning to make reports. Lucas stood up. "I want you in charge of this investigation. I think you are ready, but if you need help, ask."

Wolfstan got to his feet and dipped his head. "Thank you, Major. I will not let you down."

"I have no doubt. Just be careful and keep me informed."

"Sir."

The door swung open to admit the rest of Lucas's team, and the intriguing assignment was put to one side for the moment.

CHAPTER EIGHT

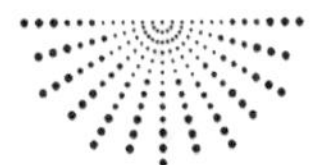

*I*dly, Madeline turned the pages of the notebook. *Whom ought she surprise next?* Her eye fell on the name, Lord Leland Castor, the Marquis of Tynnet. Disquieting though it was, she forced herself to recall every detail about the man.

In his mid-thirties, his marriage was without issue. She recalled him bemoaning the fact, his wife did not care whether he wanted an heir; she was not interested in risking her life or her sylphlike body for... in her words... his squalling progeny.

Madeline supposed the marquis might be considered handsome, in a brash sort of way but, although easy on the eyes, his features did not stir her. He had treated her kindly and with tenderness — traits at odds with the reasons for his visits — and, to Madeline's undying mortification, was one who had induced veritable waves of ecstasy during their *sessions.*

That did not excuse him. Given Tynnet had *paid* Raymond, Madeline was at a loss to understand why the marquis hadn't simply taken a mistress. Surely more logical, and far less risky than to take liberties with, nay abuse, another man's wife — whatever the justification.

"My Lord Marquis," she murmured, lifting a blank sheet of embossed paper from the desk. "Prepare yourself."

Leaving the letter until the ink dried, Madeline went upstairs to finish getting ready for the day ahead.

Leland Castor contemplated the neat stack of correspondence on the silver platter, positioned pointedly, in the middle of his desk.

His lips twitched at Mr Barnes' silent admonishment regarding what his butler considered to be his master's woefully lackadaisical attitude to his mail. Barnes took any post to the study as soon as it arrived, and Leland ignored it until after dinner.

What began as a bit of a game had become more a test to see who would capitulate first.

So far, it was stalemate.

With a resigned sigh, he would much rather be relaxing in the drawing room with his pipe, Leland plucked the first one from the pile.

"Come," he invited at a quiet knock.

Mr Barnes entered, carrying something small.

"Beggin' your pardon, my lord, but this was hand delivered this morning. I kept it apart, thinking it might be important." Barnes placed the beribboned missive on the desk. The two stared at it, the black bow taunting them.

"A trifle odd, eh, Barnes?" Leland mused. He lent closer the better to examine the package. A dead rose, a card, and a letter. His nose crinkled in distaste. "A dead rose? What sort of tomfool sent me a dead rose?"

"I'm afraid I cannot shed light on the sender, my lord. Higgins," one of the household's footmen, "reckoned it was just a messenger. He did notice the carriage had no crest. Odd sort'o letter." He bowed and turned to leave.

"Wait, Barnes. I want a witness to this. It smacks of something underhand."

"As you wish, my lord." Barnes stood by the desk respectfully.

Cautiously, Leland tugged at the ribbon. As the bow came undone, the rose rolled off the white sheet, scattering disintegrating petals which settled on the leather inlay like a bouquet of dried blood.

Both men recoiled.

Stifling an oath, Leland unfolded the letter. The card, tucked within, slid out, printed side up. He stared at it. The fine penmanship seemed to quiver under his gaze, but slowly the words came into focus.

Baffled, he turned his attention to the letter. Had he but known, it was a duplicate of the one received by Lord Holles, and the one Lord Masham handed to Lucas Withers. The only differences were the date and pecuniary penalty.

17th May

Dear Lord Tynnet,

The death of your facilitator does not eradicate your guilt. The offence was not committed against him.

You are fortunate, I am of a magnanimous nature, and will consider your sin expunged if you make an <u>anonymous</u> donation to Sanctuary

House in the amount of twenty-eight pounds. The reason I chose this charity should be self-explanatory.

Like the gentleman you purport to be, it would behove you to honour my request. While I care little for my reputation, you, however…

I expect the donation to be made no later than one week from the date of this letter. Rest assured, I shall be informed immediately 'tis paid, at which point, I give you my word, any reference to you will be obliterated from the list I hold.

Oh, and before you act rashly, should anything, anything at all, untoward happen to me, I have given instructions for your indiscretions to be broadcast.

M

Leland's jaw dropped.

Which imbecile was trying to extort money from him? He inspected the sheet to see whether there was anything other than an initial to identify the sender. Nothing. He lifted it, and the leaping flames from the fire caught the watermark. *Another* rose. This was bizarre. Was it from someone called Rose? Impossible, he knew no one bearing that name.

"Who did you say delivered this?" he quizzed.

"Cannot tell you, my lord. Shall I summon Higgins?"

Please," Leland replied absently and, picking up the card,

perused it more thoroughly, as Barnes went to find the footman.

He read the poem twice, sifting through his rapier-like brain to identify the sender. Something flittered on the outer reaches of his consciousness yet he could not pin it down. He concentrated, the fragments coalesced then crystallised, and recognition dawned.

"How dare she?" he groused, rage bubbling. "She thinks she can hold me to ransom? *Me*. The insolent chit. Pay that kind of coin to some..." he retrieved the letter and peered at the details... "home run by bleeding hearts. What does she take me for?" he ranted under his breath until Barnes reappeared, Higgins on his heels.

"Higgins, what can you tell about the messenger who delivered this letter?" Leland waved the sheet. "All of it, man."

"My lord." Higgins bowed. "I apologise but I took little notice. The man wore a long, dark green cloak, but 'e 'ad 'is collar pulled right up, and 'is topper rammed fair o'er 'is forrid... it were raining... so, I didn't catch ought but a glimpse of 'is face." He opened his hands in a conciliatory gesture.

"Average height, clean and neat. Hmmm... black hair, I think. Came in a plain, black, two-horse carriage with no coat of arms, leastways none I could see. All's I can say with any degree of certainty is that whoever sent him was not short of a bob or two. Sorry, not to be of any better help."

"Thank you, Higgins. That is actually very helpful, and I believe I have fathomed the sender." Leland smiled without humour and dismissed the pair. "That will be all. Oh, I may need the carriage in the morning."

Barnes closed the door, leaving Leland to his thoughts. This needed to be nipped in the bud. Give them... *her* an inch and she will take a mile. Blackmail was an ugly word, and he was *not* about to capitulate. To disguise herself as a man and have the effrontery to hand the letter to his footman. Oh no.

Withers, that's who he needed to see. Withers was just the man to deal with this. Honest, trustworthy, and best of all, discreet.

"Madeline Galleron, you wicked, wicked woman," he declared to the quiet room. "You will rue the day you tried to best me."

In the silence, his conscience nudged him. *She might be wicked, but did she not have cause?*

Leland ignored it. He was not the one stooping to blackmail.

What other recourse does she have? The, extremely irritating, voice of reason needled. *You cannot believe your conduct was acceptable?*

"Damn and blast it all to hell." Leland propelled himself out of his seat but, as he paced the study, muttering ominously, a quote from the bible popped into his head. *Be sure your sins will find you out…*

He sank back onto the comfortable leather, steepled his fingers together and stopped trying to justify his actions.

In general, an honest man, Lord Tynnet forced himself to face the truth. The idea of forbidden sex had been irresistible, especially as his marriage… arranged while he was in the cradle… was one he endured rather than enjoyed. When first wed, his wife had suffered his attentions with little enthusiasm, and they had not been intimate for years.

That did not excuse him. He had delighted in bedding Madeline. What red-blooded male wouldn't? A beautiful young lady, ripe for the taking — one who was *not* a whore, and, therefore, clean. That Galleron often watched, while initially a trifle… unnerving, as though his performance was being evaluated, eventually enhanced the thrill of the clandestine encounters.

He did not think the countess had been averse. Galleron swore that Madeline was a willing participant and, in fact, he thought himself rather masterful. He recalled her crying out when he brought her to the peak, conveniently forgetting her quiescence, her abject misery and the self-hatred swirling in her defeated gaze.

He slammed his palm on the desk, welcoming the sting. He would settle the debt. Twenty-eight pounds was a small price to pay but, if he detected the slightest whiff that Lady Parham expected more out of him, the letter would go straight to Major Withers.

Satisfied with his decision, he made a few notes then retired to the drawing room and his pipe.

Three days later, a terse missive was delivered.

It read; *You are absolved of your malfeasance.*

Not a man who gave credence to a higher power, Leland Castor sent up a heartfelt prayer that it was so.

On the same day, Lord Tynnet's *error of judgement* was nullified, Madeline, to her astonishment, received an invitation to a ball hosted by Lord and Lady Bennet, the Baron and Baroness Merryfield.

Mildly unsettled, she placed the gilt-edged card with its elegant script on the mantel and stood back. Hands on hips, she studied the white oblong intently, as though expecting it to explain how she came to be on the guest list. An odd and rather belated inclusion, all things considered.

Madeline had not attended anything since her husband's death; mourning provided the perfect excuse.

This ball provided the perfect opportunity. Lord Grenville Bennet just happened to be her penultimate target. His visits had dwindled during the second year, but that did not exonerate him. In his early fifties, Lord Merryfield was a childhood friend of Raymond, and — to outward appearances — a devoted husband and father.

How Bennet had been caught in his friend's web, Madeline was never able to determine, but his affection for his wife could be the reason his *visits* were over almost before they began. His rapidity implied a trepidation — perhaps of being caught in the act, while too weak-willed to extricate himself from Raymond's snare. A personable gentleman, the baron always thanked her, a courtesy at variance with his actions.

Madeline had allowed a fortnight to elapse between each letter. Regrettably, the date of the ball fell outside her schedule, however, this sparked an idea which would avoid establishing a pattern — should anyone feel moved to investigate — and add a furtive flair to her next delivery.

All it required was a little stealth, and a propitious moment.

Madeline rifled through her wardrobe and, in keeping with her supposed grief over her husband's untimely demise, chose a gown in a hue reminiscent of dense forests, so dark it was almost black. Only when the light caught the shimmering silk did the green become apparent.

Hideously expensive, Madeline had no qualms about spending Galleron's coin.

Her argument — the one and only time he queried an account from the modiste — was that if he expected her to dress like a countess, he had to pay for the privilege; moreover, it was the least he could do… under the circumstances.

Her unflinching gaze had pinned him in place until he inclined his head. While her recriminations for his deplorable conduct were subtle, they were also inexorable — and he only had himself to blame.

He never questioned her expenses again.

Madeline had yet to wear this particular gown, Raymond decreed it too sombre for Society, but she loved it, glad she had bowed to Madame Renaud's expert opinion.

At first glance, the inky colour seemed drab, but it complemented Madeline's creamy skin, ebony hair, and emerald green eyes, giving the dress a vibrance few could carry off.

Madeline lifted it out and hung it on the door of her armoire, nodding in approval. It was entirely appropriate.

An unexpected prickle of excitement skittered down her spine. Her first ball as a widow. A chance to see how she was treated and, if any of her… libertines attended, whether they would acknowledge her.

Her mouth twisted sardonically, a fascinating prospect.

CHAPTER NINE

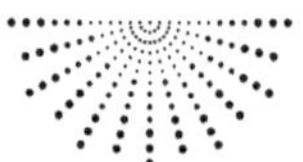

While Madeline was choosing which gown to wear at the Merryfields' ball, across town — in far less salubrious surroundings — Wolfstan Colleville was no closer to exposing Lord Swinbourne's blackmailer, than the day the earl had stormed into the unassuming office on Bow Street.

He had suffered several soirees, four musical evenings, and a ball, hoping to hear something… *anything* of value. He had even attended the theatre — twice, his least favourite pastime. The plays were dreadful and the gossip trivial.

Hours expended with nothing to show for them.

"Never assume time spent investigating is wasted," Lucas had placated when Wolfstan bemoaned his lack of success. "You never know when a snippet of information evolves into something relevant or provides a link to something crucial. It might not be connected to the case on which you are working, but vital all the same."

"I concede your point but that does not temper my exasperation," Wolfstan replied gloomily.

"Have you scrutinised his business associates, parliamentary colleagues, family members, friends?"

"Exhaustively. Everyone concurs, Swinbourne is a decent chap. Nothing underhand has come to light. Not to mention, *I* know him and have never seen a hint of impropriety. It will require a different approach. If there is even the faintest trace of scandal attached to him, no one is forthcoming. Coincidentally, one of our maids is cousin to one of their footmen. Cyril thinks the sun rises and sets with the earl. Seems he is a generous employer."

"Not everyone agrees with Cyril," Lucas said dryly.

Wearily, Wolfstan rubbed a hand around the back of his neck. "Whoever wrote the poem is referring to something known only to the recipient, yet so distressing it cannot be defined overtly." He pulled the card from the file on his desk and read it out loud.

"For the sin committed. What sin? Avarice, pride, wrath, envy, lust, gluttony, sloth." Wolfstan ticked off the cardinal seven on his fingers. "Next line. And the pain endured. What pain? Corporeal or of the mind? Has Swinbourne hurt someone, inadvertently or otherwise? That covers murder, adultery, theft."

Lucas took the card. "For the respect omitted." His brow creased. "The respect omitted. We must presume, given the tone of the poem, certain rules have been overstepped or, and more likely, flouted completely."

"Which would also secure her — we agree this was written by a woman — silence and, expanding that thread, could result in her dignity being stolen," Wolfstan mused.

"All of which would ruin a person's happiness." Lucas extended that thought to its logical conclusion. "What about 'for promises broken'?"

"I surmise she is alluding to marriage or, at the very least, a betrothal?" Wolfstan offered. "Are we looking for a lady whose chance at marriage has been ruined by a heinous act? A lady whose reputation has been irrevocably ruined. I struggle to equate that with the Lord Swinbourne we know."

They looked at each other. To cancel a wedding, while not unheard of was a rare occurrence, especially if the union was arranged. Dislike of your intended was not enough to sever an agreement your respective parents had signed years before — which was why husbands took mistresses, while their wives turned a blind eye.

"The letter, dated May third, states payment is expected within a week. Today is the twenty fourth. Allowing for that seven days' grace, recompense is a fortnight overdue. Will there be a similarly crafted second ultimatum, or will the follow-up be less… private?" Lucas pondered out loud.

"I cannot think a lady would wish the world to know of her suffering."

"I concur. I predict our esteemed Lord Swinbourne will be pounding up yon stairs in the not-too-distant future." Lucas nodded towards the office door with an exaggerated eye roll. "Perhaps it might prove interesting to call upon his lordship, to remind him of the deadline. Gauge his reaction, press him about the poem. He is hiding something. Has to be."

The two men discussed the matter a little longer then, given they could make no more progress that day, addressed any other matters requiring attention. There was always plenty to keep them occupied.

The Lodge

The morning before the ball, Mr Blake announced Mr Emory de Wilton, and was my lady receiving?

"Yes, thank you, Mr Blake, please show him in, and please organise some refreshments. Mr de Wilton does like a hot coffee." Madeline smiled at the butler, who ushered Emory into the drawing room and left, closing the door behind him with a quiet click.

"Emory, what brings you to The Lodge?"

Emory bowed over Madeline's hand, waited until she had taken a seat, then made himself comfortable in the adjacent chair. "I come to ask a favour," his tone bordered on the dramatic.

"A favour? Of me? I am intrigued. Pray, do go on." Madeline's eyes danced with mischief.

"You know Winifred Cardon?"

Madeline dredged through her brain.

"Lord Mayhew's daughter?" Emory prompted.

"Wait, 'tis coming to me. Her mother, Serena, married Baron Oakford. After his death, she wed Jonathan Cardon, the aforementioned Lord Mayhew. Her older sister, Justina, now lives in Ireland, yes?" With a jubilant beam, Madeline sat back, pleased with her recollection.

"In a nutshell." Emory grinned. "Recently, Winifred was struck down with a nasty bout of fever and is staying with her brother because Lady Mayhew had to travel to Ireland to be with Justina. First baby," he expounded at Madeline's quirked brow.

"To divert Winifred, Edward… her brother… invented a case and asked for her help in solving it. In turn, she asked for me to be included. She believes we are on the trail of a sneaky thief, who robs members of the nobility during Society events."

"That sounds a mite implausible, are you sure she does

not suspect the whole thing is a sham?" Madeline shook her head. "She must be very gullible."

"Not at all, Freddie is sharp as a blade. She would make a good spy. Very little escapes her attention."

"So, why do you need a favour?"

"I'm coming to that. To maintain the subterfuge, I have escorted her to the usual affairs. Any behaviour we determined questionable, we reported to Edward. Everything was going smoothly until Ernest set his sights on Freddie."

Madeline was cognisant with Ernest's reputation as a rake. "Oh dear."

"Oh dear, indeed. I am of the opinion, Freddie thinks she is one to tame him, but I know my twin. He is having fun, not toying with her affection as much as enjoying the game and is not in the slightest interested in having that curtailed. I have been invited to Baron Merryfield's ball, tomorrow night, and my favour is to ask whether you might be kind enough to accompany me."

"Are you not taking Freddie?"

"Ernest beat me to it. Georgina is in Town, and he is squiring the two of them. My sister is no more prudent than Freddie, and I prefer to keep an eye on the pair of them."

"In essence, you are using me to conceal the fact you are spying on your brother?" Madeline quizzed, without rancour.

"In part, and in part, desirous of observing the reactions of the other guests when we arrive together." Emory chuckled unrepentantly. "In truth, I am under instruction from Edward to watch over Freddie who does not take kindly to being… supervised. I take such responsibility seriously, and 'tis unlikely she will question my presence if I have a beautiful lady on my arm."

"Thank you." Madeline accepted the compliment graciously. "I must say, this seems to be above and beyond the call of duty. Do you perhaps harbour an affection for Winifred?" she postulated.

Emory flushed, his gaze sliding away before coming back to meet Madeline's. "I have no idea what you mean."

Madeline did not press, his reaction eloquent enough.

"As it transpires, I too have received an invitation to the Merryfields' ball. I shall be honoured to attend with you. It will make a change to be on the arm of someone I actually like." Her expression, droll.

Mr Blake entered bearing coffee and a plate of fresh ginger biscuits, which the pair consumed with gusto. They moved onto other topics, and soon Emory took his leave, affirming he would call for her at nine the following evening.

Little did Madeline know how many people would be affected by her actions, or how far the ripples would spread.

Elm Grove, Baron Merryfield's residence belied the lowly title of its owner. The grand mansion — just off Grosvenor Square and nestled in extensive gardens — took up half the street. All manner of conveyances, from magnificent coaches to modest hackneys, queued… almost patiently… until able to disgorge their exquisitely attired passengers.

Ascending the short flight of steps, guests were welcomed into a scene of light and colour.

The delicate fragrances permeating the air from the profusion of floral arrangements, complemented by the abundance of trailing greenery atop pedestals and framing the open windows, created an atmosphere of summer delight. An ambience enhanced by sparkling chandeliers, dainty wall sconces, and numerous candelabra, turning night into day.

"The baron has spared no expense," Madeline murmured to Emory as they were announced, stifling an unladylike bark of laughter at the swivelling of heads, and whispering behind fans. "Oh, I intend to enjoy this."

The couple swept into the ballroom, apparently oblivious to the stunned expressions of their peers.

Madeline, elegance personified, smiled and nodded to strangers and acquaintances alike. Spying Kitty — blooming, following the birth of her second daughter at the end of March, Adam beside her — waving madly to attract her attention, she made a beeline for them.

"Good evening, Madeline." Kitty drew her friend into a hug. "You look positively regal, that gown is sublime."

"Your compliment is reciprocated wholeheartedly. I did not expect to see you, so soon after Eleanor's birth." Madeline replied, holding Kitty's hands to admire the rich turquoise of her friend's dress; neither woman adhering to the current fashion for insipid pastels. "What a glorious gown. Good evening, Lord Teasdale," She turned to the marquis, dipping a neat curtsy.

"I refuse to lie abed for weeks on end, it would drive me to distraction, and Adam prefers I wear vivid shades," Kitty confided. "He can distinguish them better than the paler colours."

"Please call me Adam." Kitty's husband smiled, the gesture transforming his grave countenance. "I am not one to stand on ceremony among friends."

Madeline blushed prettily. "I should be pleased to, my lor… Adam, on the proviso you call me Madeline."

He bowed. "It would be my honour." He moved his head slightly. "de Wilton, how goes it?" The two men fell into conversation, as Kitty ushered Madeline into the chair adjacent to hers.

"I confess, I am surprised to see you," Kitty said. "In a good way," she added hurriedly. "I suspected large gatherings might yet be uncomfortable for you."

"My reasons are two-fold," Madeline admitted. "I am here to assist Emory in his endeavours to keep an eye on Freddie, who is attending with Ernest. The girl has developed a *tendre* for Ernest, and her brother has asked Emory to ensure nothing… unfortunate happens," Madeline clarified at Kitty's uncomprehending frown.

"Ahhh, yes. Lord Langley is every mother's torment." Kitty nodded sagely.

"I suspect Freddie thinks she might be the one to curb his wild ways. Emory and, presumably, Edward Lindsay do not share her optimism."

Kitty studied her friend. "And the second reason?"

Madeline did not answer immediately. Instead, she withdrew a little package from the hidden pocket in her gown.

"Madeline…?" Kitty's voice rose a notch. "What are you up to?"

"Merely delivering a letter." Madeline rejoined primly.

"*Delivering a letter*? At a ball? Do you think me witless?" Kitty retorted. "Madeline Galleron, what are you up to?"

"It seemed felicitous. Much easier than calling during the day and handing it to a footman. No one will notice if I slip away from the ballroom for a moment."

Recollecting their many conversations, Kitty held Madeline's gaze. "Do you not trust me?"

"I trust you more than anyone in my life, but you cannot be held accountable for what you do not know."

"Pfft," was Kitty's snorted response. "You forget to whom you are talking, my dear. Are you committing a crime?"

Madeline hesitated.

"Madeline," Kitty's subdued wail caught the attention of Adam and Emory.

"Is something amiss?" Adam moved to stand behind his wife.

"I believe there is a decent possibility," Kitty grumbled. "My delightful friend here may well be flouting the law."

Madeline looked at the trio surrounding her and shifted in her seat. "Oh, for goodness' sake, your theatrics are misplaced. I am simply seeking a soupçon of justice for past… slights."

"Justice?" Emory and Adam spoke in unison, although Emory's reaction was less startled than Adam's.

Solicitously, Kitty reached out to squeeze Madeline's fingers. "Please do not risk your freedom. You have only just regained it."

"I must do this. I *need* to do this. I will never be free until they have made restitution," Madeline countered.

"They?" Adam sounded puzzled. Evidently, Kitty had not imparted the entirety of Madeline's secret to her husband.

There was a long silence, during which three pairs of eyes skewered Madeline to her chair.

Debating whether or not to make an indecorous run for it, Madeline was conscious she would more likely trip over her skirts than escape.

With obvious reluctance, she capitulated. "Fine. If you promise not to stand in my way, or report me, I shall disclose my, for want of a better word, scheme."

Emory opened his mouth, but before he could speak, she added, "Those are my terms. This is not something I impart lightly."

Pledges sworn, Madeline, skipping the more… brutal details, divulged her revenge.

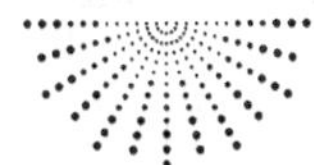

olfstan Colleville skirted the ballroom, a headache brewing. He was beginning to hate these functions with a passion. Social gatherings, never his first choice of entertainment, were wearing thin.

Worse, he did not know who he was looking for, judging it unlikely the woman behind the letter was about to advertise the fact at a ball. Subtlety appeared to be her preferred method.

Rubbing his chin broodingly, he weighed up the benefits of dallying at the Merryfields' until the early hours of the morning, or heading home for a decent night's sleep.

The latter was gaining favour when his gaze fell on a vaguely familiar figure. At the far side of the room, deep in conversation with three people Wolfstan knew well, sat a woman whose face had pestered his subconscious for weeks.

He stopped in his tracks and, drink in hand, leant against a convenient pillar to observe the lady in question.

Raven hair swept up into an elaborate twist. Alabaster skin, almost dewy in the candlelight. Her black gown, no, wait... when she rose to her feet, the material flowing around her… it was the darkest shade of green, evoking a mysterious forest under a waning moon. *Moonlight? Mysterious forests? Really Wolf,* he chided himself.

She smiled and said something to her companions who looked mildly perturbed but did not prevent her departure.

His feet took him across the floor with ungentlemanly alacrity. "My lady, Lord Teasdale." He bowed. "de Wilton, well met."

"Colleville, I did not pick you as a social butterfly," Emory jested, as Kitty dragged Wolfstan into the seat Madeline had just vacated.

"This is business, not pleasure," Wolfstan gave an exaggerated eye roll, making them chuckle.

"Goodness what a night for intrigue." Kitty dimpled. "Are you permitted to tell us."

Wolfstan pricked up his ears, while shaking his head. "Regrettably, no. I'm working on a rather sensitive case where diplomacy is key. To change the subject, because I know you want me to elucidate and, honestly, I cannot…" he twinkled at Kitty who assumed an innocent expression, "… might I ask the name of the young lady who just left?"

All three exchanged glances, piquing Wolfstan's interest further. "'Tis only that I believe we met once. In truth, an encounter so brief it was barely a 'hello,' but…" he tapped his chin thoughtfully and did not finish his sentence.

Kitty held her tongue, aware Wolfstan would not be coaxed into revealing anything unless it was pertinent to do so. Time would tell.

"Lady Parham," Emory supplied. Further details were unnecessary; all in the *ton* knew of her husband's demise.

"Thank you." Wolfstan inclined his head, his brain slotting her into a 'to be revisited' compartment. "If you will excuse me."

He was gone before they could object.

"Well," Kitty exclaimed. "Did you ever?"

"I most certainly did not," Adam mimicked her tone, which resulted in an elbow to his ribs. "Never mind young Carnforth, would you like to dance?"

"I thought you would never ask." Kitty beamed. Adam took her hand; she stood and lifted onto her toes to brush her lips to his cheek.

"I'll fetch us some refreshments," Emory said, watching Kitty lead her husband onto the dance floor.

"Thank you," her reply floated back to him over the strains of the music.

Grinning after the couple, Emory strolled in the same direction Madeline had taken, heading for the dining room, his head whirling with the latter's revelations.

While part of him, the law-abiding solicitor part of him worried Madeline would be caught, the rest lauded her resolve. It was a rare occasion when a woman was able to exact a modicum of retribution in so perspicacious a manner.

Intent on filling several plates with a selection of dainty morsels, Emory did not register the commotion at first, but a muffled disturbance seemed to be growing louder. A trifle concerned, he turned in the general direction, to see a slender figure whisk passed him in a flurry of dark silk.

Madeline.

Emory frowned, and was about to forestall her, when he heard a familiar voice. *Freddie. An affronted Freddie.* He pinched the bridge of his nose. *This did not bode well. What have you done, this time, Ernest?*

Dropping the plates onto the table with little regard for the delicate china, he hotfooted it along the corridor to see what the fuss was about.

. . .

Coincidentally, Wolfstan who, as inconspicuously as possible, was trying to find Lady Parham, happened along the same corridor. Using his considerable height to his advantage, he peered over the heads of the small crowd gathered at the door of the baron's study. Within the room, he spied a dishevelled young lady in a tussle with... wait, was that *Emory?*

He elbowed his way to the front of the group and, to a chorus of tuts, closed the door quietly. "I think perhaps a moment might be in order," he said firmly.

"He's assaulting her," an overly bejewelled middle-aged lady, with spiteful beady eyes — Wolfstan recognised as the Countess Sele — screeched.

"I sincerely doubt that," Wolfstan refuted politely, "and jumping to conclusions is presumptuous."

"She was," the woman lowered her voice to a spiteful hiss, "disrobed."

"I beg to disagree." Wolfstan stared at the speaker until she had the grace to blush, but she refused to be silenced.

"Compromised. You mark my words, she is compromised. Her poor dear mother will be distraught when she hears."

Her shrill voice echoed along the hall, leaving Wolfstan certain that the unfortunate young lady's parents would be informed with gleeful and exaggerated relish. Regrettably, rumours would be circulating already, and the gossips never permitted the truth to interfere with a good story.

Clandestine trysts were not unusual at balls, everyone knew they occurred, but to be caught in the act could result in unwanted and irreversible repercussions.

Through the heavy wood of the door, he heard the soft click of a latch followed by a heated yet muffled conversation, then felt an eddy of air drift around his ankles as though another door had been opened.

The handful of people gathered in the hall, loitered. That they might be witness to a scandal, too thrilling to miss.

"Perhaps a return to the ballroom," Wolfstan used his most persuasive tone, to no avail.

Lady Sele folded her arms across her impressive bosom and stood her ground. "I shall remain here until I know the gel has not been dishonoured."

Wolfstan prayed for patience. "Is it, perchance, conceivable the gel does not wish to suffer further humiliation? If the worst has indeed happened, to face a sea of judgement could cause her unnecessary upset."

Mutterings of agreement circled the cluster of people...

"He is correct."

"Difficult situation."

"Youngsters these days, no morals."

...and the like.

Right at this moment, the door opened with such vigour, Wolfstan nearly fell backwards into the study. He managed to maintain his footing and spun around to see Emory with a dark-haired young lady, whose gown appeared to have challenged a rose bush to a fight and lost.

A crumpled black petal clung to her tattered décolletage... compounding his impression... which she was clutching tightly, her modesty saved by Emory's jacket slung across her shoulders. Her eyes were downcast and her cheeks fiery red.

"Oh, good evening, good evening. How lovely to see you." Emory's face was wreathed in smiles. "Forgive a foolish romantic. In my joy, I had a lapse of etiquette. My apologies.

"Miss Cardon has bestowed on me the greatest honour and consented to be my wife. I confess, in our... err... enthusiasm to... errr... seal our betrothal, the button of my jacket snagged the lace on her gown. My poor dear beloved does not deserve to be the brunt of gossips. I shall escort her home... in company of her chaperone before anyone thinks me behaving without due propriety."

Wolfstan gaped at his friend. This was a patent obfuscation. The Emory de Wilton he knew had eschewed the bonds of matrimony for the bonds of the law.

Emory caught his eye, sending a silent message, which Wolfstan interpreted with a speed honed from years of distinguishing between the finest nuances employed by both Society and suspects — the former being significantly more artful than the latter.

He inclined his head in acknowledgement; he would extract the truth soon enough.

"You owe me," he said to Emory out of the corner of his mouth, before smoothing his features and flapping his hands at the spectators. "As I surmised, nothing is as it seems, and we are grateful your concern was unfounded. Instead of a crisis we have cause for celebration."

He smiled at Lady Sele and her nosey coterie who, to his relief, allowed themselves to be ushered away from the scene.

Madeline forgotten for the time being, Wolfstan wound his way back to Kitty and Adam who were none the wiser.

"I take your intriguing and toss in a dumbfounding," he said as he sat down.

"Do I sense an exposé," Kitty joked.

"Literally and figuratively," Wolfstan's expression gave nothing away.

Kitty's eyes widened. She leant closer to the viscount. "I beg your pardon?"

"Wait and see." Was the unsatisfactory answer.

· · ·

As predicted, and with indecent exuberance, Lady Sele set tongues wagging.

"Emory and Freddie?" Kitty clapped her hand over her mouth to check the nonsense about to spill over. "I cannot fathom…" she stopped, took a breath, and wagged her fan thoughtfully. "Perhaps…" she let that dangle, ignoring the curious looks from the two men. "I need to speak with my reprobate brother. Ernest."

Adam reached for her hand. "This is not your business, sweetheart. Ernest and Emory are all grown up. They need to learn to handle their own mistakes."

"When a young lady appears to have been placed in an untenable position, it becomes my business," she contradicted. "Mama and Papa are not here to be the voice of reason, 'tis my responsibility."

"Then might I suggest you wait until the morning? You know Ernest does not take kindly to his behaviour being called into question, and Emory has a sensible head on his shoulders. He does not do anything without due consideration."

"Normally, I would agree, but not in this instance. Emory's decision was precipitated by something which happened here, tonight, at this ball. Wolfstan?" Kitty turned a penetrating gaze on the viscount.

He raised his palms in a conciliatory fashion. "My dear, Lady Teasdale, hand on heart, I do not know the circumstances behind Emory's announcement, but he is a shrewd chap. For what it is worth, I believe he is acting with the utmost chivalry. I agree with Adam, sleep on it. Now," he sought to divert. "What can you tell me about Lady Parham?"

Oblivious to the furore which had exploded on her heels, Madeline leant back against the soft leather of the carriage seat and contemplated her evening. Quite successful, despite being coerced into confessing her crusade.

She had attempted to find Emory to inform him she was going home, but he seemed to have vanished off the face of the earth.

Hopefully, he had plucked up the courage to ask Winifred to dance. Picturing them as a couple was easy, if only Winifred could see beyond Ernest's seductive magnetism. Madeline heaved a sigh, falling under the spell of a man like Ernest was all but inevitable. His devil-may-care attitude — irresistible.

From the dawn of time, young women had been attracted to rogues, reprobates, and rakes, yet, from her observations, it was the unassuming, kind, honourable, and old-fashioned gentlemen whose affection never strayed, whose passion was reserved for the one to whom he gave his heart.

A whimsical smile curved her lips. *You should not touch champagne,* she chided internally, *your cynicism wanes.*

Emory's light was usually clouded by his twin's brilliance. As the quieter, and oft deemed rather stuffy of the two, Emory's qualities were disregarded, yet these were the very traits Madeline considered appealing.

Setting Freddie and Emory aside, she pondered Baron Merryfield's reaction to the letter and whether he possessed the gallantry... or guilt... to pay his dues, which reminded her — the estimable Lord Masham had yet to discharge his account.

She tapped her chin thoughtfully. The earl need not think he could ignore her request. *Hmmm, how to give him a... nudge.* A range of possibilities came to mind, only to be discarded;

Madeline conceding, while undoubtedly justified, each might be considered a tad… excessive. She was already teetering on the brink of breaking the law, the last thing she needed was to fall headfirst over the edge.

As the carriage drew up outside The Lodge, she was no closer to a solution.

Hopefully, a good night's sleep might offer some clarity.

CHAPTER ELEVEN

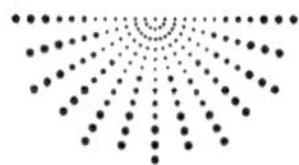

Two days later, Emory and Freddie, the ever-faithful Agatha... Freddie's personal maid and sometime chaperone in tow… entered a quiet atrium on Bow Street.

"Good morning, Mr Hughes," Emory greeted the man sitting behind the desk at the far side of the space." Is Major Withers around?"

"Morning, Mr de Wilton, No, but—" Mr Hughes started to explain.

At that moment the door at the top of the stairs opened and Wolfstan appeared. "de Wilton, we meet again. What brings you all the way down here?" His eyes widened a fraction at Freddie's presence.

"We have something for Lucas," Emory replied diplomatically.

"Come up, come up," Wolfstan invited and turned on his heel.

Agatha indicated she preferred to remain in the atrium, smiling when Mr Hughes offered to make a brew. "Thank you, sir, tea would be very welcome."

Emory ushered Freddie up the stairs and into the long desk-lined room where he had spent more than an odd day. If the law had not been his calling, Emory could see himself as a member of Lucas' organisation. Both involved deciphering mysteries in one form or another, and danger could be found in the most unlikely of places.

Wolfstan led them to his desk, which was scattered with papers and books, and brought each a chair. "Sit, sit. Nate." He addressed the man at the adjacent desk. "Might you be so kind as to rustle up some refreshments for Emory and Miss Cardon," his sharp brain recalling her name from the kerfuffle at the ball.

"Happy to," Nate replied. "I need a break from this nonsense anyway." He sent the trio a long-suffering grimace and strode away.

"Now," Wolfstan said as they sipped steaming coffee and munched on ginger biscuits. "Firstly, may I extend my congratulations?"

"Thank you." Emory grinned. Freddie lowered her gaze and said nothing, but the pink tinge stealing up her cheeks told its own tale.

Aware of undercurrents, Wolfstan, giving Freddie time to compose herself, asked, "How may I be of help?"

"As this is a rather convoluted tale, I will give you the abridged version and flesh it out should you gauge it necessary," Emory prevaricated, hoping he could avoid mentioning the puzzle, Edward Lindsay — another of Withers' operatives — had set to distract Freddie, unsure whether Wolfstan knew.

"I am intrigued." Wolfstan opened his hand. "Please go on."

"Miss Cardon noticed something untoward at Lord Merryfield's ball."

"Ahhh, and am I to assume this was the reason for the… err… scene in the study?" Wolfstan was quick on the uptake.

"Precisely," Emory paused, then launched in. "Until this morning, Miss Cardon's well-being remained my priority, but further detail has come to light, about which I have some inkling."

Wolfstan registered that Emory was fighting an internal debate. *Wheels within wheels.*

"Do you trust me?" he asked quietly.

"Of course, why do you think we are here and not next door?"

"Is the issue one of criminality?"

Emory's hesitation was answer enough.

"Perhaps you had better tell me everything. Fear not, Miss Cardon." Wolfstan smiled at Freddie encouragingly. "Discretion is our motto. Confidences shared here are safer than those told in the confessional."

Emory glanced at Freddie who squared her shoulders. "It is not as eas—"

A deep sigh accompanied by a, "Let me tell him, Emory. Thank you for trying to shield me, but this debacle is my fault," stayed Emory's equivocation.

Wolfstan noticed Emory flinch when Freddie said debacle. *Dash it all, not only is he saving Miss Cardon's honour, but also he has fallen for her. That explained the scene at the ball. What a pickle.*

Setting that aside for now, he concentrated on Miss Cardon.

"My brother had set me a task. One, I am beginning to deduce was nothing more than a ruse to keep me, in his terms, out of mischief. Tsk… he and I are due a quiet chat." She canted her head pensively.

"Sorry, yes, as I was saying, a task, which was to keep an eye on anything suspicious at the various social gatherings of the Season. Regardless of Edward's reasoning, I admit I enjoyed the challenge. Balls can be tedious, picnics full of twittering gossips, and all utterly exhausting." Her expression wry.

Wolfstan chuckled, and the hint of tension in the air lifted.

"Nothing noteworthy had happened, until two nights ago, when I spied a woman leaving the baron's study… alone. In and of itself, not particularly significant, except her demeanour was furtive, and she sidled out of the room, checked the corridor, then hugged the walls when she hurried away, as though trying to hide in the shadows, remain unseen."

Freddie shrugged. "Edward told me that if something looks out of place, there's usually a good… or a bad reason. I was with Ernest." Her colour heightened, but she continued, "I wanted a witness, you know, just in case. There was no one else in the room, but on the desk, I found this." She handed Wolfstan a crumpled and slightly torn sheet of paper.

"There was a dead rose tucked into that ribbon." She pointed to the thin band of silk tied around the sheet. "In the err… excitement, it ended up on the carpet."

Wolfstan recalled the petal clinging to the lacy neckline of Miss Cardon's gown.

A letter and a dead rose… this was no coincidence. He swallowed an impulse to yell *huzzah* and waved the letter. "May I?"

"It is not my place to prevent you," Freddie replied primly.

Wolfstan unfolded the paper and laid it on his desk to smooth out the crinkles.

26th May

Dear Lord Merryfield,

I ought to thank you for the generous invitation to this ball, although I remain confused as to your motivation. Perhaps your lovely wife suggested it might look a trifle strange if you did not include the widow of your dearest friend.

It is all about creating an impression is it not?

You probably do not wish to know my impression, and I prefer not to revive what I have tried, with minimal success, to forget.

There is, however, a way to mitigate your... misdeeds. I will consider them expunged if you make an _anonymous_ donation to Sanctuary House in the amount of ten pounds. My choice of charity should be self-explanatory.

Like the gentleman you purport to be, it would behove you to honour my request, while I care little for my reputation, you, however...

I expect the donation to be made no later than one week from the date of this letter. Rest assured, I shall be informed immediately 'tis paid, at which point, I give you my word, any *reference to you will be obliterated from the list I hold.*

Oh, and before you act rashly, should anything, anything at all, untoward happen to me, I have given instructions for your misconduct to be broadcast.

M

This letter contained various details which solidified Wolfstan's suspicions.

The writer was definitely a woman, and she was a widow. The allusion to a friendship between Merryfield and the writer's dead husband was an added element. Was he acquainted with Swinbourne too? Not beyond the realms of possibility.

Out of the corner of his eye, Wolfstan spotted Emory nudging Miss Cardon. She glowered at him, but gave a resigned huff and, rifling in the pocket of her coat, withdraw a sadly maligned card.

"There was this also," she muttered and thrust it at Wolfstan.

Hardly daring to hope, Wolfstan pried apart the corners to flatten the card. There it was… the same poem.

He gave a muffled crow of elation. "Thank you, Miss Cardon, you have no idea how important this is. Thank you." His eyes gleamed, the threads were coming together nicely.

Unwittingly, Freddie furnished him with the last strand. "There is one more thing. I forgot in the ensuing… commotion. The woman, I do not know her name, but her face is familiar. She was married to some earl or other, I think, who was much older than she. He died, hmmm, last year's end.

"I remember Mama saying she, the lady not Mama, was

seen only occasionally after her marriage, and that it was a shame because she had been a gregarious soul, despite her family being … what was the word she used," Freddie thought back, then snapped her fingers, "that was it... censorious of her." She beamed at Wolfstan.

His brain whirring, Wolfstan returned her smile. Something Kitty Teasdale had said at the ball, when he asked about her friend — the one he had met months ago — pestered the back of his mind.

She is only recently out of mourning, her husband died last year. He was much older, and it was not a happy union. Kitty's expression saying more than her discreet remarks.

Another coincidence. A widow at a ball where a letter was left. Might be nothing... Wolfstan ruminated over the scant evidence he had managed to collate. He opened his mouth to ask the question uppermost in his mind, but Emory spoke first.

"Freddie, might you give me a minute?"

Freddie shot him an arch look. "Want me out of the way so you can speak privately?"

"You read me like a book." He patted her gloved hand, and his accompanying smile would have convinced even the most jaded sceptic of his affection for the young lady.

The young lady, who seemed utterly oblivious, nodded and, dipping a neat curtsy, excused herself.

Emory waited until she had disappeared through the door. "I know more than I am able to tell, but I gave my word. While I have no right to ask, please, if… when… you think you know the identity of the sender, I beg you to discuss your findings with me before taking the next step. This is not some prank to cause a stir. If that was the case, it would not have been done in so covert a manner. The rationale behind the letters is complex."

"I have no intention of going in half-cocked, de Wilton,

what do you take me for. Wait… letters? You know there is more than one?"

Emory cursed himself for the slip. "My lips are sealed. I told you, I will not betray a confidence."

Wolfstan took a gamble. "Is it Lady Galleron?"

It failed.

Emory was in control now and did not react. "Good day, Carnforth." He offered his hand, glad when Wolfstan shook it good-naturedly. He did not like keeping secrets, but in their line of work, it was inevitable.

"I promise to contact you." Wolfstan inclined his head.

"That's all I ask."

Emory caught up with Freddie and Agatha, leaving Wolfstan to reflect on their meeting.

Why these two men? Who else had received a letter? Emory's lapse was enlightening, there must be others. Was this a serial blackmailer, the victims chosen at random, or were the targets limited by a common denominator. The latter seemed more likely, especially given the demand was not for personal gain, it was for charity.

Additionally, Lord Merryfield remained incognisant of the fact he was expected to pay the price for an as yet undisclosed infraction. What would happen if remuneration was not made?

His quick mind swung to Lord Swinbourne. His remittance was overdue. Were repercussions in the offing? It seemed probable, but in what form?

Wolfstan jotted down his thoughts on a blank sheet of paper, adding a name at the bottom.

He could not prove it, but instinct told him his guess was correct.

Madeline paced up and down the library, ruminating over what to do about Swinbourne. Why was he shilly-shallying? Did he think by ignoring the letter, he could pretend he had not received it? *Fool.*

Letters, letters, there was no point sending him another letter, he needed a sharp jolt to make him realise this was not a game or some half-hearted attempt at blackmail. *A shame I cannot administer a swift bang on the head with a skillet.*

Yes, technically it *was* blackmail, but Madeline preferred to think of it as being more along the lines of justifiable restitution.

The faintest inkling of something teased the edge of her mind but, try as she might it remained annoyingly out of reach.

"No help for it," she gave up. "I need a distraction."

The day was warm and, in place of a spencer, she opted for her favourite light-wool shawl, in the most divine shade of violet. Digging a parasol… less confining than a hated hat… out of the stand next to the coat rack, she informed Blake she was going for a walk, and headed into the sunshine.

A long constitutional ought to clear her head and she knew just the place. Hyde Park at this hour should be reasonably quiet, too early for the fashionable set to be abroad.

Her brisk stride covered the short distance quickly and, within minutes, she was wandering along empty pathways, listening to the soft quack of the ducks, the chirping of the birds, and the rustle of leaves in the pleasant breeze.

The day was too beautiful to be marred by thoughts of revenge, and Madeline pushed everything out of her mind to enjoy the tranquillity. She walked for over an hour, threading her way around the spider's web of tracks, eventually coming to a bench overlooking the Serpentine.

Sinking onto the cool wood, she let her mind roam. The idyllic scene conjured up her dream; the one she seldom had any more. Her noble knight… her lip curled sardonically. *No such thing*. Men were only interested in slaking their lust. Romance, loyalty, fidelity… love… did not rank high on their list of husbandly attributes.

She stirred restlessly. No, she was being unfair. Not every man was a boor. Adam and Hugh adored their wives and would surely die for them, but they were the exception. Even Emory would make a good, dependable husband — a man who would never stray, regardless of whether his wife bore him any affection.

Madeline blew a sigh. The lucky few. She had only just reached her majority, yet the years stretched out ahead of her, barren and bleak. Oh, to have someone love her beyond reason or explanation, what bliss, simultaneously, conceding that her ordeal left her with too many scars. Could she ever trust a man not to hurt her, or reveal the truth without fear? She wished for the impossible.

"It would be easier to snatch the stars from the sky," she announced to the foraging waterfowl… who took no notice.

The intricate patterns thrown across the ground by the sunlight through the trees were soporific, and before Madeline knew it, she was asleep.

CHAPTER TWELVE

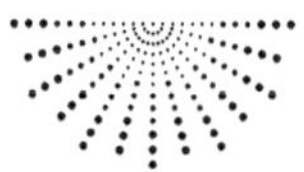

"My lady? My lady? Are you unwell?" A voice penetrated her cocoon of comfort.

"'Tis too early, leave me abed," Madeline mumbled, and tried to recapture the dream, but it was gone like a wisp of smoke.

"My lady," the voice was more urgent now and she blinked, drowsily. The lake came into focus, prompting her to squint, *what a peculiar angle.* Light dawned and she shot upright, swallowing a groan as her neck muscles protested.

"My lady?" The speaker was male and sounded solicitous.

"Forgive me. Goodness, how indecorous." Madeline felt hectic colour staining her cheeks as she rose to her feet, smoothing her skirts while striving to regain her dignity.

"No, 'tis I who ought to apologise. I should not have disturbed you, except you looked a trifle pale and I was concerned you had fainted, or worse."

Madeline looked up. The speaker was in silhouette, compelling her to shade her eyes in order to see him.

She frowned. He seemed familiar, but she could not place him.

"Thank you for your concern. As you can see, there is no cause for alarm. It serves me right for napping in the middle of the park." She offered a diffident smile.

"If you are certain, then I bid you good day." He held his topper and tipped his head. He took three steps, hesitated, and turned around.

"I beg your pardon, but I believe we have met before, oddly enough in this very park. It was some months ago. You are Lady Parham?"

"I am she," Madeline replied, a trifle warily. As she sketched a curtsy, a name popped into her head. "Wait… Lord Carnforth?" Recalling the morning to which he referred, her blush deepened.

He bowed again. "The very same. Considering the circumstances, along with the sporadic occasions I choose the longer route through the park, I might question whether this is a coincidence or Fate?" He grinned engagingly.

Madeline found herself smiling back. "It is a small world, my lord. We were bound to cross paths, so to speak, sooner or later."

"Oh, and there was I trying to instil a hint of mystery into our encounters." He chuckled. "My sister tells me, I need to stop looking for hidden meanings in everything because, in her opinion, life is not terribly complicated."

"She is fortunate indeed. I have found the opposite to be the case," Madeline replied, a trifle self-consciously. "To accept everyone, or everything, at face-value leaves you vulnerable to deceit."

Lord Carnforth showed no surprise at her remark, nor did he contradict it, saying instead, "A refreshing and unusual perspective. On that note, I shall leave you to your day. A pleasure, Lady Parham." He nodded his goodbye.

· · ·

Wolfstan did not look back, but permitted himself a small smile as he strode away. Following his intuition, and the exceedingly sparse details he had wrung out of Kitty March-main, Wolfstan had made it his business to do some digging with regard to Lady Parham.

To date, he had not unearthed much of significance, but he was a patient man and, had discovered, it was often the most trivial of details which provided the key to unravelling a mystery.

He knew where she lived and, that she seldom left the house but when she did, it was usually on foot. The woman walked everywhere, which made her reasonably easy to track. He knew her staff was loyal, and reckoned they would protect their mistress with their lives.

He had yet to gather any proof that she was the sender of the letters, but his head told him he had the culprit. What he really wanted to know was why, and what had caused such antipathy.

This morning, he had come across her by accident. Lost in thought, he scarcely registered there was anyone sitting on the bench, let alone a woman, until he was almost upon her.

His quick appraisal noted her lustrous dark hair — no bonnet to be seen — piled on her head in ringlets, and how well, despite her pallor, she suited the rich purple of her wrap.

Given his approach had not disturbed her, and genuinely concerned she had fainted, Wolfstan felt it only courteous to check her well-being. That this presented an opportunity to conduct even a brief conversation, an unexpected bonus.

He maintained the guise of vague acquaintances and did not tarry but, even so fleeting an encounter left a mark. The woman was becoming entrenched in his thoughts to a greater extent than was warranted. There was something fragile, almost ephemeral about Lady Parham, as though she might evaporate in a puff of wind. Yet Kitty had implied an indomitable strength.

He ruminated over the paradox and revised his destination.

Madeline watched the viscount until he was out of sight, struck again — as she had been all those months ago — by his confident bearing. A fine gentleman.

Shaking her head, she picked up her parasol and strolled slowly home.

One thing the episode *had* done was sharpen her wit. The glimmer of an idea nudging at the periphery of her mind had gained substance and, the moment she set foot in The Lodge, she made a beeline for the library.

Meticulously, Madeline combed the shelves, on the hunt for a book, the title of which she did not know, although she had an inkling as to where it might be among the numerous tomes.

Ignoring the dust and cobwebs showering her person liberally… *hmmm, mayhap a thorough spring clean is in order...* she removed books, checked, and replaced them.

Dawson appeared with coffee and biscuits, and she roped him in to help her.

"What are you looking for?" he asked politely, resisting the temptation to ask whether it was wise to stand on a chair to reach the shelves.

"A book detailing the consequences of adultery," she

replied without thought of Dawson's sensibilities. One did not bandy about such terms... *ever*... and especially not to your *staff*... too, *too* vulgar.

"Beggin' your pardon, my lady." With effort, Dawson, presuming he had misheard, managed to sound unperturbed.

Madeline twisted to look down at him and, brushing a cobweb off her brow, repeated herself, adding, "I believe the edition is one he found at The Wise Owl, so the volume may have Mr Abbot's name inked on the flyleaf."

To Dawson's consternation, she jumped off the chair carelessly to drop the book she was holding onto the desk.

"Perhaps we ought to collect all the books carrying Mr Abbott's name and check those first," she suggested. "Do you suppose anyone else might be willing to lend a hand?"

"Certainly, my lady," Dawson assured, aware the staff would leap off a cliff, if she asked them to, and went to rustle up anyone who was free, requesting more refreshments be organised at the same time.

The library became a hive of industry, and a neat pile of books began to form on the desk, then another, then another. The room echoed with lively chatter and, temporarily — such was the relaxed atmosphere — the task trumped titles.

For the first time in longer than she could recall, possibly for the first time in her life, Madeline had a sense of belonging. She relished the conviviality, wishing it could remain thus, acknowledging that, as soon as her staff realised how informal they were being, decorum would reassert itself.

Platters of food and cups of steaming hot coffee appeared at regular intervals. No one thought to sit down to eat it, they just munched while beavering away.

An inside picnic, Madeline smiled to herself.

By late afternoon, hot, tired, and decidedly grubby, they had accumulated four, alarmingly tall, stacks of books.

Mrs Watson opened the windows and, aided by Lottie

and Ruby, effected a thorough clean of each shelf as the books were removed, instructing Mary, the young scullery maid, to wipe each tome with a dry cloth before it was replaced.

As a semblance of order emerged from the chaos, Mrs Watson and Ruby dusted and swept until the room, spotlessly tidy now save the precarious piles of books, smelt of fresh air and linseed oil.

"Thank you very much." Madeline smiled her gratitude, unaware of the smutty smears marring her face. "I do not know what I should do without you."

Bowing and curtsying, they collected cloths, mops, buckets, and hurried out, leaving a sudden silence in their wake.

Madeline heard their banter fade as the baize door closed behind them, the cheer of the afternoon dwindling. Straightening her shoulders, she studied the books and, shaking off the momentary melancholy, set to.

An hour later, she crowed with glee. Convinced she had imagined Parham telling her about this particular work, she came upon the elusive publication.

It was old; the cover cracked with age and, given the fusty odour tickling her nose, possibly damp. Cautiously, she scanned the first page, taking care not to open it too far, for fear the binding would disintegrate.

The typeset was hard to read, but, the longer Madeline studied it, the more familiar she became with the quaint phraseology.

Avoiding the obvious question as to why her husband felt moved to purchase a book about Puritan Massachusetts — nothing about him surprised her anymore — she concentrated on pinpointing the information which must be contained therein.

. . .

She stretched her back, and rolled shoulders grown stiff from being hunched over.

Her stomach felt hollow and she glanced out of the window to see the day had been subsumed by twilight. Her gaze came back to the clock on the mantle. Seven thirty… *gracious, I have been reading for hours.* Someone, Mr Blake probably, had lit the candelabra; twinkling flames bathing the room in a comforting glow.

Pleased with her afternoon's endeavours, she slid a bookmark in between the dry pages, closed the volume, and tucked it into the bottom right-hand drawer of the desk. Standing, she shook out her skirts, and rang the bell.

Lottie appeared.

"I think a bath is in order, Lottie, if you would be so kind as to organise that for me." Madeline smiled ruefully. "I do believe I have earned it."

"Right away, my lady." Lottie bobbed a curtsy and hurried away.

Shortly thereafter, Madeline was wallowing — there was no other word for it — in a hot bath, the lightly scented water easing aching muscles.

She relaxed in the warmth, her eyes drifting shut. The dream lingered, tantalisingly close and, smiling, she permitted herself to be carried away… only to have Viscount Carnforth's face supplant that of her gallant knight.

She shot up, splashing water everywhere. *What the dickens?*

The image refused to be banished.

The household had yet to stir when Madeline, swaddled in an enormous dressing gown, trudged downstairs to the library. Slumber, never her dearest friend, had abandoned her sometime after midnight, and the hours of tossing and turning had left her tetchy.

She blamed Swinbourne and his unaccountable delay in settling the debt for her sleepless night, studiously ignoring the voice at the back of her mind insisting her insomnia was related to a certain viscount, not an earl.

He needed a sharp nudge.

Withdrawing the old tome from the desk drawer, she opened it at the bookmark, and perused the content, seeking the part she had read the previous day. At one time, a capital crime in the American state of Massachusetts, by the end of the sixteen hundreds, the penalty for adultery had become more lenient — lenient being a relative concept.

She read out loud, stumbling a little over the archaic language,

"...if any man shall commit adultery, the man and woman that shall be convicted of such crime before Their Majesties Justices of Assize and General Goal Delivery, shall be set upon the gallows by the space of an hour, with a rope about their neck, and the other end cast over the Gallows: And in the way from thence to the Common Goal, shall be severely whipt, not exceeding forty stripes each..."

With a grim smile, Madeline conjured up an image of Lord Swinbourne being flogged. "'Tis a shame such punishments are no longer considered appropriate," she mused. "I should be glad to wield the whip." Chuckling softly at her lurid flight of fancy she read on, finding the section describing the letter.

> *"Also, every person and persons so offending, shall for ever after wear a capital A of two inches long, and proportionable bigness, cut out in cloth of a contrary colour to their cloaths, and sewed upon their upper garments, on the out side of their arm, or on their back, in open view..."*

She leant back in the chair. "A most suitable penance, my Lord Swinbourne. I daresay you will not be duped into wearing a waistcoat blazoned with an A," she mulled over possible substitutes. "An embroidered cravat or kerchief, however... yes, that would do nicely. No sense in delaying." Dropping the book on the table, Madeline hurried upstairs to her husband's suite of chambers.

Opening the door onto the scene of her nightmares, she hesitated on the threshold, a flurry of images skittering through her head. With determination, she pushed them aside... *he is dead, he cannot hurt me...* and entered the darkened room.

With no spill to light the candles, Madeline drew one set of curtains. The shaft of light offered sufficient illumination for the purpose, dust motes dancing a frenzied jig along the beam. Ignoring the great four-poster bed, Madeline crossed to the dressing room, and began rifling through Raymond's belongings.

In the top drawer of one of the chests, she found his collection of kerchiefs, neatly folded, and arranged by type of material; some cotton, some linen, some silk. Rolling her eyes and grumbling, "Who on earth requires so many kerchiefs?" she extracted a decent handful and piled them on the dressing table.

In the drawer below, she located Raymond's cravats...

also arranged by material, colour, and size. She withdrew one and studied it. A stout man, Raymond had possessed heavy jowls and the cravat looked too large for Swinbourne's less rotund frame.

"Never mind, 'tis the principle which is important not the fit," Madeline announced to the quiet room. Gathering a handful, she added them to the heap of kerchiefs, closed the drawers and beat a hasty retreat.

While Madeline had every right to be in the suite, she avoided doing so unless absolutely necessary, and this was only the third time since her husband's death, she had set foot in his chambers. In truth, she wished she could burn the damned rooms, without… obviously… damaging the rest of The Lodge.

Swallowing the revulsion which never failed to swamp her whenever she ventured into Raymond's wing, she returned to her own bedroom where Lottie was waiting to help her dress for the day.

CHAPTER THIRTEEN

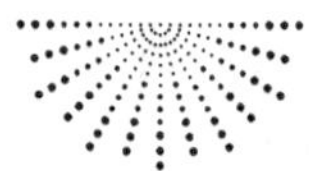

hile Madeline foraged through the Parham library, Wolfstan Colleville was accumulating evidence.

Returning to Bow Street, he spent some time scanning the file pertaining to his current assignment.

Removing the items addressed to Baron Merryfield, he slotted them into a slim leather satchel and, hailing a hackney, was soon rattling along busy streets to the leafy quiet of Mayfair.

Hopping down and paying the driver, Wolfstan climbed the steps of Elm Grove and rapped on the door.

A smartly attired footman answered. "May I help, sir?" he intoned.

"Is the baron receiving?" Wolfstan gave the butler his card.

"I believe so, come in."

Shortly thereafter, Wolfstan was ushered into a sunny study. "Good afternoon, Lord Merryfield." He bowed as Granville Bennet, his expression bland, reciprocated. "I apologise for my intrusion, but a matter has arisen about which I suspect you remain ignorant."

"Please, take a seat." Lord Bennet looked over Wolfstan's shoulder at his butler, hovering deferentially, and requested refreshments.

The two exchanged the usual pleasantries but, as soon as the steaming hot coffee had been served, Wolfstan explained the reason for his unexpected visit.

"During the ball, held here two nights past, a… for want of a better description… missive was left in this very room. It was addressed to you."

"I have received no such missive." Grenville's forehead creased in puzzlement.

"No, it was intercepted by someone who believed it to be connected to a string of burglaries. A mistake rectified when the package was delivered to Lucas Withers."

The baron's bushy brows shot under his hairline. "Major *Withers?*" Everyone in the *ton* knew of the latter's impeccable reputation, should a complicated situation require discreet handling.

Wolfstan inclined his head. "I have the letter with me." He extracted two items from his satchel and handed both to Grenville.

An uncomfortable hush fell as the baron read and re-read note and poem. He turned the pages this way and that as though this might reveal the identity of the sender, then looked at Wolfstan in wordless question.

"Apparently there was a dead rose attached to the letter by a black ribbon. Can you think of anyone who might hold a grudge?"

"Impossible, I am an honest man, my business dealings are impeccable," the baron blustered, "ask anyone. Ten pounds? To where…?"

He scanned the letter again. "Sanctuary House? Why should I want to donate anything to that blasted place? Already too many do-gooders throwing their hard-earned coin in that direction, and what has it achieved? A queue of whingers begging for alms. The dickens. They should stop relying on handouts, get off their lazy backsides and find honest work."

Lord Bennet tossed the note and the card on his desk in disgust.

Wolfstan, quelling the urge to slap some compassion into the man, parried placidly, "*Au contraire*, Merryfield. Sanctuary House is devoted to assisting those who have escaped untenable circumstances, and furnishes them with the skills required to stand on their own two feet. Mayhap a visit…" he opened his palms in an eloquent gesture.

The baron grunted sceptically but did not argue the point. "I do not see what the place has to do with me, let alone that the demand is tantamount to blackmail."

"I think it is perfectly clear, Wolfstan said, adding facetiously, "Would you like me to spell it out for you?"

"Do not patronise me, Carnforth. You may hold higher status, but you are barely out of breeches."

"It is not my intent to insult you, my lord, but you need to think hard. Why would you be sent something of this nature? The writer, a woman, is not a random stranger. She is someone with whom you are well-acquainted. She knows you were close friends with her dead husband, which has led to a breach of trust… against her at least."

Merryfield's brows knitted, but before he could speak, Wolfstan continued, "Only the most honourable among us possess the courage to admit to an incautious act. Think, man. The widow of a dead friend believes she deserves compensation for a wrong inflicted upon her.

"This is not some perceived slight at a Society function, this is a grave accusation. The letter declares she holds a list bearing your name. Where do you suppose she found that? What have you been involved in which might include others?"

Grenville Bennet scowled at Wolfstan darkly. "How do I know this is not the first of many letters, soliciting money?"

"You do not, but the implication is that, as long as you follow her instructions, your name will be removed, and your debt paid. Of course, it is your choice, but…" he left that dangling.

The baron shifted awkwardly, weighing up their conversation, then heaved himself out of the chair to pace the floor.

Despite his claim of innocence, he knew who had sent the letter. The second line was the giveaway. Madeline's distraught countenance drifted through his mind and, in that moment, he hated himself.

Until today, he had managed to blot it out, pretend it never happened, hoped it would not find him, persuaded himself she was a willing participant, that she had enjoyed his attentions.

His conscience badgered him, reminding him of those few months when common sense had deserted him… *but there was a list, there were others?* He had been unaware, the possibility never entered his head. Parham had convinced him… *and I was stupid enough to believe him. What a fool.*

His stomach roiled, as memories flitted through his mind. An aberration, induced by too much wine and the hedonistic lure of an illicit affair.

Dear lord, how have I been able to sleep at night?

Merryfield, whose marriage had been arranged when he was babe in his cradle, fell in love with his wife long before they were wed and, his brief lapse in judgement notwithstanding, his devotion had not wavered. The idea of hurting her cut him to the quick and, if she discovered he had violated their vows, their happiness was in jeopardy.

He *had* to fix this mess.

"This will be kept between us?" he asked after a protracted silence.

"You have my word."

With a resigned huff, he resumed his seat. "It will be done."

Two days later, Madeline, blissfully unaware of what had transpired since she placed the letter on the baron's desk, received confirmation from Sanctuary House regarding an anonymous donation of ten pounds.

She scribbled a curt receipt to the baron and, as promised, destroyed the page bearing his name.

In the meantime, she had fashioned a black 'A' on five of Galleron's kerchiefs. Laying them out in a row on the desk in the study, she nodded in satisfaction. *Perhaps an accompanying reminder…* she pondered that and decided in the affirmative.

"I refuse to let him skirt his obligations," she announced crossly to the quiet room. "He was quick enough to take advantage when it suited him. Hmmm, mayhap I was too circumspect."

She picked up the quill and twirled it in her fingers contemplating her choice of words.

Lord Swinbourne,
I am deeply disappointed to note, despite my

clear instructions, your debt remains outstanding. Do you suppose my decision to request recompense for your actions was taken lightly? Do you think my previous letter was written in jest?

Come, come, my lord, you are an intelligent man, you cannot expect me to believe you do not know to what I alluded. In case your conscience has suppressed the interlude, let me refresh your woeful memory.

You had a dilemma, for which a solution was offered. An agreement, whereby you, for want of a better phrase, purchased relief. Relief you were unable or preferred not to find elsewhere.

That long ago conversation and, the fact, the earl viewed her to be an adequate, albeit temporary, substitute for his wife, rankled. The arrangement concocted by her husband had left her as much a *mistress* to his friends as any woman they might pick up in a brothel.

Gripping the quill, she blinked back angry tears. "You ruined me, all of you ruined me..." she snarled under her breath, "...and do not think for one moment, I will not return the favour."

Ignoring the fact she was teetering on the brink of blackmail, she added that thought to the letter.

It would behove you to do as I ask, as your delaying tactics may come back to haunt you. You ruined me, and I am more than happy to return the compliment.

M

She read it through, waited until the ink was dry, and placed the sheet on one of the silky kerchiefs. Wrapping the little parcel in a square of brown paper, she secured it with a length of black ribbon.

A rebellious streak within Madeline induced her to don a disguise when she delivered the letter. It was something she had resorted to, sporadically, during her marriage, granting her the ability to escape the confines of The Lodge undetected.

The freedom which came with anonymity far outweighed the fear of being exposed.

She rang for Lottie, who helped her change into the street attire. Ready, she studied herself in the mirror.

"I am too clean." She chuckled and turned to the fireplace.

"My lady," Lottie's dismayed exclamation stayed Madeline's hand as she bent to scoop some of the cold ashes from the grate. "If you must, please allow me." Tutting, she swept a handful of the grey particles onto the little brass shovel and held it steady.

Madeline dabbed an old kerchief into the dust, then smeared it lightly across her cheeks, forehead, and the back of each hand.

"Do I pass muster?" she asked Lottie.

Lottie nodded. "Mind, you'll need something to cover your hair, my lady."

"I thought this one." Madeline lifted a scruffy blue cap

perched atop the pile of street clothes she had acquired; although from where, Lottie had no clue.

"Take a seat," Lottie adjured and proceeded to scrape her mistress' hair into a tight chignon, grudgingly rubbing a little of the ash onto the ends to dull the glossiness. She fitted the cap over the style, the battered brim hiding any hint the wearer was a woman — unless you paid close scrutiny.

"There, how about that." Lottie stood back to admire their joint handiwork. "Gracious, but you look so different."

"Then, we have achieved our aim." Madeline smiled at their reflections. "No time to waste. Please pass me the brown jacket. It is a beautiful day, so I shall detour through the park on my way home," she paused and squeezed Lottie's hand.

"I have not lost my reason. Yes, Lord Parham is dead, and you supposed this charade no longer necessary, but I have a task to complete. My costume allows me to move uninhibited by Society's constraints. I confess, men are fortunate indeed to wear trousers. Comfortable and practical." She shrugged into the jacket Lottie was holding out.

"Thank you, Lottie."

With that, Madeline whisked down the stairs to collect the package, Lottie on her heels.

To her staff's well-concealed consternation, she left through the tradesman's entrance with a breezy. "Do not fret, 'tis in keeping with my character."

Exiting the mews at the rear of The Lodge, she walked briskly along the tree-lined streets towards Swinbourne Place, quickly blending in with the hustle and bustle of humanity traversing the city.

.   .   .

Unbeknownst to Madeline, her steps were shadowed.

Across the road, Wolfstan, slouching against a decorative fence, spied a curious looking fellow hurrying from the mews. Assuming he was just another street urchin, something about the boy's gait caught Wolfstan's attention.

Through narrowed eyes, he watched until the inconsistency dawned on him. His lips twitched. This was no messenger boy.

"Well, well, Lady Parham. What prompts you to hide in plain sight?" He followed the countess from a judicious distance, not particularly surprised when he discerned her destination. Her drab attire might camouflage her body, but the woman's inherent grace was a dead giveaway.

He took refuge behind a tree when she knocked on the door, then handed over a package to whoever answered, and took her leave without exchanging more than half a dozen words.

Rather than retrace her steps, Madeline continued on her way, to — if he was not mistaken — Hyde Park and her regular constitutional.

Unwilling to show his hand, but concerned the countess might end up on the wrong side of the law, Wolfstan made a snap decision.

The Serpentine resembled a huge glass platter, reflecting the sky and surrounding trees so clearly it was as though another world resided therein. Madeline wound her way along its banks, breathing in the delicate perfumes floating on the balmy air from the profusion of blossoms.

Coming to her favourite bench, glad it was too early for the fashionable set, Madeline sank onto the warm wood.

"My lady."

The deep voice spoke from behind her. With an unlady-like squawk, Madeline leapt up, and spun to face… *him*.

Why, oh why, did it have to be him? Wait, he recognised me. So much for my efforts at subterfuge.

"Errr…" was all she could manage, and she sketched a curtsy, an incongruous gesture in her current garments.

Before she could remonstrate, or justify, he bowed.

"Beg pardon, my lady. It seems my lot in life is to startle you." The gentle smile accompanying his apology did funny things to her insides.

Collecting herself, Madeline contested nonchalantly, "One might be forgiven for thinking you are following me, so frequently do our paths cross, even when 'tis clear I am striving to be incognito." Ignoring the fact that this was only the third time in nearly seven months.

Wolfstan did not reply immediately, and she noted an odd expression flit over his face, gone so quickly she wondered whether she had imagined it.

"'Tis a beautiful day. Would you object to me joining you?" He indicated the bench, avoiding a direct answer.

Madeline's brow creased. *Maybe not.* She fixed him with an assessing gaze, reading nothing more than friendly polite-ness, yet there was something…

"I would not take exception to your company," she said primly.

Wolfstan made himself comfortable on the seat, ensuring there was an acceptable gap between them, despite Made-line's mode of dress.

He did not speak immediately and Madeline — who was sitting ramrod straight, hands folded in her lap — found herself relaxing.

Their companionable silence was broken only by the

rustle of reeds as waterfowl foraged along the banks, and the trill of birds as they swooped to catch busy insects.

CHAPTER FOURTEEN

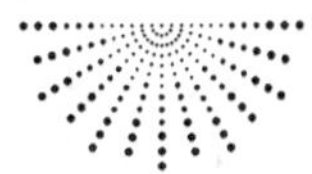

Conversation flowed with unexpected ease. Nothing of any significance, just the light-hearted banter of acquaintances.

Madeline reduced Wolfstan to helpless laughter with her humorous observations about certain political figures, which also served to demonstrate her shrewd mind and sharp wit.

In his turn, Wolfstan, avoiding any mention of his current occupation, regaled Madeline with tales of misadventures of his childhood.

Time slipped by, unnoticed.

To her surprise, Madeline found the viscount's company refreshing and oddly congenial.

A rare pleasure.

"I find people endlessly fascinating," Wolfstan said meditatively, after a brief lull in their chatter.

"You do?" Madeline smiled, wondering where this was going.

"To understand their behaviour, their motivations. To

decipher whether they are genuine or hiding behind a façade. Whether their words are the truth or a clever ruse. To define the reason, they do what they do. Quite, quite fascinating."

Something in the viscount's tone, prompted Madeline to shuffle on the bench the better to study his profile.

"Why, Lord Carnforth, are you a spy?" she teased, instilling a note of levity into her question.

He turned slightly and dropped a slow wink. "I can neither confirm nor deny your accusation."

Madeline gave a soft chuckle. "Which clearly indicates you are, or at least engaged in something covert, for otherwise you would issue a strenuous rebuttal. What encouraged you to allude to such involvement? I am a stranger."

"In some respects that is true. In others, I believe I know you better than your closest friend."

"I sincerely doubt that," Madeline refuted. "Pray, how did you come by this epiphany." She expected him to laugh it off, affirm he was jesting.

"Observation," Wolfstan's tone was benign, bland even, but seemed layered with meaning.

In the blink of an eye, their cordiality vanished.

"You have been… I am under… my lord…" vexed, Madeline rose to her feet, and reached for a non-existent parasol, momentarily forgetting her disguise.

Wolfstan didn't move. "You are the elusive M, are you not?" he posited, his tone tranquil, his gaze on the ducks.

Madeline was so shocked, she dropped back onto the bench, her legs refusing to hold her upright.

"I-I have no idea to what you are referring," she hedged.

"My dear, Lady Parham, do you suppose I plucked your name out of the air? That I came to this conclusion without investigating every piece of evidence…"

"Evidence," she murmured weakly, her carefully fabricated scheme crumbling before her eyes.

"…thoroughly? This morning, proved my hypothesis correct."

"This morning?" Madeline rounded on him. *"This morning…"* her voice went up an octave. A distasteful thought reared up. "You followed me?"

"Of course," he did not sound in the least contrite. "When members of the nobility are being threatened, it is my job to expose the culprit."

Her ire began to bubble. "So, all this…" she flicked her hand between them, "…all this, your friendly overtures, the reason we seem to bump into each other at random intervals, was naught but a ruse? You are no better than the rest of them. No, you are worse. At least they made their intentions clear, however reprehensible. You employed deception to achieve your goal."

Bristling, her green eyes flashing, Madeline heaved a stormy breath. *"Expose the culprit?* You would not recognise a culprit if you tripped over one. Shame on you."

Infuriated at being hoodwinked, at allowing herself to believe that not all men were cads, Madeline glared at Wolfstan and marched off in high dudgeon.

"Lady Parham…" Wolfstan hurried after her.

"Don't you dare Lady Parham me, you… you…" icncensed, Madeline could not think of a suitable insult and plumped for "…muddy-mottled moldwarp."

"Please…" he opened his hands in a gesture of remorse, but Madeline was in no mood to listen, and berated him in a manner which would have cowed a lesser man.

Seemingly unruffled by her excoriation, Wolfstan waited patiently for her to run out of steam.

"May I speak?"

"I cannot imagine you have anything to say that I want to hear."

"Please," he tried again, kicking himself for so egregious a miscalculation. This was *not* how he intended this moment to unfold.

Suddenly the fight went out of Madeline and, to Wolfstan — captivated by her vivid, if smudged, countenance, as she castigated him — she seemed to wilt, like a summer flower caught in a sudden frost. His chest pinched.

"Fine, I sent the letters. Are you happy now? Throw me in jail. I'll wager 'tis a picnic compared with what I suffered at the hands of your so-called noblemen." She tossed her head, and pivoted on her heel.

"For the pain endured…" Wolfstan risked quietly.

Slowly, she turned around to stare at him; her features leached of all colour, the dirt on her cheeks stark against her pallor.

"What did you say?" she whispered.

He recited the poem in its entirety, his tones solicitous.

"What happened to you?" he appealed.

She put up her hands as though warding off an attack. "Why do you care? I am naught but a chattel, of no more consequence than this stupid cap." She yanked it off, her hair spilling out of the severe style.

"To me… to us… no one is more or less important than the next. A servant is treated with the same respect as a king. I know there is more to this story than a letter soliciting a charitable donation but, until I have all the facts, I cannot proceed."

"Why did you not call upon me, request an interview?

Broach the possibility I was behind the letters? Why today, here, in the park?"

"Here, you are away from your usual, safe surrounds. An appointment, petitioned out of the blue by a man you scarcely know would raise your suspicions, put you on guard. I doubted you would confess unless I shocked you into it," Wolfstan admitted.

"My lady, no one pens a poem of that nature unless they are desperate. Desperate for some form of redress, or to regain their self-esteem, or to convey a long-buried grievance."

Madeline felt as trapped as a rabbit caught in the sights of a rifle. "Why should I trust you?"

"Because I have dedicated my life to uncovering the truth, however unpalatable. We act with the utmost discretion, cannot be bribed, and are not swayed by status."

"We?" This was the second time he had spoken in the plural.

"As you inferred, I work for a clandestine organisation, whose tasks, typically of a sensitive nature are many, varied, and always confidential."

Something Emory once said, nudged at her subconscious. She let it roll around her head for a few seconds. "Are you employed by Major Withers?"

This time it was Wolfstan's turn to be shocked. His hesitation giving Madeline her answer.

She smiled, a little sadly, he thought.

"I am acquainted with the Major's endeavours. My friends trust him and, by extension, that trust includes you. I am disinclined to bare my soul and disclose my impropriety here. I will accompany you to your offices if that is preferable or, you are welcome to escort me home, were we can… discuss the matter further over refreshments."

Wolfstan opted for the latter.

Ushered to a huge, leather, wing-backed chair, a steaming hot cup of coffee at his elbow, Wolfstan fought to contain his disgust at the depravity of his fellow man when Madeline divulged the reason for the letters.

She showed him the shabby book with its offensive lists, along with the letter, poem, and clarified why she had chosen a dead rose.

That her explanation matched the theory — minus certain details — Lucas and he had developed, was a hollow triumph. *Who wanted such heinous speculation to be proved right?*

Husbands abusing wives was not uncommon, but to sell your wife to your friends beggared belief and, given the number of brothels dotted around the city, wholly unnecessary.

Lord Parham's perversion left a sour taste in Wolfstan's mouth. He was torn between applauding Madeline on her commensurate reprisal and digging up the earl's body to inflict retributive justice. That this would be posthumous would be no less rewarding.

To treat a woman, nay any human with such disrespect spoke volumes for the perpetrator and his cronies.

"I have burnt the pages relating to those who have paid. Once the debts are settled, the whole book will be destroyed, effectively deleting any evidence of their... involvement," Madeline concluded, her voice lacking any inflection.

"Am I to assume Lord Swinbourne has yet to honour his debt?" Wolfstan essayed.

"You assume correctly."

"Might I ask what you delivered this morning?"

Madeline studied him, struck by the compassion on his kindly face. A face, she decided, which had missed being handsome — by current standards, at least — but was arresting all the same. His features were craggy, rugged, and lightly tanned, which, along with his dark hair and smoky grey eyes, gave him a slightly foreign air.

Smoky grey eyes? Madeline control yourself, she remonstrated inwardly.

She wrested her wayward brain back to the matter at hand. Her guest awaited an answer. "A kerchief bearing the letter A in black," she confessed.

Wolfstan who, coincidentally, was an avid reader of world history, barked with laughter and slapped his knee.

"Well, I'll be damned… beg pardon," he was quick to apologise. "I am impressed by your ingenuity. Do you suppose Swinbourne will understand the reference?"

Madeline shrugged. "I neither know nor care. Ignoring my request will not make it go away. He was quick enough to, how should I put it, sample the goods, with regularity. He had the audacity to inform me, as though this exonerated his behaviour, that his arrangement with Parham protected his wife from unkind gossip because he had not taken a mistress.

"What was I, if not a mistress? A nobody, little more than a thrall who could be relied upon to keep her mouth shut. Parham knew I could not complain or protest. My family have no sympathy for my sensibilities and, had I plucked up the courage to accuse my oh-so impeccable husband of misconduct, they would lay the blame at my feet."

She lifted her chin defiantly. "His death liberated me, and if their coin helps to mitigate another person's hell, I have no regrets." She placed her empty cup on the delicate table between them; the tremulous chink of china, the only sign of her distress.

"May I ask who else you intend to target?" Wolfstan ventured after a brief silence.

"Swinbourne is the last," Madeline's reply was a little too

quick and a little too emphatic, but Wolfstan knew, if he pressed the issue, it would be like hitting a stone wall. He could bide his time.

"What shall you do if he continues to ignore your... err... request?" He asked instead.

"I shall ruin him."

"I understand your antipathy, my lady," Wolfstan said slowly, "but, by destroying him, you will also destroy his family, not to mention yourself."

"Which is why I trust common sense will prevail. I cannot imagine Swinbourne wants his wife and sons to be tarnished because of his degenerate behaviour. As for me. I do not give a fig for my reputation. My friends, whom I can count on the fingers of one hand, are aware of my scheme, and will support me whatever the outcome."

She got up to pace the floor, unconsciously wringing her hands together; to Wolfstan, a sign of agitation if ever he had seen one.

"I know my actions might be preposterous, even criminal, but I need to sleep without nightmares. To hear the doorbell ring without my stomach clenching. To live without dreading the creak of floorboards—"

"You expect to find peace of mind once each debt is paid?" Wolfstan interjected.

"I do not know," Madeline flung around to face him, her eyes haunted, "but it is a good start. Doing something which will benefit women fleeing a similar ordeal is cathartic, not to mention poetic justice."

Wolfstan smiled suddenly, and the fraught atmosphere which had shrouded the room eased marginally. "Then it is incumbent on me to expedite the matter. Perhaps that might help assuage your burden."

Madeline's brow creased. "You are not handing me over to Major Withers or the Runners?"

"To whose benefit? The evidence against you is strong but deniable. You are a recently widowed and respected countess of impeccable character. I have no witnesses. Those involved will never admit to their actions." He ticked them off on his fingers. "I have no case."

"And the Major?"

"I suspect he will agree with my findings," Wolfstan hesitated.

"What?"

"My lady, might I beseech you to end your vendetta today?"

"I am not…" Madeline's expression turned mutinous.

"Mayhap, if I was to request an interview with Lord Swinbourne," he went on quickly. "You have been successful thus far, but these men are not without influence. Swinbourne will do everything in his power to preserve his honour. To underestimate him would be a grave mistake."

"You think that has not crossed my mind? Did you not hear what I said about my reputation? He, they ruined my life, stole my trust, shattered my soul, and destroyed my faith. There is nothing he can do to me. Death would be a relief." Her vehemence echoed in the quiet room, shocking Wolfstan to his feet.

"Death, my lady? You prefer death?"

"At least I would be at peace." A sob caught at her throat. Valiantly, she tried to swallow it.

I will not cry. Never again will I cry. No one deserves my tears.
Her frayed nerves had other ideas.

CHAPTER FIFTEEN

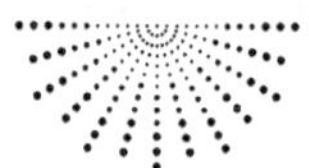

*I*rresolute, Wolfstan debated whether to ring for Madeline's maid or to offer comfort.

The latter won.

Aware of his hostess' likely disinclination to suffer the touch of any other person, let alone a man, Wolfstan hurried to where she stood, slid a hand under her elbow and guided her gently towards the warmth of the fire.

Half-way across the room, Madeline crumpled and would have fallen if not for his swift reflexes. Her wretched sobs undermined his resolve and, preparing to suffer a tongue-lashing and possible battering, lifted her into his arms to carry her to the chaise.

Desperately trying to regain her composure, and failing miserably — *weeping in front of a virtual stranger, what am I thinking?* — Madeline stiffened at the unexpected contact, but the revulsion and panic which accompanied this kind of gesture did not manifest.

Unbidden, she recalled their first meeting, when he had cupped her elbow. She had not recoiled then either.

Odd.

Unable to process whether that meant anything, she *did* register that Viscount Carnforth's proximity soothed rather than sickened.

Involuntarily, and cursing herself inwardly for her display of feeble femininity, Madeline clung to him as she was conveyed across the room. Before she could formulate even the vaguest protest, the viscount had lowered her onto the chaise, and relaxed his hold.

She felt his clasp slacken and, to her complete bafflement, did not want him to let go. Right at that moment, he was solid, immutable, and she felt herself drawing strength from him.

The sensation was as bizarre as it was encouraging. Was there *any* chance the repugnance, she believed ingrained, had begun to diminish?

"F-forgive m-me," Madeline hiccupped into his shoulder. "Y-your b-beautiful jacket." Making no move to sit upright.

"Do not fret, it is of no matter. Shall I ring for your maid?"

"N-no. P-please, if you c-can bear my nonsense…" she let that trail off, not entirely sure what she was trying to ask.

The viscount seemed to understand for he remained seated, his arm steadying her against him.

Wolfstan was in a torment of indecision. The feel of Madeline in his arms was exquisite torture, yet he had stepped so far outside the bounds of propriety, he feared they would never be reinstated.

Do I want them to be reinstated?

Shocked at the direction of his thoughts, Wolfstan

discarded them with alacrity. Undaunted, they refused to recede, creeping back into his mind, whispering seductively.

Mentally, he shook his head. This was a fool's hope. Lady Parham was more fragile than the gossamer strands of a cobweb.

She is stronger than you give her credit for, the voice of reason chided. *Today's emotional outburst aside, she is a lady of mettle, a survivor. Yes, intimacy in any form might repulse her, may even reduce her to a quivering wreck, but she is not screaming at the moment, neither has she fled the room, or demanded you leave. Perhaps your hope is not so foolish.*

The debate in his head paused… then…

A word of caution, do not toy with the good countess. If she permits you to call on her, any subsequent courtship will be protracted, and to love her might not be enough…

Wolfstan acknowledged the truth of his thoughts, however unpalatable. *Am I capable of such devotion? Do I possess the patience to nurture a courtship?*

Was it worth the risk?

He glanced down at Madeline.

Her tears had left tracks through the grubby smears on her cheeks. Her hair was in total disarray, her garb — which still made him want to chuckle — although awry, suited her, evincing an underlying rebellion.

He scoffed at his frivolous thoughts. He, Wolfstan Colleville, was not seeking a courtship, let alone a wife. Ridiculous. His life was exactly how he wanted it — no encumbrances, no responsibilities to anyone other than himself and his job.

His subconscious mocked his naïveté.

Realisation slammed into him with the force of a summer storm.

The thought of another stealing her heart was unconscionable.

Madeline Galleron, widowed countess, abused, battered, and possibly broken was worth everything.

Oblivious to Wolfstan's revelation, Madeline, by virtue of her paroxysm of weeping was sliding into a cocoon of lassitude.

Before decorum asserted itself, she was asleep.

Her noble knight took her hand and led her to the sun-drenched glade. Slowly, he peeled off her clothes, scattering kisses across her skin, as his fingers wove their magic. She stared up at him, his features teased at something in her brain.

His hair, dark as freshly brewed coffee; his slate grey eyes, glowing with affection. His claret-coloured, silk cravat hanging loosely around his neck; his matching brocade waistcoat — unbuttoned.

Wait... her knight wore armour, not the fashionable attire of the ton...

In the midst of her dream, Madeline registered something had shifted, but was too wrapped up in the joy of being adored to question it.

A dark cloud appeared on the horizon; a storm approached. This was no ordinary tempest, the swirling black mass took shape, a face was discernible.

It was him...

Madeline hissed her antipathy. "Begone, you iniquitous villain."

The world around her began to fracture, the knight splintered into a million pieces, taking her heart with him...

· · ·

"Nooooooo." She bolted upright, disconcerted to find herself in her own bed.

Her forehead creased in confusion. The last thing she remembered was talking to Lord Carnforth in the library.

She glanced around the room, half-expecting him to be sitting on the window ledge, a nervous giggle bubbling up at the absurdity. The curtains were drawn but she discerned slivers of light around the edges. Was it the same day, or had she slept the night through?

Too comfortable to crawl out from under the covers to check, she snuggled back against the pillows, and ruminated over her conversation with the viscount, several aspects standing out.

The main one being the sense of optimism he engendered. That somehow, despite how desolate her future once looked, the slimmest, the almost infinitesimal possibility had arisen — after this matter was put to rest, and assuming she did not end up in Newgate or Bedlam — of happiness.

She had neither flinched nor taken fright at his touch. Heat washed up her cheeks when she recalled her conduct… in detail. "Madeline Galleron," she lamented. "You wanton hussy."

No amount of self-recrimination was sufficient to quash the residual warmth of being in his arms.

"He was simply being kind," Madeline crushed her own kernel of hope, and got out of bed, mildly perturbed to note she was in her chemise. Before she had a chance to ring Lottie, that young woman, who surely must have a sixth sense, knocked, and poked her head around the door.

"My lady, 'tis glad I am, you have woken. You fair slept the day away."

"Better than it being tomorrow," Madeline replied drily.

Lottie chuckled. "Lord Carnforth asked me to inform you

that he's sorry to have caused you upset, and 'opes you'll feel much restored after your rest."

"'Twas not his fault."

"He seems like a kind man, if you beg my pardon for sayin'," Lottie ventured.

Madeline pursed her lips meditatively. "I am wont to agree, Lottie. A genuine gentleman. I did not think such a paragon existed."

Lottie, wise for her years, said no more.

Lost in thought, Wolfstan climbed the stairs to the office two at a time. He shouldered his way through the door, and more by instinct than actually seeing where he was going, headed to his desk.

He surveyed the room, nodding a greeting to the handful of his colleagues busy at their respective assignments, but there was no sign of Lucas.

Sitting in his chair, Wolfstan retrieved the file pertaining to Madeline from his locked drawer and opened it. He looked at the paltry evidence garnered to date and reached for his quill.

For the next hour he wrote; quickly covering sheet after sheet with his notes, impressions, and suggestions. The afternoon was almost at an end by the time he was confident he had detailed everything Madeline said. He leant back in the seat and stretched, his back protesting at being hunched over for so long.

"I wondered whether you were ever going to stop," a laconic voice remarked.

Wolfstan turned to see Lucas grinning at him from across the room.

"I needed to record this before I forgot, not that I think there is the remotest chance of that," Wolfstan's mouth twisted.

"You want to discuss it?" Lucas studied his subordinate appraisingly.

"I think that is essential. There are so many layers to this case." Wolfstan blew a sigh. "It is not pretty, not pretty at all."

"When is it ever?" Lucas' question not requiring an answer. "Show me what you have."

Wolfstan was surprised at the stillness which enveloped the office. Save Lucas and he, all had left for the day, or were out on other investigations.

The night shift would arrive shortly, for Lucas ensured his organisation was available twenty-four hours a day, every day — neither crime nor scandal adhering to respectable hours. In fact, darkness seemed to encourage shady conduct — those perpetrating it presuming the night concealed their activities. They reckoned without Major Withers and his men.

"What is your next move?" Lucas asked after he had committed Wolfstan's findings to memory.

"I confess, I am not convinced Lady Parham has ceased her crusade. There was one name left in the book, one she had underlined repeatedly. If the number written alongside, tallied with the times this person had…" Unwilling to sound crude, and despite Madeline being nowhere near, Wolfstan opted for, "…visited, he was the worst offender."

He picked up his notes, more for something to do with his hands than for any other reason. "I cannot imagine she will permit him to walk away without penance."

"Will she not suspect you are watching her?"

"I believe she thinks she can hoodwink me." Wolfstan chuckled, explaining her disguise of earlier.

Lucas laughed at Wolfstan's humorous description of their encounter.

"I thought she might faint, or worse pound me into pulp. She is a force of nature that lady," Wolfstan mused, unaware Madeline had attributed this exact same characteristic to Kitty Marchmain.

Something in the younger man's voice prompted to Lucas to narrow his eyes. "Be careful, Carnforth. She is not a client, she is a suspect, and she has suffered unimaginable torment."

"I beg to differ, sir," Wolfstan countered. "After today, even though she has not solicited our help, she is just as much a client as the men she targeted. She deserves our protection."

"You are not suggesting we let her continue with this folly?" As it happened, Lucas agreed with Wolfstan, but that was not enough. In order to facilitate an outcome which appeased all parties, they had to tread carefully.

"Not only do I believe she ought to be permitted to continue, I intend to assist her endeavours." Wolfstan, cognisant that Lucas was fair minded and would never allow injustice to triumph, outlined his plan.

Lucas listened attentively, throwing in an odd question here and there. As the thud of feet announced the approach of the night crew, he gave his approval.

"If, for any reason, you feel out of your depth, come to me immediately, and for heaven's sake, be discreet. Report back daily. A note on my desk will suffice, if I am not here."

"You have my word." Wolfstan inclined his head.

Lucas patted Wolfstan on the shoulder. "Thank you for taking this on, and once again, be careful. I sense Lady Parham is more than just a name in a file to you. Use your brain not your emotions."

"Trust me, I feel sorry for her, but that is the extent of my emotional involvement," Wolfstan strove to assure.

"I shall remind you of this conversation on your wedding day." Lucas walked away chuckling.

CHAPTER SIXTEEN

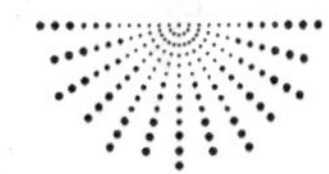

$\mathcal{B}$efore venturing back into the fray, so to speak,
Madeline decided to let the dust settle for a few
days.

She was not a fool, and half expected to see Lord Carnforth loitering at her front door every time she stepped out,
which produced an irreverent giggle when she imagined the
scene.

If their roles were reversed, she would not believe he had
curtailed his campaign simply because someone asked him
to, especially given the gravity of the grievance. No, he
would bide his time and, when least anticipated, resume his
mission.

Her strategy precisely.

A week ticked by during which she visited with Kitty and
Helena, both of whom demanded to know whether she had
abandoned her madcap scheme.

"You know I have to do this," she said to Kitty as they
supped tea one sunny afternoon.

"Are you not afraid of the repercussions if any of these wastrels catch you?" Kitty felt obliged to play devil's advocate.

"They will not catch me and even if they do, what then? Do they atone for their sins or compound them?"

"They are men, they will be the ones whose voice is heard. Women, even those fortunate to be of the nobility, might as well be mute. Their opinion, save in the privacy of their own homes, discounted more often than not. Madeline, my dear, this could end so very badly."

"I understand your misgivings, Kitty, truly, I do, but I *must* see this through. I have come too far to stop now. There remains one last individual to importune, then I promise to close that chapter of my life. You, of all people must appreciate my need for resolution."

She bent her head. "I cannot move forward until they have paid their dues.

Kitty studied her friend, recognising that Madeline's steely determination, scarcely suppressed the torment which continued to haunt her. She knew that feeling, that misery, and did not wish it on anyone.

"Fine, I accept it is your decision. I shall say no more, except please come to me if you feel overwhelmed or afraid. Remember, these men might be degenerate maggot-pies, but they are also very powerful."

"*Maggot-pies*? Why, Lady Teasdale, for shame."

"Do not try to divert me, Lady Parham." Kitty wagged her finger.

"You need to trust me, Kitty."

"I do trust you. They, on the other hand, not as far as I could throw a donkey. Beware the unscrupulous, that's all I am saying."

"When do you leave for Teasdale Mallow?" Madeline's

abrupt change of topic did not fool Kitty, but that lady was perceptive enough not to question the deflection.

"Three days hence." Kitty, with no care for decorum, leant back in her chair and stretched her body, languidly. "I am looking forward to the change of pace. I miss the countryside and the fresh air, and the absolute lack of anything to do but simply be. Evie is about jumping out of her skin to be on the way, and Oscar is bringing a friend to stay for the summer." She sighed contentedly. "Perfection."

"You might not be saying that when those children run you ragged." Madeline teased.

Kitty flapped a hand. "Oh, fear not, Adam will bear the brunt of their antics. He already thinks I ought to be wrapped in blankets and closeted away from the world." She gurgled with mischievous laughter. "I think, this time I may acquiesce to his wish, as long as he agrees to be closeted with me."

"Kitty Marchmain, you are outrageous." Madeline struggled to contain her mirth.

"I know. Is it not divine?" Kitty assumed an angelic expression.

She sobered. "Please, Madel—"

Madeline squeezed her friend's hand. "No more talk of dark things. Tell me all about Teasdale Mallow."

Conceding defeat, although making a mental note to have Adam speak to Lucas, Kitty waxed lyrical about the country estate.

Helena's remarks mimicked Kitty's although, she *was* moved to ask whether Madeline might like her to approach Hugh with a view to dropping the uncooperative nobles in the Thames. "…if they continue to procrastinate," she concluded.

"A splendid punishment," Madeline replied, "but perhaps a whit drastic."

"The offer is there." Helena's smile was sweet. "For the amusement value alone, if nothing else."

"You are as bad as Kitty. I thought I was the dastardly woman among we three. My fiats are piffling compared with the ideas you two invent."

"The blame for that lies entirely with our husbands. Mixing with the dregs of society must rub off, somehow," Helena claimed loftily.

Madeline burst out laughing, for two more upstanding citizens than Adam Marchmain and Hugh Drummond, she had yet to meet. *No…* her thoughts veered off at a tangent. *Lord Carnforth is also upstanding, as are Lucas, and Emory.*

"Not everyone is a reprobate," she murmured, almost to herself, but Helena's sharp ears caught the comment.

"No," she said softly. "Most men are decent human beings, and I hope, one day you meet one." To Helena's astonishment, a red stain washed up Madeline's cheeks. "Madeline Galleron?" she exhorted. "Is there something you are not telling me?"

"No, maybe, no… oh, I do not know," Madeline wailed, floundering.

"Come on," Helena coaxed. "A problem shared…" her voice lifted encouragingly.

"There really is naught to tell, except," despite all the bells clanging a caution in her head — very, *very* loudly — Madeline could not quash the minuscule flicker of hope that a happy ever after was not beyond the bounds of possibility, however improbable. "I am addled even to think it, but…" she capitulated and divulged the details of her interactions with the viscount.

Helena listened, gleaning more from Madeline's account

than the latter might be comfortable with. "I know Wolf, Lord Carnforth," she said when Madeline ran out of words.

"*Wolf?*" Madeline interposed. The name sat well, fitted what she knew… in truth, very little… of Lord Carnforth who, in her opinion was intelligent, kind, well organised, and loyal.

"Yes, short for Wolfstan. The whole family have archaic names, their sister is Lunette." Helena gave a wry grin. "Wolf is an honourable man. His older brother, Leofwin, married Sapphira Beresford, the lady whose sister ran off with her fiancé. Remember?"

Madeline, recalling the scandal, nodded. "I do, they live in Italy do they not?"

"They do, rapturously happy by all accounts, and another lady whose fortitude nearly ended in disaster. A tale for another day," she said, spying Madeline's wrinkled nose. "Where was I going with this? Oh yes, he is a good man. Dependable, honest, and decent, and would never, *ever* trifle with a lady's affections. If you believe there is something stirring between you, why not trust your intuition and see where it leads?"

"Regrettably, my intuition is less than reliable these days," Madeline admitted, "although, our conversation and later discussion was not arduous. Talking is one thing. It is detached, done from a safe distance. If things were to… develop, I fear I would panic, and who wants a woman already used?"

"My dear, do not forget, Wolf already knows what you have suffered. If he was repulsed," she saw Madeline wince, but persevered; the woman needed saving from herself or she would end up a lonely, wizened crone surrounded by cats, "he would not be offering to help. A service which will bring him into contact with you frequently. Give him a chance, Madeline, do."

"I shall think about it. That is as much as I can promise. Curiously, his proximity does not incite the usual trepidation, or need to flee." She tilted her head, reviewing their encounters.

Unbeknownst to her, a small smile played over her lips, which did not go unnoticed by Helena who kept her counsel, saying merely, "That is all I ask. Now, what did you think of…" changing the subject, to less… emotive topics.

As fortune had it, before Wolfstan had a chance to knock on Lord Swinbourne's door, the earl burst through the one on Bow Street.

It was a bright summer's afternoon, the warmth in the office alleviated by the breeze wafting through the windows, carrying with it a vague and not unpleasant salty tang from the Thames.

The office was quiet, save the scratching of quills and an occasional curse when a tip required sharpening.

The pounding of angry footsteps ascending the stairs was the only alert that the serenity was about to be extinguished. Seconds later a burly figure burst through the door, already voicing his displeasure.

Nodding at his colleagues to indicate this was his client, and preparing himself for an acrimonious confrontation, Wolfstan stood to greet the visitor.

He was given no chance to speak.

"I trusted you had done as I asked and dealt with this

nonsense. Now this," Lord Swinbourne fulminated, brandishing whatever he was holding in his hand under Wolfstan's nose. "Are you an imbecile? I solicited your services at no small cost, to put a stop to whoever was trying to blackmail me."

With a sense of déjà vu, and his jaw stiffening at the slur, Wolfstan watched the earl stomp up and down the office, deducing it imprudent to point out that his lordship had not paid *anything* to date. It was almost amusing, given what he had learnt but, ever the professional, he assumed a concerned expression and listened politely, glad Lucas was within earshot.

"Don't even know what this is supposed to mean." Swinbourne opened his fist, the soft material falling open across his palm, the black *A*, distinct against the white cotton. "My name is Peter. Whose name begins with A?"

"Please sit down, my lord. You will wear a hole in the soles of your shoes," Wolfstan said, his patience hanging by fewer threads than remained in the rug.

Testily, Lord Swinbourne did as requested, but it was obvious his aggravation seethed.

"May I see the letter?" Wolfstan asked, his tone mild.

The earl thrust the crumpled missive at Wolfstan who scanned it quickly, clamping his lips together in an effort not to smirk. Madeline's phraseology, sufficiently cryptic. It was *just* plausible the man was being deliberately obtuse, determined to continue with the masquerade of innocence.

Wolfstan contemplated Swinbourne, trying and failing to get a read on him; the latter was too angry.

No more prevaricating. This needed to be nipped in the bud, if for no other reason than the preservation of the office rug.

"We have investigated, as you requested, and are in possession of the salient facts. Before I divulge any more, I confess, I am disappointed. When first you insisted we find the perpetrator, I...we..." Wolfstan indicated Lucas who was, to outward appearances, engrossed in paperwork, "...asked whether there was anything which might prompt someone to extort money from you.

"You assured me, as did everyone we interviewed, you had nothing to hide, that you led an impeccable life, are a man of integrity. To behave in a manner which might bring disrepute to your name and that of your family was impossible."

Swinbourne started to speak, but Wolfstan was not finished.

"That is not quite true, is it, my lord?" he held the earl's gaze. "You are not the innocent victim you claim to be."

Swinbourne exploded out of the chair and spat a string of expletives, more suited to a dockhand than a titled nobleman.

Wolfstan did not react, his expression impassive.

"How dare you place the blame for this on me. You piddling goosecap. To suggest this is *my* fault, outrageous. I... I..." Swinbourne stopped mid-tirade, his face livid.

"It *is* your fault, and I have proof," Wolfstan replied calmly. "Do you suppose I am prone to making sweeping statements without any evidence to support my contention? We do not jump to conclusions. This organisation has done its due diligence and then some, my lord. We left no stone unturned. I repeat, this is your fault but, one easily rectified. Settle your debt."

The earl's countenance darkened, his hand twitched at his side, where once a sword hung. For a split second, Wolfstan questioned whether the man was about to call him out.

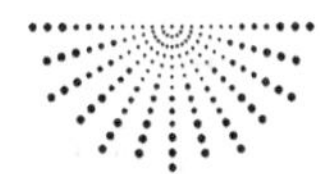

CHAPTER SEVENTEEN

"*S*it down," a voice barked from the other side of the office. Lucas, tired of the earl's theatricals, intervened.

Swinbourne spun around to face the speaker whose face was thunderous. Shocked into silence, he slumped back onto the chair, he had just vacated.

Every inch a major, Lucas stalked across the room. "Enough, Swinbourne. This is becoming a farce of epic proportions. You asked us to investigate. We have done exactly that. You were the one who was liberal with the truth.

"I do not dispute that the letters you have received are tantamount to blackmail, but the instigator had little alternative. That you profess to have forgotten your... error in judgement is the outrage here, and if you ever insult one of my employees again, a duel to the death will seem like a constitutional in Hyde Park.

"Do you understand?"

Wolfstan had never heard Lucas raise his voice. The man

was unfailingly affable, and an image of the latter leading troops into battle popped into Wolfstan's mind. A formidable foe indeed.

Lord Swinbourne seemed to deflate, shrinking into the far less bellicose Peter Masham. He jerked his head in irascible acknowledgement, his high colour fading to a healthier hue.

Lucas perched on the edge of Wolfstan's desk. "How well did you know Lord Parham?" he began conversationally.

Swinbourne straightened up. "Galleron? Why do you ask?"

"Because this mess can be traced back to him."

"To Parham? How on earth?"

Wolfstan still could not decide whether the earl honestly had no clue or had lost the use of the brains he was born with.

"Do you love your wife?" Lucas continued, in the same tone.

"What sort of question is that? Of course, I love my wife."

"So, you would do everything in your power to protect her, and your sons?"

"What kind of question is that? Yes, I would give my life for them."

"What is your opinion of husbands who do not act with such… valour?"

"Cads, the lot of 'em. Deserve to be tossed in the Thames. Where are you going with this?"

Lucas smiled, although there was no humour in it.

"What if, for example, a man thought it… entertaining to… share his wife among his friends?"

Reflexively, Swinbourne opened his mouth to vilify such conduct, then Lucas' words hit home. The healthy hue drained to waxy white. "W-what…?"

"Ahhh, now we are getting somewhere. Your memory is jogged. For the sin committed, and for the pain endured. We have deciphered the poem, and the reason we have been asking you all these questions is because we already know the answers. None of them shed you in a good light."

Swinbourne spluttered, got up, sat down, got up and circled the room, pulling on his cravat. Protesting peevishly under his breath, he resumed his seat with bad grace and glared at Lucas, his jaw grinding.

"It is simple enough. Would you want your wife to be treated thus?"

"The deuce, Withers. Never."

Lucas leant forward until he was within an inch of Swinbourne's face. "Then pay the debt, you fool. You took without recourse and, had Parham not died would likely still be taking. Did you ever consider the lady's sentiments? I doubt it. You were thinking only of your own gratification. If I was her, or your wife for that matter, I would be sorely tempted to remove your manhood with a blunt blade."

Swinbourne remained motionless, but his mind was spinning. Scenes chased through his head; scenes he had suppressed, not only because of the associated guilt, but also because he could not deny he had enjoyed bedding the countess.

He had relished being able to bring her to the peak over and over again, to hear her cry out, while studiously ignoring the self-loathing in her gaze.

"The *A* stands for Adulterer," Wolfstan interposed, "and do not think of reprisals. If I hear a whisper of a threat, or perceive the vaguest hint of danger, or if even a single hair on the head of a certain individual is harmed, there will be no escape from my wrath. By the time I have finished with you, you will beg for that duel."

"Pay the damn debt," Lucas reiterated with a growl.

The message from Sanctuary House, advising they had received the sum of forty-six pounds from an anonymous donor, surprised Madeline. She had not anticipated Lord Swinbourne would capitulate so quickly.

A face strayed into her mind. *Had Lord Carnforth kept his promise?* It seemed probable and compounded her belief, the viscount was a man of his word.

Madeline stared at the letter, relief flooding her. The end was on the horizon.

The following day, among the post delivered to Lord Swinbourne, a letter — severe in its brevity — *Your debt is rescinded.*

While Swinbourne was reading confirmation of his exculpation, Wolfstan was staring at a name. The only name without a line through it. The name — if Madeline's list was to be believed, and he had no reason to doubt it, given it was written by the late Lord Parham, not his wife — of the man who had 'called upon' Madeline, thirty-seven times in two years.

Thirty-seven. That was more than once a month. Wolfstan's lip curled contemptuously.

Was this the only reason Madeline had left him until last

or was there something else. He ran his mind back over the shabby notebook, picturing the name, underscored so many times the quill had punctured the paper. None of the other names had been treated with such fury.

He thought about Madeline's face as she narrated her sorry tale in that wooden voice. The venom glinting in her green eyes. The almost indiscernible change of inflection when she mentioned the duke.

There was definitely more to this than the number of visits. "What did you do to her, Alberforce?" Wolfstan mused, "and, is she the only one who has been subjected to your impulses?"

There was only one way to find out. Rifling through a huge armoire tucked into an alcove at the back of the office, Wolfstan donned attire which, had she seen him in it, would give his mother a fit of the vapours.

He glanced in the mirror. The man gazing back at him looked like a coal-whipper. All he needed to complete the transformation was a dirty face. Running his fingers along a high window ledge he collected a smattering of dust, patted his palms together, and pressed them to his cheeks.

"Better," he addressed his reflection with a grim smile. He penned a quick note for Lucas and left the office, immediately swallowed into the seething mass of humanity jostling its way along the streets of London.

He wound his way to the wider, cleaner neighbourhoods. Leafy squares, graceful residences, an abundance of fresh air. He passed his own home without slowing his pace and, shortly thereafter, reached Charles Street. Lined with a veritable medley of elegant houses, each a distinctive design yet the overall aspect, one of gentile harmony.

The only sound was the soft trill of bird song, and the rustle of the breeze through the plane trees which, in turn, scattered a tapestry of light and shade across the cobbles.

A most attractive lane.

He located no. 16 — the duke's residence, a charming plaque declaring it to be Hollywell House — and walked a few houses further until he found a place from where he could monitor the comings and goings, unobserved. While not a particularly comfortable niche, at least he was unlikely to fall asleep, mid-surveillance.

"Let us hope the man shows his face sooner rather than later," Wolfstan muttered to the empty street.

The traffic, both foot and carriage, was minimal, unnervingly so, prompting Wolfstan to question whether the inhabitants were afraid of the daylight. No nannies escorting children to the parks, no ladies taking constitutionals, no gentlemen hurrying out to their clubs. He quelled the urge to release a ghoulish shriek to see if that provoked a response.

About to give up for the day, he heard the slap of approaching feet. A gangling youth passed Wolfstan, shoulders slouched as though apologising for his existence.

A tuneless whistle echoed off the walls as the lad trudged up the short flight of steps to number 16 and rang the bell.

A uniformed butler answered the door; a brief discussion ensued, and the lad handed over a slim package.

Wolfstan straightened up and narrowed his eyes, straining his ears to catch what they were saying, but he was too far away.

The butler gesticulated, somewhat descriptively, prompting the messenger to shrug, descend the steps in one stride, and dart around to the mews leading to the rear of the house.

Wolfstan peeled himself out of the cramped recess and followed, keeping his distance. He squinted down the gloomy alley, spying the lad munching what looked like a slice of pie. Wolfstan's stomach rumbled, reminding him it was hours since he had eaten.

Ignoring the spasm of hunger, he spun around and sauntered away casually, just in time. Rapid footsteps came up behind him. The lad barrelled out of the alley and was gone.

Was it Madeline in yet another disguise? Wolfstan was not convinced. Despite his intuition telling him she had not accomplished her objective, nothing about the messenger's bearing likened him to the countess. Even had she tried to hide her innate grace, he doubted she would stoop to slouching… as it were. He chuckled at his own wit.

"One more port of call, then, I shall call it a day," he announced to the disinterested walls.

Recalling his pledge to Emory de Wilton, Wolfstan, enjoying the clement air, opted to walk to the offices of Dunstan, Dunstan, and Fitch, where he found his friend immersed in a pile of legal paraphernalia.

"I cannot fathom how you find this more interesting than working for Lucas," Wolfstan teased gently, picking up a sheet of creamy vellum covered in fluid copperplate, and shaking his head.

"Cannot explain it. Makes me sound addled." Emory grinned. "Sit, sit." He indicated an aging and overstuffed leather chair currently providing a home for a stack of papers. "Just put those…" he glanced around, "…on the floor."

Wolfstan chuckled. "That you know where everything is astounds me. It is a mess."

"Yes, but it is an organised mess, and I can put my hands to any document immediately. If someone tidied this up, I would be reduced to a quivering wreck." Emory waved his hand at the teetering heaps of files scattered around the room. "I doubt this is a social call, so how may I help?"

"I am fulfilling my promise... regarding Lady Parham," Wolfstan elucidated at Emory's frown.

He gave his friend a succinct account of his investigation to date, including his hypothesis regarding Madeline's intentions. "I am not asking you to break a confidence, but Alberforce has powerful allies, and Lady Parham is hell-bent on bringing him to his knees. He is dangerous, she is furious — it is a disaster waiting to happen. Is there anything else you think I ought to know?"

Emory studied his friend and sometime colleague. "This goes no further."

He waited until Wolfstan dipped his head in tacit agreement, then divulged what Madeline had disclosed the night of the Merryfields' ball. "Before you ask, I do not know the extent of the abuse but, reading between the lines, I posit Alberforce leans towards the... unorthodox when it comes to the bedchamber."

Wolfstan grimaced. "What a delightful man. My gut tells me, this is going to get worse before it gets better."

"Keep her safe, Carnforth," Emory's tone held a warning.

"You have my word. How is Miss Cardon?"

A warm smile brightened Emory's rather sombre features, then just as quickly faded and a shadow flickered behind his eyes. "I am hopeful." He did not elaborate.

"Do not lose faith, de Wilton. Sometimes, we are blind to the obvious." He hesitated, unwilling to sound pompous, but canny enough to know Emory was floundering. "You know my opinion on romance..." he lifted a brow.

Emory nodded, a reluctant grin surfacing.

"...but, I *am* exceedingly good at reading nuances, and you have nothing to fear where Miss Cardon is concerned. Your devotion will be rewarded, I have no doubt."

With that gem of wisdom, Wolfstan got to his feet, replaced the papers, and took his leave, shaking a speechless Emory's hand.

"Patience, de Wilton. Patience."

CHAPTER EIGHTEEN

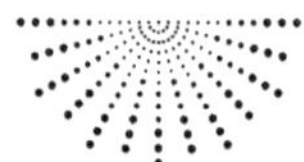

A quiet knock preceded Mr Blake, who entered at the equally quiet, "Come in."

"The message was delivered, Lady Parham." He bowed.

"Was he seen?" Madeline asked.

"As anticipated, his presence was noted, but he was not followed home. Fleet of foot is our Ned," Mr Blake was referring to Ned Dawson, the footman's fifteen-year-old brother. The youngster's official job title was stable hand, but he could turn his hand to most tasks.

"Poor Lord Carnforth. I wish I had seen his face when he realised the delivery boy was not me in disguise." Madeline smirked unrepentantly. "Now, let us see whether the Odious Knave has a conscience."

Mr Blake, who had witnessed more than he would ever reveal to his sorely beleaguered mistress, doubted that very much. The man had fewer morals than a tom cat. "One can only pray, my lady." He dipped his head.

Madeline registered the tinge of unease in his voice. "Soon, Mr Blake. Soon, this will be over and, perhaps, we can live again."

Blake turned to leave, only to hesitate.

"What is it Mr Blake?"

He vacillated, then decided to speak his mind. One thing he had learnt about his mistress was that, as long as respect was maintained, she appreciated honesty.

"Begging your pardon, my lady and 'tis not my place to say, but we are worried for you. Lottie was saying as you'd been upset after the viscount's visit." His cheeks reddened, but his gaze did not waver. The young countess was dear to her staff, all of whom she treated with friendly dignity, none wanted her to suffer any more than she had already.

"Your concern warms my heart, Mr Blake. I grant my scheme is exacting, but Alberforce is the last on my list. He was the worst of…" she let that dangle — to spell it out, unnecessary.

"I am of the opinion, I am not the only woman upon whom he has forced his…" invariably polite, she chose the less explicit, "…peculiarities. A man who required such frequent *entertainment* cannot just stop. It is as much an addiction as gambling, and I often question whether I was his only victim.

"He has not darkened my doorstep since the night Parham died, for which I am exceedingly thankful, but that does not mean he has curtailed his activities. I intend to find out who else he is abusing."

"He is a dangerous man, my lady."

"I know, and I shall take every care."

"Why not ask Lord Carnforth to investigate?"

"He has offered his assistance, but men miss much that women do not, however cunning their tactics. I will keep him informed when I judge it pertinent."

"We are at your service, my lady, please…" Blake clamped his lips together, unwilling to overstep the bounds of propriety.

"Duly noted, and thank you, Mr Blake."

The loyal butler bowed again and retreated, making a mental note to have Ned or Grantley, the groom, follow Lady Parham whenever she left The Lodge.

It was early the following evening before Lord Douglas Gould, Duke of Alberforce, had time to deal with the pile of letters he had received.

One item bore closer scrutiny.

He studied the package placed neatly on the silver platter alongside the rest of his mail. It appeared to be a card and a folded sheet of paper bound by a black ribbon, through which had been tucked a dead rose.

Intrigued, he picked it up and turned it over.

Dry, dark red petals fluttered onto the leather inlay of his desk. Mouth puckered in disapproval, he pulled one end of the ribbon. It came apart smoothly, the satin pooling around the withered blossom. He plucked the decaying stem out of the binding and tossed it into the waste-paper basket to his right.

He read the card first.

For the sin committed,
And the pain endured.
For the respect omitted,
And the silence secured.

Was this some kind of game, a puzzle set by one of his peers? He turned the card, but the other side was blank. His jovial smile faltered at the next stanza.

For the dignity stolen,
And happiness lost.
For promises broken,
You must now pay the cost.

No, this was not a game. About to move on to the accompanying sheet, curiosity got the better of him.

For the silk that restrained,
And the relentless abuse.
For the contempt sustained,
You merit the noose.

Scowling, he grabbed the paper and unfolded it. The words sliced into him.

Your Grace,

The death of your facilitator does not eradicate your guilt. The offence was not committed against him.

You are fortunate, I am of a magnanimous nature and, despite enduring unspeakable torment at your hands, will consider your sin expunged if you make an *anonymous* donation to Sanctuary House in the amount of one hundred pounds.

The reason I chose this charity should be self-explanatory.

To outward appearances, you are a man of

stature who commands respect from his peers. As such, prudence dictates you honour my request. While I care little for my reputation, you, however…

I expect the donation to be made no later than one week from the date of this letter. Rest assured, I shall be informed immediately 'tis paid, at which point, you have my word, any reference to you will be obliterated from the list I hold.

Oh, and before you act rashly, should anything, anything at all, untoward befall me, I have given instructions for your indiscretions to be broadcast.

M

Alberforce ground his teeth, under no illusion as to the sender. "Bitch," he muttered under his breath. "You think you can trick me? *Me?*"

He scrunched up the letter and was about to hurl it into the hearth when there was a knock at the door and his wife entered. He lowered his arm and assumed his most urbane persona.

"Constance?"

"Ahh, Gould you are home. Remember we have seats at the theatre this evening. Parker has drawn you a bath."

"The deuce is that tonight? I had forgotten."

His wife forbore from commenting on his language and nodded. "Do please hurry, or the water will be chilled." She waited, and her husband knew it would be a long evening if he annoyed her.

"Yes, dear." He mustered up a smile, dropped the ball of paper onto the desk, made a mental note to deal with it later, and followed his wife from the room.

Lady Constance Gould, a woman of singular intelligence, noticed her husband flick something onto the desk. His behaviour, always odd, had been more secretive of late, and curiosity got the better of her. As the duke disappeared into his bedchamber, she slipped into the study and, spotting the ball of paper, smoothed it open.

Committing the content to memory, her eyes were drawn to the card which lay on a forlorn heap of dead rose petals. Without touching either, she read the poem, feeling her cheeks blanch.

Her hand fluttered to her chest which ached, memories crowding in. *Not again. I thought he had curbed his appetite. Clearly, it is insatiable.*

Noting that the writer was determined to make the duke pay, Constance pondered her options. *Do I possess the strength to betray my husband?* Her laugh was mirthless. *Who would listen? Who would care? Gould would declare me demented and have me committed to Bedlam before I could blink.*

Sadly, she balled the missive into a lump, replaced it, and continued with her preparations for the evening ahead as though naught was amiss.

The following afternoon, Alberforce did what he had intended the previous evening. He threw the letter into the fireplace, then tore the card into shreds and tossed them on top.

Lighting a spill from one of the candles, flickering jauntily on the mantel, he burnt the offending correspondence, watching the flames lick around the edges, the paper curling and flaring red, before disintegrating into a satisfying pile of embers.

"Lady Parham, prudence dictates *you* ought not make an enemy of me."

He returned to his seat where a glass of brandy awaited. He sipped the amber spirit, pondering Madeline's impudence. The last line of her letter rolled round his head, and he spat an oath. "Act rashly? Time, my dearest Lady Parham is something I have in abundance, and I shall bide it... for now."

He glanced at the aged grandfather clock in the corner. He had an appointment, and to miss it would be... disappointing.

Striding confidently to his destination, his cane tapping the path in emphasis, Lord Alberforce failed to notice he had more than one shadow on this glorious day. Maintaining a discreet distance, a stealthy figure tracked his progress, unaware another followed mere yards behind.

Anyone watching would have been forgiven for thinking they were witness to a Covent Garden satire being played out in suburbia, so comical did it appear.

Madeline Galleron, once again dressed like a street urchin, had slipped out of The Lodge unnoticed — or so she thought — determined to catch the duke *in flagrante delicto,* even if it took weeks of trailing him around London.

On her heels, Wolfstan Colleville, his surveillance paying dividends, equally determined the countess not put herself in harm's way. Unbeknownst to Madeline, a diligent Mr Blake had given Ned his instructions, and that young lad was intercepted by Wolfstan as he dashed out of the front door in hot pursuit of his mistress.

A hurried exchange ensued, and Ned was coaxed into letting the viscount assume control.

Madeline slowed her pace and hung back when Alberforce rapped on the door with the handle of his cane, taking note of the Berkley Street address.

Whoever answered seemed to be stalling the duke's entry, to no avail. The door slammed and silence descended.

Madeline pondered her next move. She did not know the family who lived here, or whether Gould's admittance was for legitimate reasons. She was chewing her lip in a mire of indecision when a voice spoke by her ear, prompting her to smother a startled shriek.

"My lady, I thought we had discussed this."

She whirled around almost colliding with Lord Carnforth.

"Do you *want* to give me apoplexy?" she scolded.

"If it saves you from the gallows, yes," came the smooth reply.

"Do not jest about such things. I am not—"

"You are blackmailing a duke. Who do you suppose the judge will believe?"

"Oh, do stop throwing eminently sensible arguments at me. If you want me to stop, help me catch him."

"The reason I am here," Wolfstan rejoined mildly.

"How did you know?"

"When you told me Swinbourne was the last, you were too quick, too vehement."

"That was all?" Madeline stared at him in surprise.

"It is my job to recognise inflections, nuances, and reactions. Everything about your reply told me your crusade was far from over. I just had to be patient."

Madeline huffed a sigh. "Oddly, I knew you knew. In your shoes, I would not believe me either. I cannot let it rest, my lord. This man…" she bit her lip.

"Is the worst offender," Wolfstan finished for her.

She met his gaze, her eyes troubled. "This is not his residence. He may have a rational explanation for paying a call, but my instinct tells me this is not the case."

"You cannot go barging into someone else's home on the possibility of a maybe. We need to collate evidence. It needs to be irrefutable. Please, trust me, my lady. This is my job. I am experienced in unearthing that which people hope they have buried for ever."

"I feel so, so…" she spread her palms.

"Impotent?" Wolfstan offered.

"Do you take pleasure in completing other people's sentences?" She fixed him with a vexed glare.

"My apologies, you seemed lost for words."

Madeline blew an exasperated, "No, 'tis I who should apologise. You have been nothing but kind, and generous with your time. I am too impetuous. My need to exact my revenge outweighs my discretion."

"Nothing wrong with enthusiasm as long as it is channelled appropriately." Wolfstan's smile soothing ruffled feathers.

He crooked his elbow. "Given where we are, might I be so bold as to invite you to join me for an ice at Gunther's? An opportunity to make a plan."

"I am not exactly dressed for Gunther's," she demurred.

"True, but with you in that garb, we could take advantage of a shady tree and talk without attracting nosy gossips."

Madeline sniggered. "That sounds wonderful and quite

liberating, although mayhap I do not accept your arm. We do not wish to make it easy for the rumour mill."

Wolfstan had come to realise that Lady Parham was a lady of implacable will. In light of this, he had formed a strategy which allowed her to settle the final score, without ending up in Newgate… or worse.

Circling Berkley Square, they found a quiet corner away from the afternoon crowds. Wolfstan purchased an ice each and, after an awkward silence, both spoke at once.

"I am sorry for my emotional outburst…"

"I hope you have quite recovered from…"

They stopped, stared at each other and, for no apparent reason, burst out laughing.

The bout of merriment did more to dispel any vestiges of awkwardness, than trite words or gratuitous apologies. As they enjoyed their ices, the two began to chat. Mundanities quickly evolved into a serious discussion about the Duke of Alberforce.

Wolfstan was not so crass as to allude to the number, he had spied jotted alongside the duke's name in Madeline's notebook. In and of itself, the frequency was unpardonable, but he suspected this was not the only reason, she had saved the duke until last.

With consummate skill, Wolfstan pared back the layers, and, despite Madeline's innate reticence, she let pertinent details slip. He pieced them together, his astute brain adding them to the figurative cauldron brewing Madeline's nightmares.

His job brought him into contact with people from all walks of life and he knew, of course, there were men of a certain persuasion who revelled in dominating everybody around them, including women. Subjugation more exhilarating than a win at the races or at the card table, and resistance made the prize all the sweeter.

"Lady Parham—"

"Oh, do please call me Madeline. Being Lady Parham'd all the time is exhausting, never mind 'tis a name I loathe."

Wolfstan inclined his head. "It would be my honour; on the proviso you agree to reciprocate."

"I should be delighted to call you Madeline." She smiled artlessly, and tipped her cap.

Wolfstan guffawed at her wit. Sobering, he continued, "My name is Wolfstan, but my friends, and I hope that now includes you, call me Wolf."

"I know. It suits you."

"Thank you. Now, are we in accord?" He held her gaze, dove grey on peacock green.

Madeline, relishing the freedom of being dressed like a stable hand, stretched out her legs, and reclined on her elbows, her cap — covering her dark curls — perched on her head at a rakish angle.

Wolfstan's heart thudded. The sentiment which had taken root the day she confessed all, reasserted itself with significant force, and the last hurdle fell.

He could no longer deny the truth of it.

He was in love with Madeline Galleron.

Well, damn it all to blazes.

He was sure he could hear Lucas' mirth ringing in his ears.

CHAPTER NINETEEN

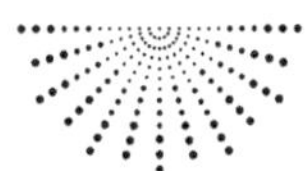

The, blithely ignorant, object of his epiphany — no bad thing — was speaking. Wolfstan dragged his mind back to the conversation.

"…whether there is a pattern."

With no idea what Madeline had said, Wolfstan cocked a brow, hoping she would expand upon her remark, which she did to his relief.

"For instance, is it their age or hair colour or status?"

He realised, she was referring to the women, Alberforce may or may not be targeting. In all fairness, Wolfstan had no proof the duke had abused anyone, even Madeline. He only had her word for it. That said, no lady in her right mind would risk the backlash from Society, never mind the repercussions from the alleged perpetrator, unless it *was* true.

Madeline might be his only victim.

Had Lord Parham persuaded those involved that Madeline was a willing participant in the carnal escapades?

Did Madeline encourage her husband?

Such… *Saturnalian* exploits were not unheard of.

If so, why exact revenge? Now her husband was dead, she

was free to play the game as often as she chose, and by her own rules — yet she had not.

Whichever way he looked at the elements of this case, however he manipulated them to fit a theory, Wolfstan always came back to the same answer. Raymond Galleron had used his young, innocent wife as a pawn in his fantasies. Everything else mushroomed from that one decision.

"I have a proposal," he said to Madeline who was waiting for him to answer her question.

"A proposal?" she echoed.

"To continue along this path, you have set yourself will, almost certainly, lead to disaster. What say we work together? I co-opt you as an investigator for the duration of this investigation. We pool information. You agree not to act alone. I agree to include you in every aspect of proceedings. We must not exceed the bounds of the law, for that makes us no better than he."

Madeline stared at him. To become a member of Lucas' organisation, even briefly was an intriguing and extraordinarily exciting prospect. "What of Major Withers?"

"I have yet to discuss the details, but I believe he will approve. Your welfare is his priority. If you and I, working as a team, precipitate a prompt and tolerable conclusion, he will action my recommendation. There will be paperwork to sign, confidentiality is key, it protects all parties."

Madeline nodded. "I have no objection. How soon might we begin?" A trickle of anticipation ran through her; that it was not entirely related to humiliating the Odious Knave, she ignored… studiously.

"If you are prepared to accompany me to Bow Street, we can complete the formalities and start as soon as we choose."

"Will the Major be offended by…" she indicated her attire.

Wolfstan chuckled. "In truth, I believe he will be amused and impressed."

"Then we have not a moment to lose." Madeline wiped sticky fingers on the lush grass and scrambled to her feet.

Madeline persuaded Wolfstan that a hackney was unnecessary. "It is a glorious afternoon. The walk will be pleasant."

"The neighbourhood around Bow Street is not the most salubrious," Wolfstan said dubiously.

"You forget, I am no stranger to the seedier side of life."

"Suffering it in your own home is one thing, quite another to be confronted with it along dingy backstreets," he replied bluntly.

"Please."

Reluctantly — and questioning whether the woman was some kind of siren, so easily did he relent — Wolfstan acceded.

Lucas, who did not seem unduly perturbed by Lady Parham's unorthodox fashion sense, took little convincing. He posed an assortment of searching questions, judging Madeline to be of sound mind… an understandable craving to give a certain duke a taste of his own medicine, aside. He amended one of the contracts to suit the circumstances, explained it in detail, and they both signed.

"If you two need assistance, I can speak to Hawk. He and Theia have just closed a case and, I have no doubt, would leap at the chance to collaborate. Their inclusion offers a certain flexibility," Lucas suggested.

Wolfstan mulled that over. "I think that is a good strategy. Those two have made melting into a crowd a fine art. Shall I approach Hawk, or will you?"

"Here." Lucas dashed off a couple of lines on a sheet of paper. "Take this, in case you see him before I do."

"Perhaps a visit on our way home is in order. Madeline?" he spoke without thinking.

Lucas appeared not to notice, shuffling documents on his desk to hide a knowing grin.

"I have no pressing engagements," Madeline said. "Who are Hawk and Theia?"

"Hawk is a long-standing member of my group," Lucas interjected. "He married Aletheia Bainard, sister of the Baron de Roumare, must be coming up four years ago. She solved a fine old mystery, which I am sure she would be happy to recount.

"As a result, I invited her to join us. A decision I have never regretted. I foresee, you and she…" he dipped his head at Madeline, "…will become great friends. You are both… hmmm… how to put this politely?" He twinkled. "Incorrigible."

Wolfstan snorted with mirth. Lucas had hit the nail on the head as usual.

Madeline tried to look affronted, but she rather liked the description, satisfying herself with a vaguely disgruntled, "harrumph."

Shortly thereafter — in the main because, this time, Wolfstan insisted they go by carriage not on foot — they were being ushered into an airy parlour in an imposing residence just off Grosvenor Square.

They were greeted by a grave-faced man who towered over the smiling woman alongside him, neither of whom seemed the slightest disconcerted by Madeline's imaginative garb.

"Well met, Wolf. My good man, to what do we owe this

pleasure?"

"Hawk, Theia, this is Lady Madeline Galleron, Countess of Parham. Madeline, Lord Joshua Hawkins, the Viscount Deincourt, and his viscountess, Lady Aletheia Hawkins. I beg your pardon for calling without prior notice, but our presence pertains to a new assignment, one to which Lucas has already given his blessing. If this is inconvenient, might we arrange another interview forthwith?"

Theia brushed off Wolfstan's apology, as she and Hawk curtsied, and bowed respectively to Madeline.

"You know you are always welcome here, Wolf," she tsked. "A new assignment. Oh, that piques my interest." She beamed at her husband who rolled his eyes comically.

"You are incorrigible." He chuckled.

His repeat of Wolfstan's earlier description, made Madeline giggle and, by the time she had clarified her response, the reserve associated with meeting strangers diminished, then evaporated altogether when a soft knock preceded a butler carrying a tray of refreshments.

"Please excuse my woeful state of dress," Madeline felt compelled to apologise. "Not my typical attire when calling on… well… anyone."

"I rather like it, it suits you," Theia placated. "Doubtless you had good reason and is, presumably, connected with why you are here."

The four savoured the treats on offer; cool lemonade and mouth-watering fruit tarts. Theia, adept at putting people at their ease, launched into an amusing monologue about her menagerie, which slid smoothly into light-hearted chatter about nothing of any substance.

Wolfstan, aware evening approached, steered the discussion back to the matter at hand.

"Your hospitality warms me but the day wears on and, irksome as it is, we have business to discuss." Wolfstan interposed at an opportune break in conversation, grinning at Theia's splutter of denial. "The pair of you have been embroiled in a difficult case of late, never mind little Violet and her needs. Time is precious, we shall not waste any more of yours than absolutely necessary."

Wolfstan, at a nod from Madeline, gave an abridged version of the latter's story. In order for his listeners to understand why their help could prove invaluable, certain elements were unavoidable.

His recital was met with silence. Hawk and Theia were not incognisant of what went on behind closed doors, but the duplicity employed by Raymond Galleron left them speechless.

Madeline's discomfiture at being obliged to lay bare what she had kept hidden was allayed by her hosts' unquestioning acceptance, unaware her tale while traumatic was not unique. If everyone lived unblemished lives, Lucas' organisation would be defunct.

"My lady," Hawk started.

"Please do not stand on ceremony with me," Madeline implored. "I hope, now Wolfstan has explained, we shall be seeing each other regularly. I accept etiquette has its place when in public but, perhaps you might be agreeable to dispensing with it in private."

Hawk grinned, and it changed his whole countenance. "For my part, I think that sounds like a capital notion. Theia?" He glanced at his wife, who nodded cheerfully.

"I am notoriously bad at adhering the rules, thus am happy to fall in with your suggestion." Theia said, her comical expression belying her prim reply. "Madeline, I am appalled you have suffered at the hands of those brutes but, I confess, I find your method of justice poetic and quite fiendishly delicious."

"Aletheia Hawkins," her husband feigned shock. "I am of a

mind to curtail your clandestine activities. Clearly, they are having an adverse effect on your sensibilities."

Theia gurgled with laughter, and elbowed Hawk. "I should like to see you try." She returned her attention to Madeline. "Ignore my beloved, he knows not what he is saying. Now, what if…"

The humorous banter was superseded by a serious debate which continued through dinner — Theia overriding the, admittedly token, objections voiced by the visitors with a breezy, "No, I shall not hear of you leaving until we have formulated a strategy. If that takes all night, so be it."

A remark supported by Hawk and, in the face of such determination, Wolfstan and Madeline had no defence.

Spontaneous it may have been but, truth be told, it was a most enjoyable evening.

Naturally inclusive, Theia refused to be deterred by Madeline's habitual reticence and, slowly but surely drew the newcomer out of her shell.

An accomplishment aided and abetted, albeit unknowingly, by baby Violet Amelia who Madeline proclaimed to be utterly adorable, endearing her to Theia on the spot. Precious treasure, Violet might be, but Theia was moved to warn Madeline, "Do not be fooled by her cherubic demeanour, she is a minx."

Violet herself remained supremely indifferent to the adoration being heaped on her downy head and, by the time the two ladies returned to the parlour, they were no longer strangers.

Later, tucked up in bed, midnight a forgotten hour, Madeline ruminated over the whirlwind events of the day. With some surprise, she realised another friendship, born of happenstance, had been forged.

This first meeting led to several more, during which tactics were discussed with the precision of a military operation. Madeline who, until now, had taken pride in her stealthy approach was fascinated listening to the professionals. The covert group's scope of operations was vast and intricate, their contacts innumerable. Her efforts seemed inept by comparison, despite the trio's assurances to the contrary.

"To confront those who have harmed you, even obliquely, takes courage, especially when you are a woman," was Hawk's considered opinion. "Moving forward, you have our support and protection."

"Do you think there is any chance he will try to misrepresent things to his advantage? Hand in the letter to the authorities, be they Lucas or the Runners, and claim he knows the writer. Will he try to ruin me further," Madeline paused, "or worse, do so publicly?"

"He may, although, I doubt it. Bullies are essentially cowards," Wolfstan said. "We shall cross that bridge if we come to it. Currently, you have the upper hand, let us try to maintain that position. If the evidence against him is overwhelming, sense ought to prevail."

Madeline gave a sceptical snort. Sense was a relative concept when it came to the Odious Knave, demonstrated by his belief he was untouchable, immune to censure, and above the rules.

Time would tell.

CHAPTER TWENTY

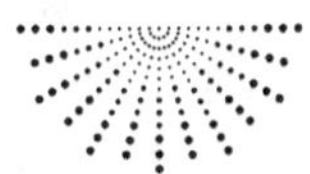

The glorious weather broke. A slow-moving storm rolled through London, lashing the city with driving rain and strong, gusty winds. The ominous grey sky was rent by jagged spears of lightning, and to step outside meant an instant drenching.

Madeline loved storms, but the timing of this one left her crotchety. She had things to do, a mission to accomplish.

"Was this really necessary?" she groused to God, or whichever celestial being was behind the tempest. The answer, a blinding flash of light and a deafening crash.

"Fine." She lifted her palms. "You win." She wandered the house, picking things up at random and replacing them, uncharacteristically at a loss. Her aimless pacing took her upstairs and, for no reason she could fathom — then or ever — came to the one suite she had never entered.

The domain of Raymond's first wife, Edith, a woman about whom Madeline knew nothing.

Madeline hardly gave the rooms or their erstwhile incumbent any thought, other than to feel sorry for her, although Galleron's inflexion when informing her they were out of bounds, had been almost tender, certainly warmer than any tone he used when addressing her.

Had he cared for Edith, maybe even loved her? Madeline's lip curled, unable to equate the man she had married with an emotion as complex as love.

Well, Lord Parham is dead, the house is mine to do with as I choose, and his directives no longer apply.

She grasped the knob, hesitated, then before her head talked her out of it, twisted the handle with some force, and pushed the door.

The heavy silence with which Madeline was greeted, brought her to a halt. Poised on the threshold, she surveyed the room, unable to shake the impression she was trespassing. The curtains were open, prompting her to speculate whether one of the staff was tasked with attending to them every day… as though the last inhabitant still lived.

The room looked spotless, but an air of abandonment lingered, the gloom matched by the leaden sky visible through the rain smeared windows.

The, what had surely once upon a time been, cosy aspect, along with the handful of chairs and a couple of ornate occasional tables, suggested this was Edith's boudoir. Madeline padded across the thick rug and, still feeling like an interloper, entered the bedchamber.

Opening the door sent dust motes spiralling in the dim light, and Madeline fought the urge to waft them away as though in doing so might banish the wisps of spectral ancestors.

She sneezed, which had the same effect.

Decorated in delicate shades of pink and plum, Madeline presumed the room reflected its last occupant. Slowly, she walked around, running gentle fingers over the sumptuous bed covers, the elaborate dressing table, the polished wood of the armoire and chest of drawers.

Sinking onto the bed, she tried to ignore the curious ache forming under her breast. The fabrics and furniture were rich, elegant, and expensive.

She recalled the decor of her own rooms prior to the recent refurbishment. Compared with this suite — adequate was the best description she could come up with.

As with everything about her marriage, Galleron had ensured she had the basics, but cared little for her comfort or well-being. This luxurious bedchamber, beseeming a countess, a prime example.

"Second best. It was ever thus, Madeline," she chided. Her parents were indifferent to their daughter; she could not recall a single instance where they showed a soupçon of interest in her, save as a means to an end. Galleron's offer of marriage, an answer to their prayers and his debt.

The spark of anger that she would never know why her husband had chosen to offer her up as some kind of toy to his friends, smouldered, followed by the question as to whether a single one of them had been a friend in the first place. Would friends treat another's wife so callously? It seemed doubtful.

"Nothing you can do," she muttered balefully. "Galleron is dead, and his cronies are unlikely to explain their deviance."

Standing, she prowled the room, checking the drawers and the armoire, combing through the exquisite garments. Her fury mounted, remembering Raymond's irascible reaction to the forest-green gown.

One wall of the large dressing room was lined with a vast array of dresses, coats, shoes, and accessories, so many, Madeline was speechless. It looked as though a modiste's shop had exploded. Clearly, money had been no object when it came to Edith and her wardrobe.

A stunning red creation caught her eye, and she lifted it

out, astonished to realise the dress, along with more than a few others, had never been worn. What a waste.

Hanging it on the door, she took a step back to admire it. The style — off the shoulder, tucked waistline, and flowing skirt — bore no resemblance to the current fashion. *Why on earth had Edith commissioned it?* Madeline mused, the silk whispering under her fingertips.

She inspected a few more, discovering them to be of a similar design; some bright, others in muted hues. A trickle of excitement ran through her. She loved beautiful clothes as much as the next woman. Unable to help herself, she pulled the deep plum cord by the bed.

Moments later, Lottie knocked and poked her head around the door. "My lady?" she asked, nonplussed at finding her new mistress in her old mistress' chambers.

"Oh, Lottie, forgive me for interrupting your day, but might you assist me?" Madeline indicated the dress.

"O-of c-course," Lottie stammered, flustered.

"Do not fret, Lottie, you are not breaking any rules. Any instructions Lord Parham gave, became null and void upon his demise, and I refuse to pander to a dead man's whims, nor do I intend to leave these clothes for the moths. Some, I may keep, if they fit. Perhaps you girls, Mrs Watson, and Biddy might see something you like.

"Yes." She wagged a finger when Lottie tried to demur. "Why not? Consider it a thank you. If they are too frivolous, I'm sure they can be adjusted to suit. The rest can be donated to Sanctuary House."

Unwilling to point out that women of her station had no call to wear pretty gowns, while a secret thrill rippled through her at the very idea, Lottie held her tongue and helped Madeline into the red dress.

It fitted as though made for her, the vivid shade enhancing Madeline's dark hair and green eyes. Madeline glanced in the pier glass, turning this way and that, nodding her approval.

"Oh, 'tis perfect my lady." Lottie clapped her admiration. "I cannot think why the first Lady Parham chose this colour. Would make her look right sickly." The maid ran a knowledgable eye over the remaining gowns hanging in the dressing room, a handful catching her attention. "As would these." She frowned in confusion. "How odd."

"Mayhap Lord Parham preferred Edith to wear bright colours."

Lottie snorted her derision before she could stop herself. "Oh, beggin' your pardon, my lady, but his lordship wouldn't know a pink ballgown from a white chemise or a blue spencer. As long as her ladyship was dressed to suit the occasion, he did not care what colour, material, or style."

"A conundrum indeed. Regrettably one which will go unsolved. The lady in question is no longer here to enlighten us."

Changing into her plain, morning gown, Madeline thanked Lottie and dismissed her, smiling as the young maid scampered off to the kitchens to share the news about the clothes.

Before the womenfolk of the household descended, en masse, Madeline took another look around the room.

Besides the clothes and a couple of oddments on the dressing table — brush, comb, a collection of hairpins — there were no personal items. Nothing to connect this room with Lady Edith Parham. No books or paintings or jewellery, not even a childhood doll perched on a chair, a link to her family. Madeline walked back into the sitting room, nothing there either.

The entire suite was soulless.

. . .

There must be something. Determined now, Madeline scoured the suite, checking under the pillows, behind the little cabinets and occasional tables, and under the cushions. About to give up, a thought struck her, and she lifted the corner of the mattress nearest the bedside table. There, tucked between the folds of a sheet, a small book.

Extracting it carefully, Madeline walked over to the window. Bound in dark brown leather, softened by age and use, the book's pages were covered in small, neat script. A flurry of rain spattered the glass and Madeline shivered.

Better to peruse this in the comfort of the library by the fire, than here where a ghost lurked.

Curled up in her favourite chair, the chill of Edith's rooms extinguished by the merry crackle of the flames in the hearth, and a hot cup of coffee within reach, Madeline began to read Edith's journal.

Two hours later, she lifted her head, her mind in turmoil. In her hands, proof of Alberforce's iniquity. While the contents would not hold up in a court of law — the victim was long dead, and any half-decent lawyer could argue the words were of a woman scorned — it was enough to establish a pattern.

That she, Madeline, was not the only one to bear the brunt of the duke's aberrant appetite offered little consolation, but she could not deny the sense of satisfaction the knowledge engendered.

She found it curious, that apparently, Galleron had not received any remuneration for whoring out his first wife or, perhaps he had and, for reasons known only to him, did not commit the details to paper.

Poor Edith, Madeline thought, her heart aching. *Did she protest? Did she weep in the privacy of her chambers? Did she lose faith in humanity?* The man who vowed, before God and family, to love, comfort, honour, and protect her, had violated every oath — almost immediately their troth was plighted, if the dates in the journal were correct.

One more innocent young woman, voiceless in her gilded cage.

The sorrow chafing at Madeline's mind was ousted by a savage fury.

Enough.

If it took 'til her dying breath, she was going to bring the Odious Knave to his knees.

Eventually, the storm blew itself out, but not before uprooting scores of trees, ripping boats from their moorings along the Thames, and dislodging a considerable number of roof tiles.

Dawn broke to a perfect summer's morning, belying the havoc wrought across the city. The azure sky, washed clean of ominous grey, seemed to sparkle.

The Lodge had suffered nothing more serious than flattened garden beds, which although a relief to most of the household was of no solace to poor Dodds who spent the day trying to save his beloved plants.

Madeline, leery of turning up at Bow Street uninvited, sent a note to Wolfstan asking whether he might call at his earliest convenience.

. . .

The day was waning when Mr Blake knocked on the door of the library.

"Come in," Madeline's distracted voice invited. Engrossed in transposing relevant details from Edith's diary into her growing set of notes, she was only half aware of the intrusion.

She looked up at Mr Blake's, "The Viscount Carnforth, Lady Parham. Are you receiving?"

It took several seconds for his question to register, then she nodded eagerly. "Most definitely, Mr Blake. Please show him in and organise some refreshments." She glanced at the clock on the mantel, startled to see it was almost half past four. "Goodness, but the day has flown."

Blake grinned, bowed, and vanished to return with Wolf-stan on his heels.

Greetings and expected pleasantries exchanged, Madeline ushered Wolfstan into the chair she had just vacated.

"You wished to see me?" he asked.

"I found this today." She handed him the journal, perched on the edge of the desk, and waited.

Puzzled, Wolf opened the book and read the flyleaf. "Edith Galleron?" he queried.

"Raymond's first wife."

"Ahhhh…" he turned the page and, briefly, a hush enveloped the room.

His reaction mirroring that of his hostess, Wolf raised his eyes to study Madeline who was staring at him, her green gaze dark, brooding.

"You are not the first." It was a statement not a question, but she nodded.

"Aside from the fact my husband was quite the entrepreneur, it is further evidence against Alberforce, for which I am heartened and disgusted."

"How did you come into possession of this?" He waved

the journal.

Madeline explained about the suite of rooms. "Parham forbade me access, and to be honest, I had no reason to enter the bedchamber of a dead woman. I suppose, yesterday, I was bored. This house is now mine. His instructions carry no weight and, in truth, I was being inquisitive...."

Wolfstan's arched brow invited her to continue.

"I think, in his own way, he loved her, or at least bore her strong affection," she described the decor and the comforts lacking in her own suite. "I was just a means to an end, a commodity not a wife." She shrugged, ostensibly indifferent, but Wolfstan was not fooled.

A beautiful young woman bound to a man twenty years her senior by arrangement, was hard enough — although such unions were not always unhappy, and often muddled along in a contented fashion, if both husband and wife found some common ground between them — but to discover your spouse's sole intention was to use you for monetary gain would be soul destroying.

The notion as to whether Madeline might ever recover from the ignominy — however private, reared in his mind again.

He studied her, meditatively, recognising the anger simmering beneath the surface and silently lauded her for the emotion. Madeline was not a woman to be cowed. Yes, she needed to heal, to be persuaded that men, in general, were not dastardly curs, but she would prevail, of that he had no doubt.

CHAPTER TWENTY-ONE

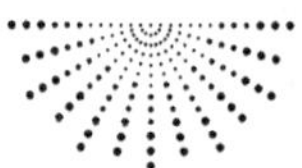

As spring slid joyfully into summer, little by little, and with the virtuosity of the most accomplished musician... or spy... Wolfstan made himself indispensable to Madeline.

Camouflaged within the scheme instigated by the quartet, made up of Madeline, Hawk, Theia, and himself, he set about shattering her carefully erected barriers.

Madeline, immersed in her determination to bring Alberforce to his knees, had no idea what was happening, and by the time she registered Wolfstan's intent... it was too late.

The more they studied their prey, the easier it became for them to predict when Alberforce, a creature of habit, was about to leave his house or his club. At least one of them trailed him from a discreet distance, often sharing the task, so as not to draw attention.

To be fair, for the most part, there was little to get excited about. Wolfstan had warned Madeline that gathering evidence, while essential, tended to be mundane. Hours of boredom interspersed with bursts of activity and, currently, the former outweighed the latter.

To outward appearances, Alberforce lived an uneventful life. Parliamentary committees, of which he chaired two and was on the board of three more, his club — every day from four until six — then home to his wife. His two sons, married with children of their own, visited periodically.

Initially, his routine did not alter, and they feared their efforts would be in vain, that the day Madeline followed Alberforce, he was on legitimate business.

Until the second Tuesday of the month.

Hawk reported that Alberforce had returned to the same house, tucked along Berkley Street, to where Madeline had tracked the duke, less than a month previously.

Was it a coincidence?

Possibly.

When it happened again the following Saturday, the four were encouraged and saddened. While it appeared to reinforce Madeline's supposition, none wanted it proved correct.

After catching Madeline outside the house, Wolfstan had discovered it was the abode of Lord and Lady Ffinch, Earl and Countess of Bayling. They had two sons and a daughter, only one of whom — the latter — remained at home.

Daphne Ffinch was barely more than a child. At seventeen, she was enjoying her first season and, as far as Wolfstan could determine, was inherently shy and a bit of a wallflower.

"Which is why he targeted her," Madeline pointed out, grimacing ominously. "Anyone who is popular and outgoing, who has a number of friends cannot be cowed or inveigled easily. They are not vulnerable. I wonder whether her parents know. Oh, give me five minutes alone with him. Yes,

yes, I know what we agreed." She caught Wolfstan's expression. "I am not addled."

Wolfstan did not expect the elbow to his ribs. "What was that for?" he protested.

"I heard your thoughts," she narrowed her eyes at him.

"I cry foul." Wolfstan could not prevent a roguish grin.

"Of course, you do, Viscount Innocence."

They bantered back and forth, conversation no longer a chore, but an amusing diversion.

Neither noticed Hawk and Theia swap meaningful looks.

To Hawk's good-humoured resignation, Theia cajoled Madeline into helping her dress like a street urchin. The two spent gleeful hours perfecting a Cockney drawl and coming up with imaginative ways of applying soot and dust, the results evoking chimney sweeps.

The ploy worked. No one suspected the pair of giggling ruffians were two well-bred ladies of the *ton*.

Evidence was collated, noted, and filed. No one was under the illusion Alberforce would ever be called to account for his malfeasance and the idea of him facing a judge was laughable.

Their aim, by presenting him with undeniable proof of protracted abuse and extortion, was to impress on him that terminating his exploits would be beneficial to his health — without actually saying so… of course.

Time drifted on; dazzling days of uninterrupted sunshine combined with summer's heat prompted many in Society to contemplate their remove to cooler country estates for the duration. The end of the Season loomed, triggering a flurry of balls; a handful to which Madeline was invited.

Among them — to her undisguised astonishment — one from the Duke and Duchess of Alberforce.

Never was it clearer that the lady of the house was in charge of organising entertainment. Madeline envisaged Alberforce's reaction at her name being floated past him as a possible guest.

A sardonic smile played over her lips as the now familiar warning bells clanged in her head. She ought to decline, but an imp within overrode her common sense.

Could she go alone? Yes, she was perfectly capable of attending *any* Society event on her own, but to arrive on the arm of a handsome escort might silence the catty lips of the gossips.

Unbidden, Wolfstan's face swam over her vision, and an image of them dancing together sent sublime tingles up and down her spine. *Really Madeline,* she chastised herself, *what was that about silencing the gossips?*

Never mind them, would he *be amenable?*

Leaning against the desk, tapping the invitation on her palm, idly, she ran her mind over the previous few weeks, recalling every gesture, every conversation, evaluating every interaction with shrewd deliberation.

As adroit as Wolfstan believed he was, he lacked feminine intuition. Fleeting indications, imperceptible unless you dissected the scene with the finesse of a surgeon, became blindingly obvious and, once seen, coalesced into a pattern which created a most intriguing picture.

Again, Madeline was confounded that the idea of spending time with Wolfstan in a more intimate setting did not frighten or disgust her… rather, it enticed. The vague sentiment, the one which had teased her when first they crossed paths returned to tantalise.

Do I not deserve some happiness, a romance… maybe something more…?

She waited for the strenuous denial to reverberate around her brain.

Silence.

Interesting…

She smiled. This was definitely worth exploring further.

The next day, Madeline and Wolfstan were leaving the office on Bow Street after a brief meeting with Lucas to update him on their progress.

"Do you consider it presumptuous for a lady to ask a gentleman to escort her to a ball?" Madeline threw out the enquiry artlessly.

"Beg pardon?" Wolfstan stopped abruptly to stare at her, not sure he had heard correctly.

Madeline repeated her question.

"I suppose it depends on the lady and gentleman. Are they known to each other? More than passing acquaintances? Friends by family association? Related? Why?"

"I should like to invite you to accompany me to the Alberforce ball two nights hence but am concerned it will be viewed as audacious." Madeline blushed furiously.

Wolfstan felt his jaw drop. This *was* an unexpected turn of events. His chest tightened as he searched her face. Cheeks rosy, eyes wary.

He removed his topper to sweep a flourishing bow. "It

would be my honour, but are you sure you wish to set foot in his home?" His tone solicitous.

"I deem it essential. He always had the advantage, I think 'tis time the tables were turned."

"He is a powerful man, Madel—"

"Do you think me a fool?" she interrupted. "I just want him to see me, fully clothed, somewhere other than my husband's bed." She choked out the words, humiliation washed over her, but it needed to be said. "To show him I am no longer his pawn to be intimidated, that I have thrown off his invisible shackles."

Wolfstan looked troubled.

"What?" she challenged, uncaring how impolite she sounded.

"Have you?" he asked quietly.

Madeline gaped at him. *What does he think I have been doing these last months? Sitting on a chaise, drowning my sorrows in laudanum?* She opened her mouth to give Wolfstan a piece of her mind when he spoke first.

"I am not denigrating what you have achieved thus far. You are a lady of indomitable strength and character, and your determination not to succumb is laudable, but he continues to haunt you. I humbly postulate that attending this ball is not a chance to demonstrate to *him* that you have triumphed, but to yourself."

"Me?" Madeline scoffed, then paused to mull this over. "Me...?"

"Do you care one fig for Alberforce?"

"Not even half a fig," her reply, emphatic.

"In which case..." He left that dangling.

"The point I am proving is to *me*..." a note of wonder laced her tone. "I am the one who has permitted him to dog my steps when, 'tis unlikely he gives me a moment's regard, never mind allows me to consume his every waking moment.

I am the one who has granted him dominance. He would be jubilant if he knew," Madeline growled her aggravation. "Why has it taken me so long to see?"

Wolfstan shrugged. "I wish I had the answer. I am sure I could sell it." He grinned. "More importantly, you have recognised it."

"There was I thinking I was being oh so clever with my poem and my black rose, and my behests for recompense. What a waste of effort."

"Not at all. You have forced them to confront and make amends for their actions. That is never a waste. To permit them to continue without recourse is tacit approval of their behaviour. Too often have lips remained sealed when they should have shouted the transgressions to the skies."

"Do you think facing him is the right thing to do?" Suddenly unsure, Madeline could not quite quash the tremor in her voice.

"I think it will be a very solid start, and you will not be facing him alone."

Madeline twisted to look at him and their eyes met.

They stared at each other, oblivious of being buffeted by the crowds of passers-by.

A tacit message winged between them.

Madeline's heart skipped a beat.

No more words were necessary.

Madeline might have been surprised and perhaps secretly amused to know that, contrary to her supposition, she *had*, of late, become somewhat of a fixture in Lord Alberforce's thoughts.

Her bold missive, bristling with suppressed outrage,

taunted the duke. He had relished trying to tame her spirit, to quash her natural exuberance, only to have his entertainment curtailed by Parham's inconvenient death. Their arrangement had been most expedient; to be compelled to seek fresh meat… so to speak… was not only irritating but also arduous.

Lady Madeline Parham needed reminding of her place. She would rue the day, she tried to blackmail him into parting with a farthing never mind one hundred pounds. The nerve.

He would bring her to her knees… a sneer curled his mouth… the perfect position for what he had in mind.

When his wife suggested they host a ball to mark the end of the Season, it presented the opportunity he was looking for. Dragged into a discussion regarding the guest list over breakfast, Alberforce had interjected a seemingly disinterested remark about his dear friend Parham's widow, resulting in Madeline's invitation — despite the latter's assumption he had no involvement.

He left the house that morning with more of a spring in his step than usual, completely unaware those steps were shadowed by the subject of his musings.

The Lodge

Wolfstan stood at the foot of a sweeping staircase watching Madeline descend… or rather glide down the richly carpeted flight.

Her unorthodox, off-the-shoulder, vermillion gown ought to have shocked him with its flamboyance in an era when pastel hues were favoured, but it had quite the opposite effect. The vibrant silk complemented Madeline's creamy skin and accentuated the deep red tones — reminiscent of an expensive claret — threaded through her ebony hair.

Lottie followed Madeline down, carrying a delicately patterned, fine woollen wrap, which she draped artfully around Madeline's shoulders.

Wolfstan swallowed, once, twice, coercing his brain into coherence.

"My lady." He bowed. "You quite take my breath away and will be the belle of the ball."

Madeline, slightly flustered by Wolfstan's reaction, blushed. "Thank you," she whispered.

He crooked his arm, and she slid her gloved hand through it, gripping his sleeve.

"Ready?" He smiled then, and the momentary hesitancy hovering between them, evaporated like dawn's mist.

"As I'll ever be," she replied.

The evening was warm, but Madeline drew the wrap around her like a cloak, then thanked her faithful maid, adding, "You have worked wonders this evening."

"Go on with you, milady." Now it was Lottie's turn to blush. "You always look beautiful."

Madeline chuckled. "I think you may need a quizzing glass, but I appreciate your sentiment. Enjoy your evening."

"I hope yours is magical, milady," Lottie opened the door and watched her mistress walk down to the waiting carriage. Aware of where the ball was being held, she uttered a heart-felt plea under her breath, "Please do not let him 'urt 'er."

CHAPTER TWENTY-TWO

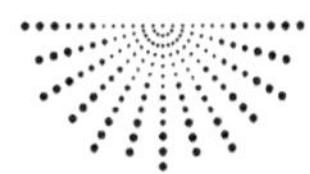

Hollywell House
The Alberforce Ball

As befitted a duke and duchess, the ball was a lavish and glittering affair. Huge bouquets of exotic flowers adorned every surface, marble plinths displaying a veritable medley of colourful plants were scattered throughout the rooms, delicate greenery was entwined around elegant columns, all bathed in the glow of innumerable candles.

Lady Alberforce had transformed her home into a summer garden.

Alighting from carriages lined up around the square, expensively attired lords and ladies entered through the great double doors, which stood open to allow the evening breeze to drift in keeping the interior cool and fresh.

Announced by a smartly liveried footman, the guests greeted their hosts, then followed a short corridor to the ballroom.

. . .

Leaving her wrap in the retiring room, Madeline joined Wolfstan who was lounging casually against a balustrade. He straightened up when he saw her coming towards him, his breath — as was becoming a habit — catching in his throat.

She was enchanting.

Madeline met his eye and dropped a slow wink, which did nothing for his heart rate but served to corral wayward thoughts.

"A sumptuous display," she murmured. "The duchess has ensured her ball will be remembered for many months."

"A success indeed," Wolfstan replied. "I suspect, her husband will remember it for a completely different reason, but I trust you will not mar her Grace's endeavours." He studied Madeline's face.

She swatted him gently on the chest with her fan. "Please afford me a little credit. I am not so crass as to spoil a lady's evening. This is merely a chance for me to retrieve my dignity. If an opportunity does not present itself, I am confident there will be another."

He smiled and took her arm. "Come Lady Parham, might you grant me the honour of your first dance this evening?"

"Why, Lord Carnforth, I should be delighted."

The couple waited in line to be announced and exchanged the requisite formalities with their hosts.

Prettily, Madeline curtseyed and thanked Lady Alberforce for her generous invitation, then pinned the duke with a look designed to flay him. He appeared unmoved, returning her glance with scarcely veiled contempt.

Before Madeline could react, Wolfstan pressed his hand against her back, urging her along the hall to a set of open doors leading to the ballroom.

Strains of music, snatches of chatter and laughter and clink of glasses wafted towards them, and they walked into a scene of light and colour and movement.

In one corner, an octet was playing a lively waltz, encouraging couples to take a turn on the dance floor. Whirled around by their partners, the ladies' gowns created a shimmering blur of pastel rainbows.

At the far side of the ballroom, Madeline spied — through a series of arches — tables laden with food, and more people milling about. To her right, French doors opened onto a broad terrace overlooking the rear gardens of the mansion.

There was no denying, this was an impressive house and, despite her antipathy towards Alberforce, Madeline had to admit the place possessed a welcoming ambience, as though the inhabitants loved it.

That the Odious Knave appreciated *anything* was so at odds with her evaluation of him, she almost laughed out loud… making do with a wry chuckle.

"Something amusing?" Wolfstan asked.

She enlightened him.

"Contrariness personified." He grinned. "Now, put him out of your mind and enjoy the evening."

Usually uncomfortable in any large group of people, and especially amongst the oft snooty members of the *ton*, Madeline realised to her amazement, she *was* enjoying herself.

Not unknown among her peers, she was drawn into conversation with a handful of acquaintances with whom she once shared a warm rapport. She was even persuaded into a dance or three.

Mid-evening found her perusing the laden banqueting table, unable to decide between sweet or savoury.

Deciding to have a mix, she was filling a plate with an interesting array of tasty treats, when her hand was stayed by a familiar voice. Unwilling to place either of them in an awkward situation, discretion advised she disappear, only to pause when she heard her name.

"Lady Parham."

Reluctantly, she turned, her gaze meeting that of a somewhat shamefaced Lord Holles.

"My lord." She curtsied, schooling her features.

"Lady Parham, I know this sounds like a hollow and belated platitude, but I wish to extend my sincere apologies for my unconscionable behaviour.

"Regardless of how your late husband couched his…" a flare of red stained Lord Holles' cheeks, but he continued delicately, "offer, my acceptance made me worse than he.

"Nothing can undo what I have done, and I do not expect your forgiveness, but I pray one day you find some peace… it is the very least you deserve after what you endured."

He bowed and made to walk away.

Well, that *was unexpected.* Madeline stared at the earl, nonplussed. *Do I absolve him, or let him stew in his shame?* Her own words came back to her; holding onto the anger, however righteous, did not affect them, only her.

She steeled herself.

"Lord Holles."

His puzzlement evident, he stopped and waited… undoubtedly anticipating a well-justified roasting.

"Thank you for your candour, it took courage and speaks to your integrity, as did your generous donation. I accept your apology, for to reject it wounds only me and not you."

She was about to leave it there, when she felt impelled to add, "I am reminded of the old proverb about the grass being greener. It is almost never true but teaches us to appreciate what we have. If we don't, it can be lost in the blink of an eye." She smiled slightly, dipped her head, and walked away.

Lord Holles watched her go, admiring her fortitude,

endlessly glad common sense had prevailed, preventing him from compounding the biggest mistake of his life.

Wolfstan appeared by Madeline's elbow. "Is everything all right?" he asked solicitously. "That cannot have been a comfortable encounter."

She recounted the conversation. "I admit to being surprised, pleased, and oddly relieved. I acknowledge they are quite separate reactions but, for so long, forgiving has been tantamount to forgetting, and to forget implied their behaviour was of little importance."

"And now?"

"That brief conversation reminded me, one does not stipulate the other. A most liberating experience." She grinned quite unselfconsciously, her eyes gleaming, her demeanour serene.

While Wolfstan wanted nothing more than to whisk her into his arms and kiss her senseless, he made do with, "An encouraging corollary," and diverted her by pinching one of the miniature cakes on her plate.

It did the trick.

"Lord Carnforth, for shame, stealing a lady's food, get your own," she admonished, without heat, which led into a gentle repartee about the delicious fare.

The clock had long struck midnight when Madeline, about to tell Wolfstan it was high time she found her bed, came face to face with the scourge of her existence as she took the air on the terrace.

"Ahh, the valiant Lady Parham," Alberforce's voice spoke from beyond her line of sight.

Spinning on her heels, she watched as he peeled out of

the darkness below the terrace, climbing the steps to where she stood.

"Your Grace," Madeline's tone was nothing short of derisory. "Skulking in the shrubbery? Why am I not surprised?"

"Tsk, tsk, my lady. Given your recent quest to extort money from me, that is rather like the pot calling the kettle black." Oozing hostility, he stationed himself between his prey and the glass doors.

Even knowing Wolfstan was probably within screaming distance, Madeline could not prevent the foreboding which slunk down her spine. Currently, she was quite alone save the man in front of her.

Quashing it, she leant against a pillar, wafted her fan, and reflected, "Nothing wrong with being a pot, they are most useful implements, both for cooking and bashing people over the head."

Alberforce was not amused. "If you pursue this infantile venture, I shall make your life a living hell."

Madeline snorted with laughter. "You mean it is not already? You snivelling plague sore. Two years… two years of my life lost because you and Parham's miserable rooting hogs refused to visit a brothel. Yes," she goaded, seeing the duke's shock at this revelation, "you think you were the only one? His special friend? An exclusive invitation to fornicate with his supposedly willing wife?

"Pah," she spat, "his treachery was not limited to me. Go on, I challenge you to do your worst."

Madeline flipped her hand dismissively.

In a flash, Alberforce reached out to clutch her flailing wrist in his left hand and jerked her closer to him. He bent his head until their noses almost brushed. "You are no better than a cheap strumpet—"

"One you were only too happy to bed," Madeline hissed.

She twisted her arm, but his fingers were too tight. "Release me you rotten piece of pondweed."

He carried on speaking as though she had not interrupted. "—and you will end up in a pauper's grave when I am finished with you." His right hand lifted to circle her throat, relishing the leap of her pulse under his thumb, as his palm bruised the tender skin.

"Oh, and to finish you would give me such pleasure," he almost crooned, his voice hypnotic.

Motionless, Madeline fought to stave off an icy terror.

"Such pleasure." He increased the pressure around her neck. "Preferably while you are restrained. To see your body bow as you gasp for air would be... bewitching."

That he could do exactly as he promised was indisputable, but she refused to give him the satisfaction of betraying her apprehension. The fact they were in his own home, practically in full view of his guests, steadied her nerves.

Surreptitiously, using her free hand, and without moving her head, she rifled through the hidden pocket of her gown, withdrew a piece of white cotton, tucked it into his waistcoat pocket, and patted it.

Distracted, he took a step back, and Madeline wrenched herself free.

Rubbing her throbbing wrist, she glared at him with undisguised malevolence. "*You* are the fool. Had you paid your debt, I would be nothing more than a temporary aberration, consigned to your past but, noooo, you cannot comprehend the notion, a woman might best you, or have the tenacity to demand redress.

"'Tis *you* who ought to be careful. Secrets have a curious way of being unearthed, and sins rarely remain quiescent. Rest assured, *mine* will not be the pauper's grave."

Alberforce removed the square of cotton and shook it

out. The black *A*, stark against the pristine white of the material. For all his faults… and they were too numerous to list… Alberforce was a well-educated and well-read man and knew to what the single letter referred.

His eyes widened then narrowed to angry slits. Recognising his attempts to intimidate had failed, he released a string of expletives, interspersed with threats of bodily harm, to which Madeline reciprocated in kind.

Their raised voices attracted the attention of those guests near the French windows, including Wolfstan who was observing the antagonists from a judicious distance, ready to intervene when he deemed it pertinent…

The duke's hand lifted to Madeline's throat.

…like right now.

Unobtrusively, he skirted the ballroom, and walked out onto the terrace, just as Madeline delivered a resounding slap to Alberforce's cheek.

"You do not own me, you… you… *lickspittle*. Your reign over my life ended with Parham's death, but," she jabbed her finger at the duke, "watch your back, you never know when I will strike next."

Deliberately, she paused for dramatic effect. "Do you believe me?" Her question catapulted the pair back to the night Galleron died.

Alberforce, rendered speechless by her audacity, recovered himself, and Wolfstan had no idea what might have happened had he not appeared.

"Is this entirely necessary?" he interjected equably. "Arguing like a pair of drunken dockhands at so prestigious a ball is unbecoming… for both of you. Lady Parham…" He did not wait for Madeline to reply, merely hooked her arm through his, and escorted her into the house through a door at the end of the terrace, avoiding the ballroom altogether.

He marched her along a dim, carpeted hall and opened another door. The room was in darkness, save one candelabra standing on the mantle, the trio of candles almost burnt to stubs.

Madeline glanced around. They were in the study. A large desk dominated the room at one end, the other a great fireplace, laid but not lit. Between the two windows framed by deep green curtains, a bookcase. A dark rug in shades of russet and sage graced the floor, and four chairs placed at random angles completed the space.

The understated, minimalist decor was in contrast with the parts of the house Madeline had seen thus far. A very masculine space. This was the Odious Knave's domain.

She shuddered in distaste and prepared to beat a hasty retreat.

Before she could take a single step, Wolfstan swung her to face him. "What did we discuss, not three hours ago? What happened to, 'Please afford me a little credit. I am not so crass as to spoil a lady's evening'? Madeline…" he perched on the desk behind him and opened his palms in a *what the hell were you thinking* gesture.

"The man accosted me on the terrace, spewing all manner of obnoxious drivel. What was I supposed to do? Walk away?" Madeline retorted, in high dudgeon.

"Yes," came the emphatic reply.

"I could not," she huffed. "He barred my way back into the ballroom. Neither was I going to scuttle away like a scared mouse." Madeline strode up and down the room, ranting about the duke's iniquity, none of which was erroneous to be fair. The soft silk of her gown swirled around her and caught in the candlelight by her erratic pacing, the hue morphed from scarlet to flame to crimson.

Wolfstan did not move, content to let her expend her ire in this quiet study away from the gossipmongers.

Eventually, her spleen vented, Madeline came to a halt in front of him, hands on her hips, cheeks flushed, and seething like a cat who's dinner has just escaped down a hole.

She was magnificent.

"Well?" She drew in a breath, presumably preparing to release another tirade.

Without a word, Wolfstan rose, took her hand and, as she opened her mouth, he kissed her… hard.

Madeline froze.

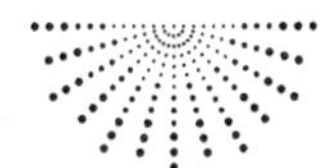

CHAPTER TWENTY-THREE

Madeline's immediate impulse was to punch Wolfstan or, better still, knee him in the groin. *He knows what I endured, what the dickens is he doing? Has he lost his mind?*

Hot on the heels of those thoughts, others tumbled into the churning confusion. *Where was the habitual abhorrence at another's touch? Where was the bubbling urge to scream, to flee, to escape?*

Her hands bunched into fists as she prepared to beat him to a bloody pulp then summon Lucas to finish the job.

Even as outrage warred with something else — one arm already arcing around to deliver a solid wallop to his back — *the* most wonderful sensation began an exquisite glissade from the top of her head to the tips of her toes, as heavenly ribbons of heat spiralled out along her veins.

She swore her heart was singing.

In a flash of dizzy delirium, it came to her.

This was the first time she had been kissed… ever!

· · ·

Since her marriage to Raymond, throughout the tortuous two years of being used for the pleasure of other men, not once had she been kissed. Kissing was too personal, it suggested a deep connection, a romantic bond, an intimacy… not emotions associated with *any* of those slaking their lust.

Her fist fell to her side as Wolfstan's hands slid up her back, tangling into her hair, mussing it with delectable unconcern. His lips moved over hers, teasing, tasting.

Involuntarily, she clung to him, moulding her body to his; unable to stop, unable to think, unable to breathe… as her heart missed a beat then tripled to a frenzied tattoo.

Wolfstan knew this was too soon, that he might terrify Madeline, might stir up repugnant memories, but his heart overrode his head and, as he felt her move into him, knew he was right to trust his intuition.

Day by day, he had watched Madeline's impenetrable barriers begin to crumble and, although his current *indiscretion* was precipitous in the extreme, it was worth the risk.

Madeline, her inner self admonishing her reckless behaviour, was certain hours had passed, surprised when the clock on the mantel chimed half past one. Flushed and trembling, she broke their kiss, and leant back in Wolfstan's arms.

"My, my, Lord Carnforth, that is an… interesting way of ending a discussion."

"I do find it a useful tactic, circumstances permitting."

Her mouth fell open in shock, only to curve into an impish grin when she spotted the roguish glint in his eye.

"Tactic?" she feigned affront. "Do I take it, I am not the only... casualty of this technique?"

"Lady Parham, do permit me to retain a little mystery."

Recollecting where she was, Madeline gathered her composure and, her smile fading, stepped out of his embrace, patting her hair abstractedly. "Thank you, your lordship. You may inform Major Withers, I approve of his methods."

"Madeline." Wolfstan grasped her hand, drawing her close again. "I know I ought to beg your forgiveness for kissing you without permission, for overstepping the bounds of propriety, compounded by my knowledge of your life, but I do not want to apologise, save if I frightened you. I have wanted, yearned for this moment, this glorious, unrestrained, unexpected moment for weeks."

"I-I..." Madeline stammered, coercing her contrary brain to focus.

"I cannot, will not deny my affection. Madeline... Lady Parham, I concede this is neither the time nor the place, but might you be prepared to consider my suit, sometime... in the future? Hopefully the not *too* distant future."

"I-I..." Madeline parroted her own words, utterly floored by Wolfstan's admission.

He lifted her gloved hand, and peeling back the cuff, pressed his lips to the inside of her wrist.

"Before we met, my longest commitment was to my work, my greatest loyalty, to Lucas. Our encounter on the Serpentine wrought a change in me I was unaware of, until recently. Your face never leaves my thoughts, you haunt my days and stalk my dreams... in a good way," he hastened to add at Madeline's furrowed brow.

"Dash it all, this is not the way I wanted to declare my hand. I had a well thought-out argument, complete with sound reasoning, you would not be able to rebut. I rehearsed it until I was word-perfect too." Wolfstan ran a hand through his unruly hair, his expression — self-recriminatory. *Have I ruined it? Have I rushed in too soon? Yes, of course, I have, what a fool...*

Madeline studied him and, despite seeing the apprehension which crossed his features, found herself biting her lip to prevent an irreverent giggle. He looked so endearing in his badly masked anguish.

A little devil within, prompted her to let the silence stretch out until the air almost vibrated with tension, before taking pity on him.

"It might please you to know, my lord, you are better at this than you think."

"I am?" disbelief etched his reply.

"Indubitably. I do, however, require further substantiation of your intent." Deliberately, Madeline instilled a prim note into her voice, unable to credit she...*she*... was teasing him this way. In part it was because she needed time to process his words... his bewitchingly, seductive words... but, in the main, she wanted to monitor her own reactions. Was she ready?

"Errr..." Wolfstan laboured to make sense of what Madeline was suggesting.

She looked him dead in the eye and spoke slowly, leaving no room for doubt. "It is imperative you repeat your tactic, in order that I may evaluate the evidence."

"E-evidence," Wolfstan croaked, his usually sharp brain not catching up.

"Goodness, me, I fear your wits are failing. I presumed, being a covert operative, you would recognise a cue when you heard it. Oh dear... such a waste."

Madeline, praying her instinct had not let her down, dipped a curtsy, and turned as though to leave, just as her remark registered. Its import, galvanised Wolfstan into action.

"Lady Parham," the rich timbre of his voice hummed through Madeline.

She paused to look over her shoulder. "Yes?"

He was at her side in an instant, his arms circling her. "This tactic?" His lips grazed hers, soft as a butterfly's wing.

She canted her head in contemplation. "Hmmm... again."

He repeated the gesture, this time not so gently.

Madeline stopped questioning her motives, and responded, losing herself in the bliss Wolfstan was inducing. She could not comprehend that a simple... *nothing about this was simple...* kiss could be so life changing.

Yet it was.

Reality merged with her dream. Refusing to heed the strident carillon sounding the alarm in her head, reminding her, she was in the Odious Knave's study, and the duke might burst in at any moment, Madeline's fingers swarmed under Wolfstan's jacket.

"Madeline," Wolfstan felt he ought to stop this madness, but her touch sent his senses reeling. Never in his life did he imagine, love could be so... all-consuming.

He had not confessed the depth of his devotion to the woman in his arms, for he wanted to take this gradually... the irony of that not lost on him... but it radiated off him, as he cradled Madeline against him.

"We must stop," he husked, his breathing uneven.

"I know," came the equally quiet reply, "but I do not want to." She tilted her face until their eyes met. "What if..." she paused... vacillating.

He took her fingers and kissed the tips. "What if what?"

"What if this is an illusion, a moment of magic wrought by circumstance? That when next we are together, I... I..." She trailed off.

"…cannot bear my touch." Wolfstan finished for her.

She nodded miserably.

"There is only one way to find out, and even if that is the case, you have taken the first step. You did not faint or scream or flee. I call that a win."

She smiled shyly, "I would like to find out very much."

They did not see Alberforce again, but did thank their hostess for a wonderful evening, who chose *not* to remark upon Madeline's tousled hair and slightly swollen lips, or that Wolfstan's cravat was badly askew.

Without questioning her motives and aware she was breaching etiquette, Madeline reached out and gave the duchess' hand a gentle squeeze.

Something akin to sorrow flickered across Lady Alberforce's face, as several snippets of seemingly random information coalesced.

An emotion neither of her two departing guests registered at the time.

Madeline's concern that the carriage ride home would be awkward was alleviated when the couple fell into their usual friendly chatter, as though a momentous event had not just occurred.

Mr Blake was there to welcome them home. Wolfstan escorted Madeline inside, and was turning to leave when the butler, as he took Madeline's wrap, asked whether she and the viscount would like a cup of hot cocoa.

"Knowing as 'ow you enjoy it afore bed, Biddy has some milk heating on the stove."

Madeline glanced at Wolfstan questioningly. "Lord Carnforth?"

"It is late… or rather early, perhaps…" He wanted to stay but it had been a long night fraught with a veritable symphony of emotions.

"We have a discussion to conclude, my lord. One cup of cocoa will not interfere with my beauty sleep, unduly."

"Then, I would be happy to stay. I am partial to hot cocoa." Wolfstan bowed and smiled.

"The library please, Mr Blake." Madeline crossed the hall, Wolfstan on her heels. As soon as they entered the darkened room, she closed the gap between herself and the viscount.

"I cannot wait. My behaviour borders on the wanton, but I need to know." She clutched his lapels.

"Your wish, my lady…" Wolfstan bent his head to hers, relieved to note Madeline did not panic or jerk away. Channelling all his love but tempering the swirling passion, his kiss was intoxicatingly, heartbreakingly sweet.

A quiet knock forced them apart, but no sooner had Mr Blake placed the tray on the table, lit the candelabra on the mantelpiece and left, closing the door with a soft click, than the two were back in each other's arms.

Safe in her own home, Madeline gave into her craving and tugged at his jacket, sliding it off his shoulders. His waistcoat and cravat followed in quick succession, as her remorseless fingers sought under the cotton of his shirt to explore warm skin.

Wolfstan, careful not to succumb to his base urges, let Madeline take the lead. This was about her reclaiming what had been stolen, not about his own gratification… but it was a hard-fought battle.

Relishing the realisation that, with this man, her fears did not manifest, Madeline relaxed under Wolfstan's masterful touch, and began to heal.

The cocoa went cold.

During the subsequent weeks, the investigations into the Duke of Alberforce and his questionable activities lapsed; supplanted by, in Madeline's opinion and to her unending astonishment, much more interesting... research.

Wolfstan courted the countess, treating her with the utmost chivalry. He did not rush, content to let their romance unfold at Madeline's pace. They had their whole lives ahead of them and, as he reiterated whenever Madeline faltered — which, in the early days, happened frequently, "Darling, why leap ahead to the destination, when half the fun is experienced on the journey."

Neither was naive enough to presume there would be no setbacks. Madeline's history was multifaceted, and it would take more than Wolfstan's kisses... sublime though they were... to eradicate her ordeal.

Possessed with an abundance of patience, Wolfstan did not care how long it took. He loved Madeline and, if it took until his dying day to free her from the invisible chains, so be it.

This is not to say, in the privacy of her home, propriety was observed to the letter.

As Madeline reasoned, mimicking Wolfstan's analogy, "If this venture has any chance of success, 'tis essential we get to know each other on every level. All our foibles and idiosyncrasies. It would be foolish to miss something vital because we were not thorough in our... inquisition."

This sedate invocation was ruined when Madeline pulled a truly gruesome face and dissolved into giggles, which became a gasp when Wolfstan kissed her soundly... just because he could.

The sound of merriment, missing for so long, now reverberated around The Lodge with joyful regularity, and all in Madeline's household knew the source.

Viscount Carnforth had saved their mistress... and they hoped he would go on saving her for the rest of her life.

CHAPTER TWENTY-FOUR

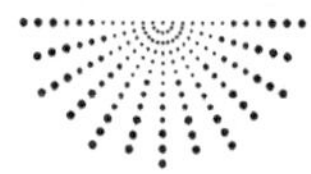

*A*utumn was almost upon the city before there was any respite from the stifling temperatures usually associated with August. The weatherwise across the land muttered about the protracted summer being a portent — although, of what, they could not be sure.

Reluctantly, those of the *ton* who had extended their sojourns in the country to escape the oppressive heat, trickled back into London as October loomed, summoned by responsibility.

The cooler days triggered a spate of crimes, which kept the members of Lucas' organisation, including Wolfstan and Hawk, busy for the duration.

Determined not to neglect her quest, Madeline coaxed Theia into resuming their surveillance while suitor and husband, respectively, were unavailable.

Madeline hoped Lord and Lady Bayling were oblivious to what was happening under their roof. If they *did* know, she had every intention of shaming them along with Alberforce.

That their staff might be complicit, badgered her, then recalled the impotence of her own household in the same situation. They had tried to protect her as far as humanly possible, but had no authority over men of status, especially given Galleron was the instigator.

That begged another question, or two. Did Alberforce have something over Lord Bayling? Was the reason the earl and his wife departed, like clockwork, on those particular days by design or coincidence?

Frustrated, Madeline decided to take matters into her own hands.

"You cannot," Theia tried to prevent her friend from overstepping their instructions, while they loitered in a corner, across the street from Ravenscourt, the Bayling residence. "Lucas was very clear. We are not to interfere, simply watch and report."

"I am tired of standing on the sidelines while this man ruins another's life," Madeline replied with asperity. She grasped Theia's grubby fingers. "What if this was Violet? How would you feel if you knew someone was hurting her for their own gratification without thought or care?"

Theia's features darkened. "I would tear them limb fro... ahhhh, I understand."

"You see? This is not just an assignment related to strangers, this is personal. I cannot stand back and do nothing. Who knows how long it will be before Hawk and Wolf are available to help. Are you with me?"

It was clear Theia was torn; loyalty to her husband and Lucas, warring with Madeline's reasonable, if emotionally charged, argument.

"We ought to wait, exercise patien—"

"What do you think we have been doing these last months?" Madeline interrupted. "We know his game. We know this girl is already ruined. What if he tires of her and seeks a new victim? Could you live with yourself if we did nothing to prevent it?"

"Suppose I was to agree. What can we do?" Theia asked and Madeline knew her friend was persuaded.

"All I intend to do is speak to the staff. If we can get them to believe we have Miss Ffinch's best interests at heart and that we are working with Major Withers to foil Alberforce, perhaps they might grant us access to the house when the duke is here, and we can trap him in the act.

Theia gaped at Madeline. "Y-you want to catch him red-handed, as it were?" she croaked. Theia was a courageous woman, but her husband had been very clear, Alberforce was not a man to be provoked. "Hawk believes Alberforce has dangerous tendencies, that he could be unhinged. He cautioned me against any direct confrontation."

The duke's threats the night of the ball came back to taunt Madeline. He would not hesitate to carry out every last one, given half a chance, but she was not deterred.

"I have no doubt that his mind and prudence have gone their separate ways, attested to by his words and behaviour at the ball. All the more reason to stop him before this gets any worse."

You think this could possibly get worse?" Theia contended.

"Theia, he would have choked me in front of a hundred guests… what do you think?"

"Fair point, but we cannot knock on the door… any door, unless it is a tavern in the Rookeries, dressed like this." Theia grinned.

"Fair point," Madeline echoed. "Tomorrow."

To Theia's chagrin, although she loved working alongside her husband, Hawk asked for her help on his current assignment, leaving Madeline to wait until her friend became available, or to strike while the iron was hot.

Madeline, being Madeline, chose the latter using the fact, the second Tuesday of the month was imminent as justification. To delay prolonged Miss Finch's agony, and *that*, she could not condone.

Gaining the trust of those with whom she wished to speak was likely to require an enormous amount of tact and diplomacy, not traits which came naturally to Madeline. She prayed the unvarnished truth would suffice.

This was a visit, she preferred to keep to herself until it was over. Wolfstan, once apprised, might feel obliged to accompany her. While his presence *might* loosen tongues, it could have the opposite effect, and Madeline believed she would receive a more sympathetic hearing if she went alone.

The Ffinch family was not home when Madeline, dressed in keeping as a countess rather than a street urchin, rapped on the imposing front door, which opened to reveal an aging butler whose face seemed pre-disposed to smiling.

A good sign, she hoped.

"Good afternoon. My apologies for the untimely hour, but I wondered whether you might spare me a moment?" she greeted genially.

Her request floored the butler, he stared at her, at a loss for words. His mouth opened and shut like a fish stranded on a riverbank, and all she heard was a baffled rasp.

Sending up a quick prayer, Madeline leant closer. "My

name is Lady Parham, I should like to talk to you about Lord Alberforce and his… calls," she finished delicately.

The man's implacable façade slipped, confirming what she suspected.

"I know when he calls, and I know what he does, for I was subjected to his immorality also." Madeline had decided, prior to leaving The Lodge, that honesty was the best way to persuade these good people, despite the humiliation her admission might cause. "He must be stopped before his actions result in even graver consequences."

She watched as he dithered between protecting his family, and seeking justice, recognising the instant the latter won. As the butler stepped aside, granting her entry, she refrained from heaving a sigh of relief.

"Thank you. I accept I am placing you in a difficult position, but his delinquency has ruined two lives that *I* know of. Who knows how many more have suffered at his hands."

The house was silent, not even the usual bustle of maids or footmen attending to their duties could be heard, but it was not unwelcoming. The ambience which enveloped Madeline when she crossed the threshold was tranquil; this was a home not a showpiece.

She followed the butler across the main hall — admiring the grand staircase, rainbows reflected in the polished oak from the sun streaming through a huge, arched, stained-glass window high above — and along the corridor leading to the green baize door.

Ushering her into the warmth of the domestic sphere, he waved a hand at the long, well-scrubbed table. "Please take a seat, I'll gather everyone."

Shortly thereafter, introductions made, Madeline explained the reason for her visit. She was careful to divulge only those details necessary to convince her listeners that her claim was genuine, because he had inflicted the same on her.

"We try to stop 'im," one of the maids, Dolly, said, wringing her hands, "but we can only get away with it so often. 'Tis strange, like 'e 'as some kind o' power o'er the master. Poor Miss Daphne, she'm never be wed now, if the mite can ever bear to let any man near her."

"Hope is not lost…" Madeline began.

"Beggin' yer pardon, lovey, but yer a widow. "Certain things are expected of unwed ladies," this from Mrs Merrick, the cook.

"I am conscious it will not be easy, but do not consign her to spinsterhood yet. She may be fortunate to meet a man whose love is unconditional and, if all else fails, a fictitious marriage and sudden widowhood is not too hard to contrive. I have discovered men will overlook much when they want something badly enough. Present company excepted, of course." She smiled at the affronted expressions of the men around the table.

Her cheeky, and wholly un-countess-like grin won over the staff. Within minutes they were embroiled in a discussion about how to end the duke's visits once and for all, causing as little additional distress to Daphne as possible.

"To curtail his overtures here is insufficient. Thwarted, he will merely seek out another victim. We need to confront him in a manner which makes it clear, he cannot continue his… game."

"How'll we manage that, milady?" the butler, Mr Elton, asked.

Madeline pondered his question, while Mrs Merrick poured everyone a strong cup of tea. "We must be subtle, but not too subtle. It needs to be witnessed by someone other than the family or you staff… someone independent of all involved. That way he cannot deny his behaviour."

She took a sip of the brew and was momentarily diverted. "Oh, my goodness, this tea is excellent, Mrs Merrick, and I am partial to these beakers." She eyed the large cup and nodded. "So much more satisfying than a tiny china cup, not nearly enough in those to quench a person's thirst. I believe I shall purchase some for my own use." Beaming at Mrs Merrick who was startled into a beam of her own.

"Thank-ee kindly, milady, naught sets things to rights like a good cup o'tea."

"My sentiments exactly. Now, back to business."

Their chatter went back and forth, ideas from the sublime to the ridiculous, tossed out, each one stymied because of the nature of the duke's actions.

Then one of the footmen spoke, "What if…" he stopped, face reddening when all eyes swivelled his way.

"Come on Toby, spit it out," Mr Elton encouraged.

"Please," Madeline urged gently.

"At the end of the day, it's quite simple ain't it? The only way to stop him, and begin yer pardon for bein' blunt, is to actually catch him in the act." Unwittingly echoing Theia's remark of the previous day.

"Yes, but how can we do that, without embarrassing Miss Ffinch?" this from Dolly.

"We cannot," Madeline conceded. "I hoped there might be another way, but I fear 'tis impossible. He will challenge any accusation where there is no definitive proof. Even happening upon him when he leaves her bedchamber is not enough. He will have the perfect excuse ready… and who will believe a giddy debutante over a duke?"

Nods all around. None in the room was naive.

"Everything he does is planned down to the last detail; every element covered. He has taken extraordinary measures to avoid being exposed but, for him — and this might be his Achilles' heel — the risk is half the thrill, a part of the game, something he relishes."

She suppressed a shudder, memories threatening. She

squashed them, no time for that now. "You are correct, Toby, we are complicating the matter unnecessarily. Simple is usually best, and less to go wrong."

One possibility kept circling her mind. One she had ignored because of the ramifications. Accomplishing it without humiliation was unavoidable but, perhaps, it could be mitigated. It only required one independent, trustworthy, discreet witness.

She knew just the person.

"What do you think of this?" Madeline outlined her plan, fleshing it out here and there. "We know when he visits, and how long he stays. Timing is key, a single delay might be all it takes to show our hand and lose our chance." She paused to let her words sink in, hoping she did not sound overly dramatic.

"Do we dare?" She looked at the expectant faces, keenly aware that if she failed, Daphne was not the only one she would let down.

As one, they chorused, "Yes!"

CHAPTER TWENTY-FIVE

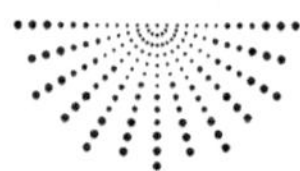

"A stroke of genius, and no mistake," Wolfstan declared the next morning when he and Madeline were enjoying a promenade around Hyde Park. "I would have escorted you, you—"

"I know, and the reason I did not mention it beforehand. You had more important duties demanding your attention, and I think your presence might have been more hindrance than help. I mean no offence," she hastened to soothe, "but, sometimes it is easier to unburden oneself to a woman rather than a man."

"No offence taken," Wolfstan reassured. "When are we going to put this plan of yours into action?"

"If Major Withers is agreeable, this coming Tuesday." Madeline had no need to elucidate on why that day.

"We shall secure his attendance forthwith. Might you accompany me to Bow Street this afternoon?"

"I should be glad to."

"Now, let us set the wretched duke to one side for the time being, and focus on more congenial topics."

"Such as?"

"How much I should like to kiss you under the shade of that willow tree," Wolfstan spoke quietly, his words eliciting a warm glow.

"Why, Lord Carnforth, have you no shame?"

"When it comes to you, my dear, not a single scrap."

Madeline affected a long-suffering sigh and fluttered her fingers against her chest like a fan. "You desire this?" Her tone, deliberately languorous.

"Like a starving man desires food." Wolfstan grabbed his throat theatrically.

"Get away with you." Madeline laughed.

"Would my lady bestow on a dying man the kiss of life?"

"Wolf, you are outrageous."

"I know, is it not exhilarating?" Wolfstan registered this was the first time Madeline had referred to him by his diminutive. One step closer.

Rolling her eyes, she allowed herself to be led into the comparative seclusion of the weeping willow. The early morning sun turning the curtain of leaves, their green hue already fading, to shimmering bronze.

"Madeline." Her name barely a sigh.

She stared at him, her heart thrumming in anticipation.

Wolfstan grazed his nose leisurely down hers, then kissed the tip. "Sweetheart, your nose is cold, mayhap…"

He got no further.

Impulsively, Madeline gripped the lapels of his greatcoat, and rose up on tiptoe to steal his lips, cutting off the rest of his oh-so-sensible sentence.

With a groan, he abandoned his tentative approach and pulled her flush to his body. Nothing mattered, save this woman in his arms, and he wanted to kiss her until the end of time.

"I have no objections," Madeline whispered against his mouth.

"Beg pardon." Bewildered, Wolfstan angled his head to look at her.

"To you kissing me until the end of time."

"I said that out loud?" he was aghast. *Numbskull. Talk about precipitous,* mentally, he slapped his forehead.

"You did, and, as such, cannot retract it. Your words came from your heart not your head," she smiled, and pressed gentle lips to his cheek, "and your candour speaks volumes."

"Are you sure?" Wolfstan searched her face, reading in her eyes what she was not ready to enunciate. It was all there — the rest of their lives reflected in her sparkling green gaze.

"I love you, Madeline Galleron. I could wax lyrical about the host of ways for hours, but I do not believe you need flowery words and chivalrous speeches, although I am happy to flood you with them. I do not want to sound like a moonstruck youth, or a character from one of Shakespeare's plays. I want this to be unequivocal."

Madeline gaped at him. "Wolf…"

"Yes, I declared my hand the night of the… that night… but I hesitated to confess the strength of my affection for fear you would run screaming for the hills." He heard Madeline give a soft chuckle.

"That was my mistake. You deserve to know. You deserve to be told every day."

He took her hand and went down on one knee.

Madeline could not control a startled gasp.

"My love, let me be the one to heal your heart."

Madeline sank to the ground in front of him, heedless of the damp grass smudging her gown. Had Wolfstan alluded to her past, and how hard she had strived to overcome it, or mentioned her current aspirations, or spoken of trials and tribulations, suffering and loss, his petition might have fallen on deaf ears.

She did not need any reminders of what had gone before,

she needed someone to promise it would never happen again.

His plain, unadorned, unembellished proposal persuaded her as little else could.

The emotions Wolfstan had awoken in her, mirrored those of her dream, but this was no nightly illusion. To deny them was to deny any chance of happiness, and she had no doubt, he was the only man who could extinguish harrowing memories, the only one to understand that it might take forever to bring her back to life yet loved her enough to be patient.

He was waiting, his expression guarded.

She seized his hands, her smile wide as the Serpentine.

"Nothing would give me greater pleasure."

His kiss seared her soul and sealed their future.

Sitting on the edge of his desk, Lucas Withers listened to Madeline, impressed, once again, by her persistence. Her dogged determination reminded him of another young woman, now an invaluable member of his organisation. Might Lady Parham be similarly disposed?

He wrested his attention back to the matter at hand.

Madeline was looking at him, hopefully.

"I cannot permit you to confront the duke alone. Deranged lunatics are more predictable."

"Major, I have no intention of going alone, but our approach must be coordinated. For this to work, we cannot burst in like a herd of stampeding cattle. He will hear us and vanish like a rat down a hole. Stealth is key. What I propose is…" Madeline drew a verbal picture of her intentions, leading to one or two smothered guffaws from the handful of men around the table.

"You are confident the staff are on board?" Lucas asked.

"Absolutely certain." She leant forward in her eagerness to convince the major. "Alberforce has become complacent, lowered his guard, thinks he is invulnerable, beyond the reach of the law for what he does. We women are the property of men, starting with our fathers, and continuing with our husbands. I am fortunate, widowhood released me from my boorish spouse."

Madeline's lips curled into a sneer. "He knows no woman will testify against him. Any case would be laughed out of court. If she cries rape, he will claim she seduced him, inveigled him, begged him to set aside his wife for her. Her reputation is torn to shreds, while he emerges like some badly maligned hero.

"He does not deserve the accolades his peers will heap on him for refusing to be lured into her trap. Neither does his family deserve to bear the brunt of malicious gossip. No, he needs to be made aware that his every move is monitored, and his first false step will be his last."

"Blackmail again, Lady Parham?" Lucas interposed.

"Again? Why, Major Withers, I have no idea what you mean." She smiled innocently. "I am merely proposing, this gentleman ought to be reminded that it is in his best interests to behave like… well… a gentleman. A friendly… suggestion if you will."

Shaking his head, Lucas pushed himself off the table, heaved a long-suffering, "Hmmm," then, addressed his men and, with the efficiency born of his military experience, initiated preparations.

Finally, Madeline could see a speck of light at the end of a long dark tunnel.

Tuesday, 19th December 1820

Madeline had vacillated between wearing an afternoon gown, or the garb of a mudlark. On one hand, she wanted to comport herself as a countess, with accompanying sophistication; on the other, the temptation to confront the Odious Knave clad in grubby, threadbare rags was irresistible.

In the end, at Theia's urging and with Wolfstan's approval — not that she asked for it — she chose the latter.

Wolfstan had agreed, under protest, not to escort her.

"I cannot be distracted," Madeline had placated. "You turn my brain to mush, and I must have my wits about me."

"I turn your brain to mush?" He puffed out his chest and gave a rakish smirk. "How delightful."

"Careful you do not get stuck in the doorway with that swelled head." She wagged an admonishing finger. "Smug does not become you."

"Come here,"

"Why?"

"I need to test your allegation."

"Wolf…"

"Madeline…" he teased and, ignoring her squeaked — and, it must be said, perfunctory — objection, conducted an extremely thorough evaluation.

"I do enjoy research." He chuckled when, eventually, he let Madeline continue with her preparations, dodging a jab to his ribs from her elbow.

"You are outrageous."

"So you keep telling me. Want me to stop?"

She paused to look at him, a puckish smile playing about her lips. "Never."

Ravenscourt

Lucas and his men in place, Madeline slipped along the mews to the domestic entrance of Ravenscourt.

Pre-warned as to her arrival, her soft knock was answered immediately, and she was ushered into the kitchen, where the stunned expressions on the faces of the staff reminded her of her unorthodox attire.

"An experiment," she said, by way of explanation, which demystified matters not one jot.

"He is here?" she continued, with no time to dally.

"He is," Mr Elton affirmed.

"Miss Daphne?"

"Could not deny his visit. Lord, but I wish I knew what hold he had over this family," the butler bemoaned.

"We may never know, but to prevent further distress will be enough."

"What if…"

Madeline pressed a hand on the butler's uniformed arm. "After today, his evil will be over. Trust me. Trust Major Withers."

Mr Elton held her gaze for a long moment, then nodded.

"Everyone ready?" Murmurs of assent reached her, as Mrs Merrick handed over a large saucepan and a heavy platter.

"Are you sure, about this?" The cook frowned, confused as to why this elegant countess was first, dressed like a ragamuffin, and second, wanted to take cookware upstairs.

"Oh, I most certainly am. The duke and I disagree about the importance of pots and pans."

"Whatever you say, lovey." Mrs Merrick shrugged and busied herself filling a large kettle pan with water. "'Like as not we'll be needing tea," she said to the room in general, receiving nods of agreement in return.

"Wish me luck." Armed and resolved, Madeline followed Mr Elton along the passage, and into the quiet entrance hall. "Major Withers will be at the back door momentarily. Heed his instructions and all will be well."

"Be careful, milady," Mr Elton exhorted. "He'm a bad'un."

"And I have two years and a lifetime of fury itching to be unleashed upon him," Madeline countered.

"Third door on the right." Mr Elton jerked his head at the floor above. "I oiled it last night."

"You are a saint, Mr Elton." Without thinking, Madeline kissed his cheek, then dashed off.

Up the stairs she sped on silent feet, slowing when she reached the door. Pressing her ear to the wood panelling she strained to hear anything from the other side.

A dry smile curved her lips. Miss Daphne was no shrinking violet. The litany of curses muffled by the thick door was unmistakeable.

Putting down the pans, Madeline turned the knob. Just as Mr Elton had promised, there was no creaking of the handle or squealing from the hinges.

Retrieving the cookware, Madeline crept inside, shaking her head frantically, when Daphne Ffinch, in an all too familiar position on the bed, spotted her.

To her credit, the young woman resumed her tirade with scarcely a pause, jerking her wrists and ankles, trying to break the bonds restraining her. Trying to dislodge the man straddling her.

The duke was too keen on satiating his lust to register the fleeting hesitation.

Madeline wanted to tell her it was futile, Alberforce's knots did not fail, but Daphne must already know. This was not the first time.

Steadying herself, Madeline stepped forward.

CHAPTER TWENTY-SIX

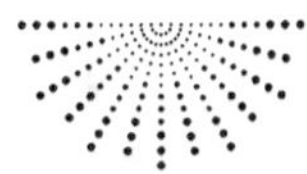

"Why, Lord Alberforce, good afternoon. What pray tell are you doing here? Wait, how silly of me, 'tis obvious. You are forcing your unwanted attentions on this poor young lady, the same way you forced yourself on me." Madeline announced herself with airy insouciance.

Alberforce glanced over his right shoulder, brows knitting at what appeared to be a bedraggled ruffian loitering in the doorway. "Who the hell a…" incredulity left him momentarily mute, but he did not relax his punishing thrusts.

Madeline removed her cap, tossed it casually on a chair, and swept a bow — her dark hair freed from the confines of the hat, uncoiling around her shoulders. "Yes, you Odious Knave, 'tis I, your nemesis."

"Madeline Galleron, you interfering harpy. Get out at once or suffer the consequences." Presuming this would effect Madeline's retreat, he turned back to Daphne, his rhythm increasing.

Madeline's sharp ears caught the soft pad of approaching feet.

Lucas!

It was imperative he witness the duke in the act of abusing Daphne.

She felt a hand on her arm and stepped to one side, granting the major full view of the scene.

Beside her, Lucas stiffened, and she sensed his suppressed rage.

"I am afraid I cannot abide by your wishes, my lord. Consequences there will be, but I shall not be the one suffering them."

"I should have throttled you when I had the chance and blamed your pathetic husband." Alberforce spat.

"Get off me, you ogre," Daphne hissed, and bucked her hips, to no discernible effect.

"Have you met Major Withers? He is a decorated soldier who served in the recent wars and is now terribly important to the government." Madeline interjected, her tone dripping with honeyed sweetness.

Lucas strode into the room. Already tall, he towered over the duke's somewhat awkward and hunched position, placing the latter — who had not yet seen the major — at a disadvantage.

Spent, his chest heaving, Alberforce, with obvious reluctance, wiped himself on the sheet. "What are you prattling about woman? Major Who? Government what?"

"Good afternoon, your Grace." Lucas bowed.

"What the deuce?" He gripped Daphne's jaw. "What have you done, you stupid bitch?"

"Miss Ffinch has done nothing. This is a blunder of your own making," Madeline bit out scornfully. "I repeat, this is Major Withers."

"I wish I could say I am pleased to make your acquaintance, Lord Alberforce, but honesty prevents m— "

Lucas had not finished speaking when the duke whipped out a pocket pistol and aimed it at Daphne.

"Are you mad?" Madeline cried.

"Your Grace," Lucas' shock echoed off the walls. "Do not make this any worse than it already is."

"Ha, you think you can trick me. *Me?*" His free hand slid around Daphne's throat and squeezed.

Daphne's eyes widened in fright, and she fought against the bonds holding her fast.

"What did I say about consequences? Edith defied me once, and she paid the price. Do not interfere."

Edith? The ramifications of his remark struck Madeline like a blow, as she recalled how often Alberforce's fingers had circled her own throat.

"You… *you* were responsible…" aghast, she could not say it… *dear Lord, surely not.*

"Our game became a trifle over-enthusiastic, and she was a weak-willed milksop. Now, get out," he roared.

Tears spilled down Daphne's cheeks. Her terror, palpable.

"Game? Over-enthusiastic? *Over-enthusiastic!*" The fury Madeline had tried to control, exploded and a red haze descended over her vision. She felt the cool handle of the large pan, she still clutched and, shrieking like a banshee hurled herself across the room.

"You murdering coward," Madeline bawled and swung the pan with all her might, rewarded by a wrist-jarring thwack as copper smote flesh and bone, then followed through by smacking the platter against the other side of the duke's head. "What did I say about pans?"

His ears ringing, Alberforce howled in pain, but released Daphne and levelled the gun at the two intruders.

"You are the trespassers here. I have permission."

"Liar," Daphne's scream was cut off by a sharp slap across her mouth.

Lucas tried to defuse the chaos, but no one was listening.

Incensed, Madeline picked up everything she could lay

her hands on and threw them at the duke. Hairbrushes, tubs of powder, books, fire irons, everything… trying not to hit Daphne in the process.

Alberforce ducked to avoid the onslaught, but Madeline was relentless. It would take more than two minutes to extinguish two years of exploitation.

"Enough," Lucas bellowed, and slammed Madeline's pan against the platter, which quivered with the impact, the room reverberating with a dissonant clatter.

Madeline paused; her arm raised.

Daphne bit her lip to smother her sobs.

Alberforce, seeing his cunningly constructed double life unravelling in front of him, rather lost his head and pulled the trigger.

The deafening bang was followed by absolute silence, as the occupants of the room were enveloped in a cloud of white dust and fragments of plaster.

Three pairs of eyes bore into the duke.

"You, blithering idiot, Alberforce." Lucas recovered himself first and, unable to see any obvious wounds on either woman, covered Daphne with her sheet before snapping his fingers.

Two of his team materialised. "Restrain him," Lucas instructed wearily.

"You cannot arrest me or charge me. You have no proof. *She…*" Alberforce jerked his head at Daphne, "… will never testify against me, and *she…*" nodding at Madeline, "…is a widow, driven mad by grief. Any magistrate will laugh you out of court. Not that it will ever reach court."

He barked a merciless laugh. "You will not get away with this, *Withers*," he scoffed. "I have friends in high places."

Lucas drew himself up to his not inconsiderable height and glared down at the duke. "Your Grace, I *am* high places."

Lucas, Madeline, and Daphne were huddled around a roaring fire in the Baylings' library. Lord and Lady Bayling were due home shortly, and Lucas wanted a statement before they arrived.

"We must tell them," Lucas said gently. "Your parents deserve to know the truth about Alberforce. It is unfair to keep them in the dark."

Wringing her hands together, Daphne blushed fiery red. "I concur, but I do not want Papa to… what if… I cannot…" she faltered.

Madeline stretched out to press her hand over Daphne's. "Does your father love you?"

"He does, very much, which makes this even wors—"

"I think you will find, he is more understanding than you expect. His ire will be directed at the duke, not you," Madeline hesitated, then jumped in where angels feared to tread. "Might I be so bold as to enquire why his Grace called upon you at a time when your parents were out?"

Daphne sat quietly for so long, Madeline expected a polite refusal.

"Not only is… was…" Daphne shrugged helplessly, "… he a trusted friend of Papa's, he is related to Mama. They are second cousins, or something like that. Uncle Douglas has always been a part of my life. Mama and Aunt Constance are very close. My brothers and I spent a lot of time with their children when we were younger." Blithely ignoring the fact, she was scarcely out of childhood herself.

"And now," Lucas interjected.

"I wanted to learn about Papa's estate, especially his horses. I love horses," she said dreamily. "He has a racing stud, which is much more involved than just breeding carriage or riding horses. It is testament to how much Papa loves me, or perhaps is prepared to indulge me," she smiled, just a little, "because when I begged him to teach me all he knew, he agreed.

"Papa does not have the best head for business and has stewards who manage that side of things. That was where Uncle Douglas came in."

She paused, and the colour in her cheeks which had ebbed, bloomed again.

"You are safe now," Madeline reminded. "He cannot and will never hurt you again."

"Are those trousers comfortable?" Daphne went off on a tangent, registering that this poised countess could rub shoulders with dockhands, and none would be the wiser.

"Surprisingly so. I wanted to catch the duke off guard."

"It worked."

Madeline was pleased to see Daphne's pinched lips twitch in amusement.

"Sorry, I digress. Uncle Douglas is a fount of knowledge about all matters pertaining to racing, from horses to betting, to the tracks, the riders, the grooms and everything. He knows what to feed the horses leading up to race days so they can give their peak performance. Where to buy the best tack, the best straw, hay, oats, the lot."

"And his relationship with your mother meant no one questioned you two being alone." Lucas knew where this was going.

Daphne dipped her head. "He was so clever. At first, he made sure mother or father were about. He left the door open to the study, where we worked. I had no idea what he was planning. Papa never suspected. Why should he? This is a duke, a lifelong friend."

"His Grace is well practiced at subterfuge," Madeline said dryly. "I shall tell you later," she added at Daphne's quizzical expression.

Daphne resumed her tale. Before long, her trusted uncle was forcing her to submit to his attentions, which, once the earl and his countess deemed it acceptable to leave their daughter unchaperoned, moved from the library to the bedroom.

"He was my uncle, family. Mama did not think a chaperone was necessary. How little she knew," Daphne rasped, sobs clawing at her throat.

"Why did you not denounce him to your mother?" Madeline asked, they had to know.

"He threatened to ruin Papa. A word from Alberforce is enough to destroy a person's reputation. His influence is far reaching. I could not imagine Papa being involved in anything scandalous but was not prepared to take the risk, and he knew it. The rotter played me."

"You are not the only one he played, and you *will* get through this. I know at the moment, it seems he has sentenced you to a life of solitude, spinsterhood but, he has not." Madeline placated.

"No decent gentleman will want me now. I am spoilt, ruined." Daphne hiccupped like a bereft child, tears raining down her face.

"Oh, you, poor dear." Madeline, unable to help herself, drew the younger girl into a warm hug. "There are always ways, none of which involve marrying you off to some aging toad. Now, sip that brandy, it is a great soother."

. . .

Lord and Lady Bayling were horrified when apprised of the afternoon's events and what had led up to them. Lord Bayling was all for challenging the duke to a duel.

"I'm a crack shot," he blustered as he marched up and down the study. "How dare he deceive us, hurt my daughter, for his own sordid gratification. I'll have his guts for garters."

It took Lucas some time to calm the earl who, grudgingly, agreed to leave matters in the Major's hands.

Madeline spoke with Lady Bayling at length, then brought Daphne into their conversation and, eventually, felt able to leave mother and daughter comforting each other.

She detoured via the kitchens to acquaint the staff with the outcome and thank them for their invaluable help. "If not for you, he would still be at large. You are a credit to this household. They are blessed to have you."

The sun had set by the time Lucas and Madeline left Ravenscourt, but their day was not over. They had one more call to make.

Lucas asked his driver to take his carriage to the Alberforce residence and wait there. The short journey between the two houses gave the pair no chance to set aside the drama of the afternoon, collect their thoughts, and steel themselves for what could be a harrowing, if not acrimonious conversation.

The duchess might refuse their request for an interview and, even if she deigned to receive them, could reject their assertions out of hand. After all, her husband was a duke, a peer of the realm. His position left him vulnerable to malicious rumours, and certain members of Society never let the truth spoil a tantalising snippet of gossip.

A person's reputation was their life and, to outward appearances, the Duke of Alberforce was an honourable man, above reproach.

Their sole purpose was to disclose the facts.

Whether the duchess accepted them was another matter.

"How do we broach this?" Madeline appealed, as they walked through darkening streets in the chill of a purple dusk.

"With the utmost tact," Lucas replied.

"Do you think Lady Alberforce is aware of her husband's activities?"

"Possibly. I have come to realise that, as a rule, the ladies of the *ton* have more awareness in their little fingers than the population of London put together."

"I wish this was over." Madeline blew a sigh.

"As do I. I am starting to think there is not enough water in the Thames to wash the taint of that man from my mind, and I have only had dealings with him recently." He glanced at Madeline striding out alongside him. "You deserve a bloody medal."

Madeline chuckled, and the underlying tension eased. "I should have grabbed his gun and shot him between his legs. Highly effective method of curbing one's enthusiasm," she said, pertly.

"Lady Parham you are…"

"Yes?" she met his amused gaze.

"…not to be crossed."

Their laughter drifted on the evening air, a momentary reprieve.

CHAPTER TWENTY-SEVEN

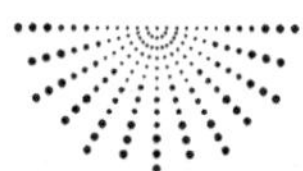

Hollywell House seemed to glower down at them in the gloom or, perhaps the forbidding aura reflected the severity of their task. Curtains drawn tight, no soft glow spilling out; the black painted front door with its brass knocker, defied the strangers to disturb those within.

Madeline hoped it was not a portent.

Lucas rapped, once, twice, three times.

They waited.

The door opened on oiled hinges. A butler bowed and tried not to turn up his nose in distaste at the two on the step, one of whom looked more than a trifle unsavoury.

Lucas handed the man his card. "I am Major Lucas Withers, this is Lady Madeline Galleron, Countess of Parham. I realise the hour is late, but it is imperative we speak to her Grace without delay."

The butler appraised Lucas, then studied the card.

"It is a matter of life and death, my good man." Lucas was not afraid to resort to the dramatic if it served his purpose.

Certain he was admitting ne'er do wells, but professional

to the core, the butler asked them to wait in the hall while he spoke with her Grace.

Madeline glanced around, once again appreciating the welcoming aspect of the residence with its restful palate of muted colours. An ambience, the duchess might well be glad of in the coming days.

At his mistress' behest, the butler ushered the visitors into the drawing room.

Lady Constance Gould was standing by the fireplace, her fingers playing with the ornate setting of her necklace, in much the same way as Madeline knew Catholics fingered the beads of their rosaries.

The duchess was nervous.

As well she might be.

"Please, take a seat," Lady Alberforce invited, covering her incomprehension at the countess' attire with aplomb.

"Our apologies for calling so late, but circumstance dictates we inform you without delay." Lucas said, choosing a comfortable wing-backed chair as Madeline sank onto the adjacent one and folded her hands on her lap.

"Is this anything to do with his Grace?" Lady Alberforce, who remained standing, asked before Lucas had corralled his thoughts.

"Regrettably, it is."

"Lady Parham has accompanied you because…"

"What we have to divulge is distressing, your Grace. I have some experience in the matter at hand and a woman's presence might be beneficial." Madeline said, her tones kind.

"*You* are the mysterious *M* of letter and poem." The duchess' expression softened marginally at Madeline's stunned gaze.

"I am… but… how…?"

"I saw them. Oh, Gould did not know. I was careful." She shook herself, almost as though shedding a burden.

"I am not unacquainted with my husband's… peculiar obsessions. I thought, hoped, he had discontinued the practice. It has been decades…" she trailed off, her vision turned inward, her expression indicating her memories were less than congenial.

"You suffered too?" Madeline murmured.

"Until I was with child. Then he stopped. I supposed he got a thrill from dabbling in the hedonistic, the salacious. It was confronting, but he never hurt me or forced me to partake. I believed if I let him do those things to me, he would not stray to a brothel, or take a mistress." Her face contorted, briefly.

Never one for beating about the bush because, in general, he believed the unvarnished truth was easier to digest than prevarication, Lucas said bluntly, "It is my sad duty to inform you, I apprehended Lord Alberforce this afternoon, after witnessing his… activities.

"Apprehended?" the duchess looked confused.

Lucas instilled a note of compassion into his voice, "To arrest him exceeds my authority, but he was caught in a situation, the seriousness of which, he could not deny. I doubt the matter will go any further in a legal direction but felt it important to familiarise you with the circumstances."

Lady Alberforce collapsed into the closest chair, her usual poise deserting her. To perceive a misdemeanour was one thing, to have it enunciated so baldly, quite another. She closed her eyes, seeing the faces of her children, her family, their friends. *How could he be so stupid?* If she was shunned for his folly, she would never forgive him. *You mean forgiveness was on the cards anyway,* her subconscious mocked.

"Seriousness? Explain yourself," she exhorted Lucas, a trifle unsteadily.

"If you would permit me?" Madeline intervened gently.

After a long moment, the duchess nodded.

As sensitively as possible, Madeline recounted the duke's misconduct, taking care not to be excessively graphic. Her listener was an astute woman and knew how to read between the lines. Neither did Madeline, who had no mind to be cruel, consider it necessary to chronicle every sordid detail.

When she reached the end of her summary, the room was utterly silent.

"He debauched Daphne Ffinch? My cousin's daughter?"

"I am afraid so."

The duchess gripped her necklace again. "The poor child, I must call upon her, offer my support."

"I am sure she will appreciate that, your Grace." Lucas smiled.

"Oh, please call me Constance, that title is becoming less desirable by the second." She waited until Lucas nodded his acknowledgement, then turned to Madeline.

"Lady Parham…"

"Madeline," that young lady urged.

Constance inclined her head. "Madeline… please accept my sincerest apologies for my husband's," she sought a suitable term without resorting to foul language, settling on, "knavery. What?" when Madeline smothered a snort, "What did I say?"

"Forgive me, but you might find momentary levity in the midst of a discussion where amusement is perverse, to know, in my head, I christened your husband The Odious Knave." Madeline replied diffidently.

Constance stared at Madeline, her mouth working.

Madeline wrinkled her nose and gave a contrite shrug.

There was a sort of strangled gulp then, without warning, and in an unprecedented display of spontaneity, Lady Alberforce burst into peals of laughter, startling her guests, who joined in, although with rather less gusto, relieved not to hide their own mirth.

"Oh, my goodness, I needed that," Constance said, her equanimity restored. "I never expected to find humour in so nauseous a subject." A hush descended again, broken when she continued, "What is the next step?"

"I cannot detain your husband. He will be released immediately we leave here. Do you think he poses a threat to you or any in your household?"

It was Constance's turn to snort. "Not him. I may have little autonomy in this rarefied world, but in my home, I rule supreme." Diluting her imperious speech with a very un-duchess-like wink.

"Thank you, your Grace… Constance," Lucas amended, "for your welcome and forbearance, given the hour, and reason for our visit. Please do not hesitate to contact me if you require assistance or have any further questions."

The duchess smiled her appreciation, then addressed Madeline, "May I call upon you, in a day or so?"

Madeline prevented an impolite exclamation by drawing on every ounce of etiquette she possessed. "Of course, I should be delighted."

"There are things I wish to discuss, and I believe you are the only one who holds the answers, but not tonight." She had no need to elaborate.

Madeline squeezed the other woman's hand. "Whenever you are ready. Goodnight Constance, I look forward to our next meeting."

"As do I." Lady Gould walked over to the cord by the fireplace and gave a light tug. Almost instantly, the butler appeared. "Please, show my guests out, Williams. His Grace will be home shortly, but he will not require his usual hot drink."

His affable expression unchanged, Williams bowed, then escorted Madeline and Lucas to the front door.

"I'll wager you would like to be privy to *that* conversation," Madeline said drolly when Lucas helped her into the waiting carriage.

Lucas grimaced. "I would not want to be Lord Alberforce for all the tea in China."

Shortly after Lucas' carriage rattled away, the Duke of Alberforce strode into the drawing room of 16 Charles Street.

His wife raised her eyes from the needlepoint she was working on to fix him with a flinty glare. "I am astonished you think it appropriate to set foot in this house," she said, her voice as cold as her gaze.

"You believe some desperate chit over the man you married nearly thirty years ago." He did not waste time dissembling.

Constance merely stared at her husband, quirking one finely arched brow pointedly. Ladies of her stature were too well-bred to argue; it achieved nothing and gave one a headache. It was enough that the knowledge of what he had done hung between them.

"Perhaps it would be better if you slept at your club tonight." Her tone implacable.

"Constance…" His use of her name attested to the emotions swirling around the room. He only used her given name when in the most intimate of settings.

"Are you aware of who called here this evening?" She cut him off.

"Withers?" he all but spat.

"He was not alone. He was accompanied by one of your victims. Douglas, how could you?" Her hand fluttered to her throat, but she gathered herself. "There is no excuse you can give to exonerate your actions. Not once did you consider anyone but yourself. Rest assured, I shall never refer to this matter again, however, until further notice, I suggest you make yourself scarce."

"Constance," the duke repeated. "Surely, banishing me from our home, is extreme? The whole thing will be written off as a misunderstanding. Girlish histrionics."

Constance leapt from her chair, her needlepoint tumbling to the richly pattered carpet. "Misunderstanding? *Misunderstanding*! Histrionics?" she railed.

"You are addled indeed if you think this can be pushed under a rug and forgotten. Daphne is your niece for goodness' sake, and what of Lady Parham? What lunacy exploded in your mind which gave you leave to think your behaviour was in any way acceptable?"

She circled the room. "I saw the letter, the one she sent you. Have you the slightest notion what that did to me, to what we once shared?"

She looked at him then, the depth of her pain clear in the haunted blue of her eyes. "You betrayed me, you betrayed our marriage vows, and you betrayed our children."

About to snarl a denial, the desolation in his wife's voice, struck a chord. At last, the Duke of Alberforce perceived the gravity of his circumstances. His affection for Constance, regardless of his extra-marital indulgences was sincere.

"Too late, Douglas. I loved you, I probably still do, despite this…" she opened her palms in a gesture which required no words, "…but you make it very hard for me to summon up a single crumb of affection. Williams has packed you a bag. For tonight, at least, you need to leave."

She picked up her embroidery and, without further acknowledgement, resumed her seat as though he was already gone.

Blissfully unaware of the confrontation between duke and duchess, Madeline trudged into The Lodge, divesting herself of cap, jacket, and cravat with rather more verve than care.

"Forgive me, Mr Blake," she said, spotting the butler following behind and picking up the discarded items, "that was inconsiderate of me but suddenly, they seemed constricting."

"Was your mission successful, milady?" Mr Blake asked.

Sinking onto the sofa, Madeline put her feet on the ottoman and gave a contented sigh. "How wonderful to be home, and yes, our endeavours were successful. Miss Ffinch has been unencumbered and, I'll hazard, Alberforce is sleeping in the coal house."

Mr Blake gave a dry chuckle. "I reckon even that's too good for the likes of him. Let us pray 'tis the last we hear of 'is nibs. Now, Biddy has something on the stove for you, and would you like a bath drawn?"

"Mr Blake, you read my mind. Oh, and please ask Dawson to inform Lord Carnforth, I am home safe. He was quite anxious."

"Of course, milady," Mr Blake affirmed, thinking *quite anxious* was the understatement of the year.

. . .

After indulging in a long soak, Madeline all but inhaled the delicious stew, Biddy had prepared, and was tucked up in bed, fast asleep, long before the clock struck ten.

Wolfstan called the next morning, eager for an update on Madeline's encounter with Alberforce.

Her comprehensive account left him impressed and, especially when she mentioned the gun, relieved — inordinately grateful the damage was confined to the ceiling; the alternative did not bear contemplating. To his credit, he kept his counsel, surmising — correctly as it happened — she would refute any suggestion she was in the slightest danger.

"I am fine, although they may require a new pan, and probably a new platter. Most efficacious utensils."

Wolfstan chuckled.

"Now," she said, her tone languid, "enough of him. Yesterday was exacting. My spirits need reviving. Do you know of anyone who might be interested in assisting?"

He did.

"Is it over?" Wolfstan asked, sometime later.

She pondered his question, astonished to register the dark cloud which had hung over her for more than three years had, in fact, lifted.

A frisson of joy simmered through her, and she smiled up at him.

"Yes, for me, it is, although I doubt his wife feels as liberated. I had not given it a great deal of thought, too many other things crowding my mind, not least that Daphne and Constance, already linked by blood, share a rather more sinister bond because of one man's perversion.

"That link includes you, my dear," he reminded.

"Peripherally perhaps," she allowed, "but I am a stranger, it makes the knowing less personal somehow. That her husband has treated her niece thus, must be soul-destroying. The duchess has asked whether she might call on me."

"To what end?" Wolfstan was perplexed.

Madeline shrugged. "I cannot say, save mayhap we are kindred spirits and, is it not oft said, to confer about a burden, alleviates it. In my case, talking with Lady Teasdale, and sharing my secret with you proved beneficial."

"I imagine there will be some interesting conversations in your future." Wolfstan smiled gently.

"From the three of us affected by his actions, directly, Lady Alberforce has the heaviest cross to bear."

"Because?" Clearly sceptical.

"Daphne and I are liberated from him. Yes, we will always carry scars but, given time and the love of family, or, in my case, a certain viscount," she brushed a kiss to his cheek, "hopefully, they will fade. Constance is bound to him for life, fully cognisant of what he has done. That is a bleak future. If we can be of comfort to each other, I am happy to offer a sympathetic ear, and a shoulder for her to lean on, should either be required."

He tightened his embrace. "My shoulder is forever available, as are my ears."

"And the rest of you?" artlessly asked.

"Has been yours since first we met, even though I had not the wit to recognise it immediately."

"You say the nicest things."

"I know… ow," he protested when she nudged him in the ribs. "No need for violence."

"What did I say about being smug?"

"Me, smug? Never. Now hush."

"Why?"

"This."

Her delighted, "Oh" was muffled by his lips as further conversation was temporarily suspended.

CHAPTER TWENTY-EIGHT

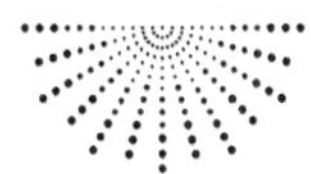

True to her word, Lady Alberforce called on Madeline, the two discovering a connection, foisted upon them by circumstance, morphed, quite unexpectedly, into an affinity.

Initially, conversations were, perforce, stilted, skirting the topic both wanted to discuss, decorum curbing their tongues. Eventually, Madeline... being Madeline... stopped equivocating and threw caution to the winds.

That was the moment, cordiality blossomed into a genuine friendship.

Occasionally, they included Daphne, whose association with a duchess and a countess did her no harm whatsoever; a queue of eligible bachelors vying for her attention.

While none, privy to what had occurred, imagined everything was rosy, the signs were positive.

A brief sojourn abroad, a young widow... there were ways to smooth the path, when the time came.

. . .

Madeline and Wolfstan spent every spare moment together. The former still astonished at how far she had come, the latter treading carefully.

Not so subtle caveats from Emory, Kitty, and Helena, were wholly unnecessary, but Wolfstan appreciated their concern. He had no intention of jeopardising the best thing that had ever happened to him.

Loitering in the wings, the embittered Lord Alberforce.

Constance, with no power to deny him entry to Hollywell House, greeted him the day after the debacle with a frosty, "This is your home, and I do not wish to prohibit your access, but you have shattered my trust, taking with it, any lingering affection. I propose, from this day forward, we live separate lives."

"Your Grace, Constance," the duke began, a thread of panic curling in his gut.

Constance shook her head. "There is nothing more to say. I doubt any of…" she flicked her hand at him dismissively, "… this will see the light of day, but that is to the merit of those involved. They prefer my reputation not be sullied by association. You tossed yours out with the bathwater years ago. I cannot believe I was so blind. More fool me."

"A chance…"

"A chance? To do what? Redeem yourself? How on God's green earth would you even begin? Perhaps, in time, we might reach an *entente* but, at the moment, I have no desire to face you across the table, or the fireplace.

Alberforce tried again, but Constance had run out of sympathy.

"I beg your pardon, your Grace. Silly me, of course,

please let me welcome you with open arms after hearing that, what I hoped had been a temporary aberration was, on the contrary, a life-long compulsion," her sarcasm, withering.

"To discover you were up to your ears in gambling debts, or addicted to opium would be less distressing. Innocent victims, Gould, innocent. How could you?

"Somehow, we have to navigate this mess. You have destroyed us, but I am not the one to whom you should be atoning." She sank onto the closest chair, her head in her hands.

For once in his selfish life, Alberforce was at a loss. Tentatively, he reached out to pat his wife's shoulder awkwardly.

Constance straightened up sharply, dislodging his hand. "I refuse to give the rumour mill any more fodder than it already has. Major Withers has guaranteed his absolute discretion, as has Lady Parham. My cousin will not subject Daphne to scandal, but her husband may call you out. If he does, I suggest you decline. He never misses.

"I have decided to retire to the country for the next few weeks at least. Please do not feel moved to join me." With that, she swept from the room.

Alberforce stood, motionless, watching his world collapse in front of him with no one to blame but himself.

December 31*st* 1820

Christmas had come and gone; for Madeline, the first she could remember with joy. Surrounded by her small group of friends and her ever-devoted betrothed, she had no time for melancholy.

Festivities of any kind were dismissed as too frivolous when she was growing up, and she had little to celebrate after her marriage to Raymond Galleron. While her dearly departed husband had not curtailed seasonal revelry, it was on his terms not hers.

To do as she pleased without criticism was an unexpected boon, and one she embraced.

Wolfstan was gratifyingly attentive without overwhelming her. They took long walks, went to the theatre, raced their horses along Rotten Row, enjoyed carriage rides, sat for hours over dinner, and talked. In fact, the more Madeline talked, the happier Wolfstan was, and those conversations became Madeline's catharsis.

In her opinion, one of Wolfstan's most endearing traits was his ability to listen, genuinely listen. To coax from her seemingly insignificant issues, she presumed forgotten or dealt with, only to find they were festering in her subconscious. To encourage her to open up, rather than keep things tucked away.

No judgement, no trite observations, just unconditional love, and support.

"New year, new me," Madeline said, as the couple kicked through snow-covered streets after an evening with Theia and Hawk. "Brrr, it is so cold."

Wolfstan squeezed her hand hooked around his arm. "Soon be home, and I think you have been a new you for some considerable time."

"You say the nicest things." It was becoming her catch cry.

"I know." Which was becoming his.

He waggled his brows.

"You are also a rogue, a rascal, and a tease," she chastised.

"You wound me." Wolfstan clutched his chest dramatically, as Madeline slid on the icy path, Wolfstan's quick reaction preventing an ungainly tumble. "Ahhh, see what happens when you malign my character."

"Do you need a kiss better?" Madeline's tone nothing short of dulcet.

"Why, Lady Parham, I am of the understanding, it is the *only* remedy."

"See… rogue," she reiterated, and planted a perfunctory kiss on his cheek.

"No, that was not nearly enough to assuage the injury." With a wicked grin, Wolfstan whisked her into his arms and — uncaring that they were in the middle of the street, that it was snowing, and that they were in full view of anyone else who happened to be abroad, or indeed peering through their windows — bestowed on her a kiss which threatened to undo her completely.

"*That* is how you heal a wound," he husked when they came up for air.

"Good sir," Madeline righted her winter bonnet, now all askew.

Neither moved.

Transfixed by the moment, bathed in the ethereal glow of moonlight, their eyes locked, and Madeline saw her reflection in Wolfstan's beautiful grey gaze. His love for her brimmed over, almost tangible in its intensity.

Something shifted; something elemental, something profound.

The last, minuscule but tenacious, vestige of doubt vanished like a snowflake on a flame.

She removed her glove to cup his face, grazing her thumb along the seam of his bottom lip.

"Then I declare, several, nay innumerable demonstrations

of this method will be essential." She smiled, her green eyes luminous.

"Your wish, my love." Wolfstan's illustration began immediately.

Wolfstan did not go home that evening, nor any subsequent evening thereafter.

Not ready for true intimacy, Madeline had no desire to sleep alone, brushing off Wolfstan's, frankly half-hearted, concerns about her reputation, with a nonchalant, "What reputation? My life, my choice."

Aware of how she affected him, she had moulded herself to his tall frame. "Do you prefer to leave at the end of the day?"

"Hell, no." He had chuckled. "Neither do I want to rush you into something you are not ready for. It is a huge step, one, I have not taken either."

Madeline stared at him. "You mean?" *Hmmm, how does one phrase* this *question?* She blushed furiously and lowered her gaze. Despite all she had experienced, discussing so personal a subject did not come easily.

Wolfstan's soft laughter brought her eyes back to his. "To answer the question, you prefer not to ask, no, I have not lain with a woman." A tinge of colour washing up his cheeks.

"But I am not…" she twiddled her fingers… "Oh drat." She turned, only to be caught and spun to face Wolfstan, who ran a gentle finger along her jaw, then pressed a light kiss to her lips.

"My love, just tell me. I surmise you are getting all knotted up over something for no good reason."

"I am not sure I can explain this properly, so, please, bear with me. Wolfstan, I have never shared my bed… not once, not even when wed to Galleron. He summoned me to his suite when…" she had no need to expound on *that* chapter of her life.

"I accept this is unconventional, but we are to be wed, and I do not want us to live separate lives, to have separate bedchambers. I cannot countenance a marriage where we only come together when you wish to have… to…" she stumbled, scouring her brain for a less crude description of the act.

"Make love?" Wolfstan supplied, raising a brow.

"Thank you." She beamed. "Yes, make love… ohhhh." An image popped into her head of them lying on dishevelled sheets, limbs entangled, and heat coiled through her. Discarding it, for now, she coaxed her wayward brain back to their discussion.

"Yes, so if it is something you are amenable to…"

"Amenable? Nothing would give me greater joy, bu—"

"A wise man once said, why leap ahead to the destination, when half the fun is experiencing the journey?" she interrupted, reminding him of his own words. "If this is not part of the journey, I am at a loss to know what is." Her expression telling him he was caught in a net of his own creation.

"A wise man indeed. Well, there's nothing for it, I cannot argue with myself."

And as Madeline, equally shrewd, had anticipated — he capitulated.

The healing continued.

Friday, 19th January 1821

A loud banging penetrated Madeline's dreams. She grumbled something incoherent and pulled the bedclothes over her head.

The banging continued unabated, if anything, becoming more insistent.

"Mr Blake," she mumbled optimistically, given her butler was downstairs, and doubtless already hurrying to the front door.

Movement and a cool finger stroked down her spine. "Go back to sleep, my love, I shall investigate the cause of the racket." Wolfstan pressed a kiss to her shoulder and slid out of bed, his nightshirt as rumpled as his hair.

Shrugging into a banyan, and ramming his feet into his slippers, he hurried out.

The knocking gave way to blessed silence.

Madeline's drift back into slumber was arrested by Wolfstan's, "Madeline, you ought to read this."

"Later," her reply muffled by the pillow.

"Sorry, sweetheart, now."

"Fiddlesticks," she griped, rolled over, sat up, and narrowed her eyes. "What?"

Wolfstan bit his lip. Delectably awry, Madeline still managed to exude the aura of a countess. A paradox which never failed to enchant him. He bent over and kissed her soundly, then shuffled her across the bed.

"My lady, this was delivered." He handed her a note.

It bore the Alberforce seal.

"What?" Madeline repeated, frowning in puzzlement.

"I have no idea. The messenger is awaiting your reply."

Breaking the seal, Madeline unfolded the single sheet and stared at the hastily scribbled words. They danced before her sleepy gaze, and she had to blink once, twice, three times before they came into focus.

"Wolf," she whispered. "Oh, by all the saints, Wolf."

"What?" he echoed.

"See for yourself." She thrust the paper at him and threw back the quilt. "I must go to her."

A hush fell on the room, as Wolfstan read the note and Madeline rang for Lottie.

Dressed in more sombre attire than was usual, Madeline hurried downstairs where she paced the hall, while she waited, less than patiently, for Wolfstan.

"Grantley is out front with the carriage, milady," Mr Blake, forewarned by Lottie, helped Madeline into her cloak. "'Tis a sorry business."

"It certainly is, Mr Blake. I do not know when we shall return, please apologise to Biddy about breakfast."

Wolfstan came down the stairs two at a time and took his great coat from the butler. "Thank you, Blake."

Seconds later, they were being conveyed through quiet streets. The only other people abroad at this hour, street cleaners, sweeps, and tradesmen.

Wolfstan took Madeline's hand, and she looked at him, her classical features twisted with sorrow.

"This is not how I wanted it to end. Not for her. She does not deserve this."

"I doubt it will become common knowledge. The *ton* have a way of protecting their own."

"I cannot imagine her distress." Madeline leant against him, seeking comfort.

Wolfstan, gathered her close, choosing *not* to add that, perhaps, mingled in with the distress, a modicum of relief.

CHAPTER TWENTY-NINE

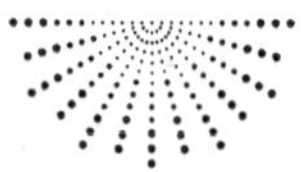

The carriage drew up outside Hollywell House. No indication of what lay behind the door.

"Are we intruding?" Madeline hesitated.

"Of course, we are but, in this instance, I think Lady Alberforce will overlook etiquette. Why else send the note. Come on." He alighted and held out his hand to assist her down.

Madeline's quiet rap was answered immediately. "I thought her Grace might..." She got no further; the butler ushered the couple inside to the drawing room.

"Lady Parham and Lord Carnforth." He bowed, and left.

"What a morning." Constance was silhouetted by the window in front of which she stood, her stiff posture testament to her iron will.

Madeline flew across the room to envelop the duchess in a hug. "Come and sit by the fire, you are frozen," she cajoled. "Wolf, please ring for hot drinks," she implored.

Shortly thereafter, the three were ensconced around the

blazing fire, sipping steaming hot coffee, Lady Alberforce's fortified with a healthy dash of brandy.

"Do you feel able to tell us what happened?" Madeline asked quietly.

"The fool could not face himself in the mirror." The duchess' jaw tightened as she strove not to succumb to a surfeit of emotions.

Aware there was more to come, Madeline and Wolfstan did not speak.

"So, he smashed it, and used a shard to slit his throat." The words came out in a rush. Constance took a large gulp of coffee, then compressed her lips. Without asking for permission, Wolfstan went to the drinks cabinet, and poured a good deal more than a snifter of brandy into a glass, which he handed to the duchess.

"Drink this, your Grace. It will help."

"Th-thank you," she stammered, and tossed the measure back in one mouthful. "Ooof," she hissed, "that *is* potent." Her eyes watered from the fiery spirit, and she dabbed at them with a cream lace handkerchief.

"He did not survive?" Madeline ventured, after a brief silence.

"He did not and, as has become his habit, left the mess for me to clear up. Selfish clod. I should have stayed in the country." Her tone hard, empty.

"Is there anything we can do, assistance you require, people you need to inform?" Madeline asked.

"Thank you, my dear. I have sent for the boys. Yes, there are numerous people who must be advised, but not today. Today, is for contemplation. For a life wasted when he had the intelligence and potential to work towards the greater good. I blame myself."

"What on earth for?" Madeline expostulated.

"I turned my back on him when he needed me. Mayhap if

I had been more caring, my sons would not have to adjust to the loss of their father."

Dismayed, Madeline was on the verge of contradicting this, when Wolfstan shook his head. "Let me," he mouthed.

With a skill honed by years of seeing the worst man can do to his fellow man, Wolfstan counselled Lady Alberforce. Madeline too, listened intently as he explained about survivor's guilt, the exercising of free-will, making choices, and taking responsibility for your own actions.

"I posit Alberforce was this way long before you wed. Sometimes, he deviated from the perverse to walk the same path as you but, I think, his corruption was not something he could control. It was as much a part of him as, say, the colour of his hair, or the shape of his nose. A trait he was born with, one he surrendered to, rather than resisted.

"Do not shoulder his guilt. As difficult as it is to accept, his Grace signed his own death warrant, the first time he granted ascendancy to his dark nature. The only question was how and when."

The news of Alberforce's death could not be contained; he was a duke, a peer of the realm, an important man.

Speculation ran rife for days. Articles about his parliamentary career, his racing stud, his numerous estates, his munificence to all and sundry, peppered the various broadsheets, and were discussed *ad nauseam*.

What *could* be stifled, to the duchess' abounding gratitude, was the manner of his death.

With studied casualness, Wolfstan remarked to an acquaintance in passing, "What a shame about the duke, I thought he was on the road to recovery. Pays one not to neglect a fever."

The acquaintance did the rest. No one questioned it.

A harsh winter often resulted in insidious ailments. One day, a person looked hale and hearty, the next, dead as a doornail. To ignore symptoms, however minor, was irresponsible. Fever had no respect for class and, once it took hold, recovery was rare, even amongst the privileged who had access to the best doctors.

Eventually, the gossip dwindled, in the main because neither Lady Alberforce nor her family made any comment about the duke's demise, and those who interested in such things assumed the funeral had been a private affair.

Wednesday, January 24th 1821

Content to let the public make up their own minds, Lady Alberforce was determined her husband should be buried as befitted his crimes.

With Lucas' help, she obtained the pertinent warrant, then called upon Madeline to explain her intentions, mentioning, almost as an aside, the legalities which must be observed.

"Legalities?" Madeline echoed, perplexed.

Constance recited, "Any person who dies by their own hand is required, by law, to be buried at a crossroads with a stake driven through the heart to prevent the shade from walking. This must take place between nine in the evening and midnight, and no prayers may be said."

Madeline thought she had misheard. "I beg your pardon?"

Constance repeated herself.

"Yes, but as far as anyone else is aware he died of a fever. Why go to all this trouble?"

"He does not merit eternal rest in consecrated ground, and purgatory is too good for his soul. His status should not elevate him above the law. He escaped retribution so our family is not discredited, but justice must be served, even if only symbolically."

"Ignoble and anonymous. Perfect," Madeline approved wholeheartedly.

"Might you be so kind as to accompany me? I have a place in mind, but it is some distance from London, perhaps two days by carriage."

The Duchy of Alberforce owned a hunting manor in a remote corner of Buckinghamshire near the aptly named hamlet of World's End, which stood at a crossroads, not far from a site the locals called Gibbet's Hill.

As far as Constance could recall, any gallows which may have been there, were long gone. She was prepared to acknowledge, however, that although not the reason behind her choice of gravesite, the coincidence *did* give proceedings a certain grotesque dénouement.

"I consider it a privilege," Madeline accepted graciously.

"Excellent. I shall arrange our travel and confirm once everything is organised. Lord Carnforth is welcome to join us. I have a feeling he is loath to let you out of his sight any longer than necessary," Constance said wryly.

"He is very protective but not to the point of suffocation and, I confess, I would not have it any other way."

Constance eyed the younger woman. "Is it true, you two are living together outside matrimony?"

"I neither confirm nor deny. Please allow me to retain a little mystique." Madeline's radiant smile telling the duchess all she needed to know.

"I am happy for you, and your secret is safe with me."

"In all honesty, I care little for the rumour mill, but discretion is never misplaced."

A quiet knock admitted Mr Blake, carrying a tray laden with tea and cakes, and the rest of the afternoon was taken up with conversation circling brighter subjects.

Friday, 26th January 1821

The Lodge was quiet. Wolfstan had left for Bow Street, and the staff had completed their morning tasks.

Madeline vanished into the library where she spent the morning composing something she believed would fit into Constance's plan.

She showed it to Wolfstan on his return.

"The consummate valediction," he approved, then paused before adding. "Mr Blake advised luncheon will be served in ten minutes. Shall I ask him to delay?"

"A hot chocolate would be lovely," she replied absently, staring at the sheet.

Wolfstan, familiar with Madeline's tendency to answer an unasked question when her mind was elsewhere, understood what she had not said and left the room.

Madeline heard the quiet sneck of the door and looked up. She was alone.

A faint smile played about her lips. *Wolfstan reads me like a book.*

A final perusal, and she rolled the sheet of vellum, tied her last piece of black ribbon around it, placed it on the desk, doused the candle, and followed her betrothed.

. . .

Her efforts of the morning had sparked another craving; this one was nothing to do with erasing memories — more about creating them.

Madeline knew Wolfstan was treading carefully, courting her as any gentleman should, letting their romance unfold slowly.

Yes, they shared a bed but, beyond a few kisses… passionate though they were… he had not tried to take their relationship to the next level.

A status quo, she was ready to change.

As evening approached, recalling the night of the ball, and conceding she was not playing fair, Madeline asked Lottie to prepare her red gown.

When she entered the dining room for dinner, Wolfstan's eyes all but popped out of his head, and he nearly dropped the glass he was holding.

He took her in his arms to scatter kisses, butterfly soft, across her exposed throat. "My love, you are exquisite."

"Why thank you, kind sir." She stepped out of his embrace to dip a deep curtsy. "Tonight warrants something special."

He frowned searching his mind for what he might have forgotten. "What did I miss. Your birthday, mayhap? Are we expected at the theatre?"

"No, although, I hope tonight will be cause for celebration long into our future."

"Sweetheart, I am at a loss. Every night we are together is to be celebrated."

"This more than any which have gone before or will come after."

His frown deepened. "I need a hint."

Glancing around, she saw the room was empty save the two of them. "My greatest wish is to banish the ghouls lurking in the far recesses of my mind. You are the only one who can make that wish come true."

The import of her words sank in.

Wolfstan's breathing hitched. He had dreamt of this moment.

His voice dropped to a whisper. "My darling, to vanquish your demons, would afford me the greatest pleasure."

She canted her head, admiring his angular features in the glimmering candlelight. Her fingers stroked the fine material of his jacket.

"Our journey advances apace and, although, I cannot promise a smooth voyage, when I am close to you, the turbulence recedes. My aversion to touch evaporates, and I ache to feel your skin against mine. For an age, the only place my innermost desire could be quenched was in my dreams, where I believed it would remain forever confined," she paused.

"Until you."

He kissed her then and… tenderly, sensuously, weaving a magic known only to him… known only to them… opened the page to the next chapter of their lives.

Dinner became the next day's lunch.

CHAPTER THIRTY

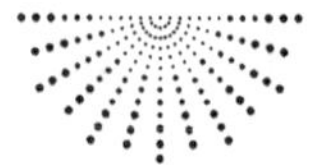

*T*he night was moonless, the stars veiled; the only light came from the four lamps, swinging wildly as the carriage lurched along the rutted road.

Madeline could just make out a layer of mist, vaporous tendrils coiling from the damp earth like withered fingers. She shivered, her imagination running amok.

Why did I agree to this? Middle of the night in the dead of winter. Nary a sheep to be seen, let alone habitation. Lunacy. I wish Wolf was with us.

Mindful he had no part in this moment, except peripherally, Wolfstan had stayed at the manor, his anxiety appeased by the knowledge, there were six eminently trustworthy men protecting the two women.

Madeline glanced across the gloomy interior at the duchess — huddled into her cloak, her face pinched — and mentally kicked herself. So, what if it was dark and miserable, it suited the mood and was *not* a grim message from Hell.

The horses slowed.

Constance pulled down the window and poked her head out, letting in a gust of cold air.

"We have arrived. I can see the beam of another lamp." She looked at Madeline. "Are you ready?"

"I hope so. 'Tis a long way to come otherwise." Madeline's attempt at levity barely raised the ghost of a smile from her travelling companion.

The body of the duke awaited them, transported here by two burly groundsmen, who had offered to undertake the task with badly concealed relish. Lord Alberforce, it seemed, had not endeared himself to his staff either.

The carriage rolled to a halt.

One of the groundsmen... "Phineas," Constance informed Madeline under her breath, "and his brother Elias," ...came to the door to assist the ladies down.

"Thank you, Phineas." Constance greeted him and nodded at the other man. "Elias. I appreciate your help."

Both men removed their caps and bowed.

"Our pleasure, your Grace. Tad nippy, mind," Elias said, stamping his feet.

"It is but, under the circumstances, far preferable to a bright sunny day," she replied, dryly. "Any problems?"

"No, your Grace. Everything's ready."

"Then, let us not tarry. This is not a venture over which, I wish to linger."

Aided by the guttering flames from the handful of rush torches, thoughtfully scattered around, Constance strode to the mound of earth at the edge of the road and inspected the adjacent hole.

"More than suitable," she murmured.

Grunting with exertion, Phineas and Elias, aided by two more men who materialised out of the darkness, hefted the casket from the back of the cart, lowered it to the ground next to the hole and, as instructed by the duchess before they left the house, removed the lid.

In the weak glow, Alberforce looked peaceful, despite the manner of his death.

Madeline glowered at the waxen features. In general, not a bloodthirsty person, she was beset by a gruesome urge to restore him to life, specifically so she could be the author of his demise. A slow, painful, and protracted demise.

"It is time." Constance's declaration broke into Madeline's rumination, and she gathered herself.

Phineas picked up a stake, sharpened at one end, and a large mallet.

"Your Grace." He handed over the stave, concern evidenced by the deep furrows marring his forehead.

"I may not have the strength to wield the blow, Phineas, but I must be a part of this ritual, otherwise my journey is for naught."As the duchess drew herself up to her full height, her blood-red cloak billowed around her, teased by the frigid breeze, evoking an avenging angel.

"Madeline?" she invited.

With no small amount of trepidation, but determined not to show it, Madeline stood alongside her friend. Sharing a long look which required no interpretation, they gripped the shaft of wood.

Praying he did not miss, Phineas swung the mallet, hitting the top of the stake with an almighty *whump*.

A mass of tiny splinters erupted, as the wood quivered, vibrations pulsing along the arms of the two holding it steady, setting their teeth on edge.

"I reckon that's done it." Phineas propped the mallet against his leg and rubbed his chin, studying the corpse thoughtfully.

Elias joined him. "'Appen," he said sagely.

Madeline felt an impious giggle threatening at the macabre scene, not daring to make eye contact with Constance, for fear she would convulse with mirth.

By sheer force of will, she regained a modicum of composure but hilarity… or was it hysteria… lurked.

At a sign from the duchess, the two men slid the coffin into the hole, then Phineas drove the stake deeper until it had pierced the thin wooden base and was inextricably anchored into the earth beneath.

The lid secured, the brothers stepped back to join the curious cortege creating a human shield around the two by the grave — six silent sentinels.

Madeline removed something from the inside pocket of her cloak. Under the flickering torchlight, she undid the ribbon and unrolled the sheet of vellum, covered in her flowing script.

"Do you want to read it with me?" she asked Constance. "It is the antithesis of a prayer or benediction."

The duchess took a moment to scan the page. "I think it imperative." She grasped one side, holding the sheet flat.

Their voices melded in a dissonant harmony.

"For the sin committed,
And the pain endured,
For the respect omitted,
And the silence secured.
For the dignity stolen,
And happiness lost,
For promises broken,
You have paid the cost.

For the silk that restrained,
And the relentless abuse,
For the contempt sustained,
You merited the noose.
For those you subjected.
To heinous misdeeds.
This place we selected.
To provide some reprieve.

No headstone is cast,
To mark where you lie,
The stake holds you fast,
And your soul cannot fly.
No grief at your fate,
Only our liberation,
As we commit your black heart,
To eternal damnation."

The last word reverberated across the inky darkness as an owl hooted somewhere above them, doing nothing to alleviate the eerie atmosphere.

Madeline went to the closest torch and held the vellum to the flame until it caught, then tossed the burning page into the grave.

She walked away and did not look back.

EPILOGUE

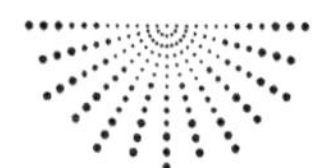

The Lodge
Five years later

Hair plastered to her head, the sheen of perspiration on her skin, her chest heaving from the hours of exertion, Madeline stared at the tiny bundle in her arms…

…and promptly burst into tears.

Since the night at the crossroads, Madeline had done everything in her power to put the past behind her.

At Helena's urging, she had consulted with a certain Doctor Theo Elliott, renowned expert in trauma and — in Helena's opinion — an excellent doctor, all round decent gentleman, and trustworthy friend.

Rarely in the city, it was fortuitous that Theo and his family were visiting his mother. After conferring with

Helena, who acquainted Theo with more details than Madeline would ever reveal, he pronounced himself glad to help.

Initially embarrassed to divulge her innermost secrets, eventually — at Theo's tactful coaxing, aided and abetted by Grace, his wife, a lady whose history was not dissimilar — Madeline unburdened herself.

To discuss her plight with an objective professional was beneficial, but Wolfstan's patience and tender devotion had gone a long way to expunging her emotional turmoil.

What continued to hold her captive, despite all rational argument to the contrary, was a gnawing guilt associated with those occasions her *callers* had brought her to a climax.

Gradually, Theo was able to convince Madeline that what she had experienced was an involuntary response, nothing she could control.

Under his gentle guidance and Grace's compassion, Madeline began to recognise that what had been a forced reaction, paled in comparison with the myriad sensations of love, desire, and passion, Wolf aroused.

While not naive enough to presume the nightmare was extinguished entirely, when spring stole in with its air of promise, Madeline's outlook was equally optimistic.

In a quiet ceremony, surrounded by their closest friends, Madeline and Wolfstan were married, which — given they were already living together — made little difference to their lives, save it silenced the gossips.

Invited to become a member of Lucas' organisation, Madeline accepted but, rather than join her husband and friends in covert operations, discovered a penchant for the numerous office-based tasks… something most personnel avoided like the plague… to Wolfstan's secret relief.

Life moved on.

Slowly, but surely, Madeline's trauma faded, supplanted by more joy than she believed possible, and she embraced every moment.

Her heart no longer shrouded.

The day Madeline, who never fell victim to the usual maladies or ailments, complained of an aching back, ongoing nausea, and an inexplicable increase in weight, took to her bed… an unheard-of event… Wolfstan called Dr Smythe.

The physician's diagnosis left the countess speechless… another unheard-of event.

"You are increasing."

"I am with child? B-but… thus far… no sign… thought… how?" she dried up, her mouth hanging open in the manner of a beached fish — most unladylike.

"Lady Carnforth, I should not have to explain the how." Dr Smythe had studied her over his spectacles, making her blush sheepishly, "I suspect about four months, give or take."

"That explains my swollen belly," she muttered, the annoyance of asking Lottie to adjust her gowns evaporating.

Happy to play indulgent aunt to her friends' children, Madeline had felt no burning desire to be a mother.

"'Tis lovely to play with them, then hand them back to

their doting parents and walk away," she had said to Wolfstan. "If we are blessed, we are blessed, but it is out of our hands and, after what I have seen, I am not sure I want to bring a child into this world. It is a daunting place for innocents."

She did not expect her husband to agree. To produce an heir was ingrained in the psyche of men; as though they were lesser beings if they did not father a child.

To Madeline's surprise, Wolfstan concurred with her opinion.

"To be brutally honest, I enjoy the freedom of being able to disappear with you, into the wild blue yonder, without considering anyone else. Not everybody's odyssey includes children."

"You do not mind, if we are forever two? Am I enough?" Madeline's tone was diffident, as searched his face, reading the truth in his eyes.

"My darling, you are more than enough, quite the handful in fact. Can you imagine if we had miniature versions of you… gracious, we would never get any sleep… or…" he leered lasciviously.

"Oh you…" Madeline smothered a giggle and aimed an elbow at his ribs.

"You are making this too easy." He chuckled and dodging the jab, grasped her around the waist, then stole her lips in a bruising kiss…effectively shelving their discussion.

Now, with three words, the doctor had turned their world upside down.

That was five months ago.

"We have a daughter," Madeline rasped through her tears, her throat dry, more from cursing up a storm and calling Wolfstan every name under the sun than from her bout of weeping.

Wolfstan stared in awe at the infant swaddled in layers of soft muslin.

"She is the image of you," he whispered, for to speak any louder seemed sacrilegious.

"She has your eyes." Madeline smiled up at her husband, cheeks damp.

"Here…" he wiped her tears with his handkerchief. "Do you know this is the first time I have seen you cry."

"I felt the occasion called for something momentous." She gave an exhausted wink and reached for his hand.

He chuckled quietly, and kissed her palm, then interlaced their fingers, holding both against his chest. "I love you more than you will ever know," he murmured.

The erratic thud of his heart matched her own. "Oh, I think I have a fair idea," she replied, "and is a sentiment, I reciprocate one hundred, one thousand fold." A hush descended on the room, the couple caught up in adoration of what they had created.

"Do you know, given my brand-new status as mother, you must pander to my every whim?" Madeline broke the quiet, a mischievous glint in her green eyes.

"Is that so?" Wolfstan bit his lip in amusement at his wife's sauce.

"So, I am reliably informed."

"What does my lady require?" Wolfstan did a half bow from his seat beside the bed.

"For you to squeeze in here. I am very tired but am also desperate for you to hold me."

"I am not su—"

"I shall raise a fuss," Madeline warned, not entirely in jest.

"Goodness, you mothers, so demanding." Shuffling his wife carefully, Wolfstan made himself comfortable on the bed.

"Get used to it." She grinned, nestling into his embrace. "Oh, that is bliss."

The midwife returned with a platter of tasty delights to tempt the new mother's palate, to find Madeline and her daughter enfolded in Wolfstan's arms — fast asleep one and all.

Without disturbing the trio, the older woman took the babe and tucked her into the cradle, drew the blankets over the slumbering parents, and left them in peace.

Madeline was dreaming.

Her noble knight lowered her onto a bed of flowers in the sun-drenched glade, removed his armour and lay alongside her, scattering kisses across her heated skin.

Balanced on one elbow, he traced her shape — slowly, inexorably — from the curve of her thigh to the dip of her waist, fingers tiptoeing up her arm to caress her shoulder before coming to rest on the pulse leaping in her throat.

Their eyes met.

The strength of their love enswathed them like an aura.

A soft whimper made them turn to look at the small cradle, rocking gently in the dappled shade of a sprawling beech tree.

Madeline's heart swelled as she took her husband's hand and pulled him to his feet, leading him across the lush grass to peer at the tiny little girl staring back them, fists bunched in infant indignation.

Her knight scooped up the child, then brought Madeline close.

A family.

Safe in Wolfstan's arms, a sweet smile curved Madeline's lips.

It was no longer a dream.

ABOUT THE AUTHOR

Rosie Chapel lives in Perth, Australia with her hubby and three furkids. When not writing, she loves catching up with friends, burying herself in a book (or three), discovering the wonders of Western Australia, or — and the best — a quiet evening at home with her husband, enjoying a glass of wine and a movie.

Website: www.rosiechapel.com

Elusive Hearts - *An Unexpected Romance*: Book One

His Fiery Hoyden

A Regency Christmas Double

Fate is Curious

A Christmas Prayer *with Ashlee Shades*

Luck be a Pirate

The Highwayman's Kiss

The Lady's Wager

Winning Emma

A Love Impossible

Unravelling Roana

Love Kindled

Moonbeams and Mistletoe

<u>Fairy Tale Romance</u>

Chasing Bluebells

<u>Contemporary Romances</u>

Of Ruins and Romance

All At Once It's You

Cobweb Dreams

Just One Step

His Heart's Second Sigh

<u>With Rori Bleu</u>

Evie's War

Vindicta

Corrupt Covenant

Lesser of Two Evils

Deadly Incision

Echoes and Illusion - *A Dystopian Romance*

The Sela Helsdatter Saga

A Flip of The Coin - Book One

Conceived Chaos - Book Two

Odin's Bane - Book Three

Valhalla's Doom - Book Four

Arcane Alchemy - Freya's Fate: A Helsdatter Saga Novella

The Pomegranate Tree

Hannah's Heirloom - Book One

Hoping to trace the origins of an ancient ruby clasp, a gift from her long dead grandmother, Hannah Wilson travels to the fortress of Masada with her best friend, Max.

Strange dreams concerning a rebel ambush begin to haunt Hannah and following a tragic accident, she slips into the world of Ancient Masada.

A woman out of time, Hannah must rely on her instincts and her knowledge of what will befall this citadel to survive.

Will she escape, or is she doomed to die along with hundreds of others as Masada falls — and what does any of this have to do with an ancient ruby clasp?

Echoes of Stone and Fire

Hannah's Heirloom - Book Two

Pompeii - a vibrant city lost in time following the AD79 eruption of Vesuvius. Now rediscovered, archaeologists yearn for an opportunity to uncover the town's past.

Some things, however, are best left alone - revealing the secrets hidden beneath the stones could prove perilous.

Hannah and Max are brought to Pompeii by a surprise invitation to join an excavation team who are trying to uncover the city's long history.

After entering an excavated house that bears a Hebrew inscription, Hannah's two worlds collide, and she falls back through time to ancient Pompeii. A place where her ancestor is a physician to gladiators engaged in mortal combat, where riotous mobs run amok and where a ghost from the past returns to haunt her.

Will Hannah and her loved ones manage to escape the devastation she knows is coming, before the town is engulfed in volcanic ash? Will she ever find her way back to Max the love of her life, waiting not so patiently millennia away?

Or will echoes be all that remain?

Embers of Destiny

Hannah's Heirloom - Book Three

AD80 - Hannah and Maxentius must embark on a new journey to Northern Britannia.

This harsh frontier is far from the comforts of Rome and danger lurks where least expected; a garrison of soldiers, some unhappy with their isolated posting; local tribes, outwardly accepting of their Roman occupier, but who may still resent the seizure of their lands.

Millennia away, Hannah Vallier finds a familiar item while working in a museum near Hadrian's Wall. It is the pomegranate; carved by Maxentius on Masada. Before Hannah can discuss it with Max, disaster strikes!

Believing her husband has been killed, Hannah retreats into the past, her soul melding with that of her ancestor, but with little idea of what they could face. Is the risk from the conquered tribes, or much closer to home?

As rebellion threatens to shatter a fragile peace, Hannah's heart whispers that just maybe Max isn't dead and that he is calling her home.

Can she trust her heart, or will she remain caught out of time, her destiny floating away like embers on a breeze?

Etched in Starlight

Hannah's Heirloom - Prequel

Maxentius - a Roman soldier fresh from the battlefields of Armenia, arrives to take command of the military outpost of Masada, Herod's isolated citadel in the Judaean desert.

A seemingly mundane posting after years of warfare, Maxentius finds it more challenging to maintain a focused garrison than to face the wrath of the Parthians across a disputed frontier.

Hannah - a young Hebrew physician spends her days dealing with injuries from street brawls, deprivation, disease and loss. As her beloved Jerusalem plunges into chaos, her brother — who belongs to a band of rebels determined to drive out their Roman occupiers — tells her of their plans to storm a desert fortress and steal the weapons stored there, persuading his reluctant sister to go with him.

Masada - following the ambush, Hannah finds and treats three badly wounded Roman soldiers. In the aftermath and against impossible odds, Hannah and Maxentius realise that they are more than healer and captive, their fate already etched in starlight.

Prelude to Fate

For Lucia, staring into the jaws of an horrific death, escape seems impossible.

Rufius Atellus, a veteran Roman soldier, is appalled when he recognises one of the victims about to be executed. Surely this is a ghastly mistake?

A ferocious she-wolf, anticipating a tasty meal, suddenly finds herself under a human's control.

In an unexpected twist, and as danger threatens, the lives of all three become inextricably entwined.

Was it chance brought them together in that theatre of bloodshed, or simply a prelude to fate?

Legacy of Flame and Ash

A Hannah's Heirloom Story

An unremarkable family ring — lost when its owner was killed in the catastrophic eruption of Vesuvius — is excavated after nearly two millennia buried under tons of pumice and ash, setting off an extraordinary sequence of events.

A brazen robbery, and the ring is lost again. The theft and

subsequent investigation, inspire twelve-year-old Cristiano Rossi to dedicate his life to the search and recovery of stolen artefacts.

Fast forward twenty years. Whispers of a rare item being offered for sale on the black market, initiates a joint operation between the Italian and British branches of the, colloquially named, Art Squad.

Hannah Vallier and her tech savvy assistant, Bryony Emerson — whose abilities to track down the untraceable, led to them assisting the UK Art and Antiquities Unit — have unearthed an intriguing thread.

Reluctantly, Cristiano agrees to team up with the pair to thwart the traffickers, retrieve the artefact and, hopefully, dismantle the site.

What ought to be a routine assignment is complicated by a rogue operative, an unexpected romance, an ancient connection, and a *very* angry ghost!

A Guardian Unexpected

The Nettleby Trilogy: Book One

August 1914: Europe is on the brink of catastrophe. In a small village in rural Lincolnshire, a wife kisses her husband goodbye.

Childhood sweethearts, Eliza and Joe have only been married two years. They could not have imagined how soon they would be torn apart by war, nor that the most unexpected of guardians would offer them hope during their darkest hours.

Under the Clock

The Nettleby Trilogy: Book Two

England 1908: Under the clock, on a sleepy station platform nestled in rural Lincolnshire, an unexpected romance blossoms.

Maisie: Every Friday, at precisely five to six, a handsome young man arrives at the station. I know the time because I can see the clock. The train pulls in, punctual as always, and among the alighting passengers is an elderly gentleman. The young man greets him with a smile and a handshake, then tucks his arm through the older man's and they leave the platform.

Every Friday.

Occasionally, we exchange a glance or two and, to be fair, I suspect I notice him more than he notices me.

Fred: I count the hours until Friday afternoon comes around. Not only because this marks the start of the weekend but also, and more importantly, I get to see the flower girl. I am clueless as to her name, yet my heart begins to race the minute the station comes into view. I almost run up the steps onto the platform, hoping for a glimpse of her bright smile.

Every Friday.

I doubt she ever notices me. I'm just a village lad, one more faceless person in the throng.

Then again, you never know what might happen… in an innocuous corner of a quiet platform…

…under the clock

REGENCY ROMANCE

Once Upon An Earl

Linen and Lace - Book One

When Fate saw fit to intervene in the life of Giles Trevallier, the very respectable Earl of Winchester, by dropping a female — soaked to the skin and with no memory of who she is or how she came to be there — literally at his feet, no one could have predicted the outcome.

While uncovering her identity, Giles realises he is falling hopelessly in love with his mystery guest, who unbeknownst to him, is succumbing to similar emotions; but, when the heart is involved, a thoughtless word or gesture can thwart even Fate's best-laid plans.

Faced with misunderstandings, whispers of scandal, secret documents and foreign agents, their chance at a happy ever after seems elusive, but fairy tales often happen when least expected, and love — however inconvenient — usually finds a way to conquer all.

To Unlock Her Heart

Linen and Lace - Book Two

Abused by a duke, and shunned by Society, relief seems at hand when Grace Aldeburgh is bequeathed a house in a small village, far from malicious gossips.

Once there, a tentative friendship blooms between Grace and Theo Elliott, the local doctor, who has already resolved to be the man to unlock her heart.

Just when happiness appears to be within her grasp, her erstwhile tormentor once again stalks Grace. After a failed kidnap attempt, the duke's quest culminates in an acrimonious confrontation, and the reason for his venal pursuit becomes agonisingly clear.

Love on a Winter's Tide

Linen and Lace - Book Three

Every day, Helena disappears into a world few acknowledge, helping the poor, downtrodden, and abused. A husband is the last thing she can be bothered with.

Busy managing his shipping line, Hugh Drummond sees no need for a wife, whose only joy is dancing and frivolity. If — and it was a huge if — he ever married, it would be to a woman as capable as he, not some giddy society Miss.

Then, Hugh meets Helena and despite their resolve, fate, it seems, has other ideas. As their attraction deepens however, treachery threatens to tear them apart. Will they uncover the perpetrator in time, or will their love be swept away, lost forever on a winter's tide?

A Love Unquenchable

Linen and Lace - Book Four

Jessica Drummond, a bright and cheerful young woman, rarely gives romance, let alone love, a thought. Long hours working in her brother's shipping office affords little chance of her ever meeting an eligible bachelor.

Duncan Barrington, veteran of the Napoleonic Wars, believes himself wounded in both body and soul. He has no intention of inflicting his demons on anyone, certainly not a beautiful and, in his opinion, irresponsible city lady.

One cold and snowy morning, the plight of a bedraggled puppy throws Jessica and Duncan together and, as a spark of something indefinable yet wholly unquenchable begins to burn, it is unclear who rescued whom.

A Hidden Rose

Linen and Lace - Book Five

After witnessing his mother's grief at the loss of his father, Nick Drummond resolved never to cause someone he loved such distress. Even the happiness of his siblings would not sway him — until he met Rose.

Rose Archer was almost content assisting her doctor father in a tiny fishing village in the north of Yorkshire. To experience the world beyond, a tantalising dream — until she met Nick.

Unexpectedly, the impossible becomes possible, and the renounced — desired above all things, but the shipwreck that brought them together, may yet tear them apart. Will Nick learn to trust his heart, or will his love for Rose remain forever hidden

The Daffodil Garden

Horrifically scarred during the war, William Harcourt - Marquis of Blackthorne - prefers to spend his days in the quiet of his daffodil garden; plants do not pity, turn away, or judge.

Lucy Truscott, whose life is far removed from that of the *ton*, has no idea that by saving the life of a young woman, to whom she bears an uncanny resemblance, her own will be placed in mortal danger.

A chance encounter leads to something more. William begins to trust that Lucy sees the man beneath the scars, while Lucy is persuaded that love might actually transcend status.

Unfortunately, before their courtship has really begun, someone has every intention of ending it - permanently.

The Unconventional Duchess

Refusing to suffer the humiliation of her husband flaunting his mistress at Society events, the newly married Duchess of Wallingstead, Ella Lennox, takes control of her life. She leaves London for the family's country seat in remote Yorkshire.

A woman alone, Ella spends the next four years turning a cold, grim house into a home, and transforming the fortunes of the estate. Not afraid of hard work, she soon earns the respect of those around her with her determination and unconventional attitude.

Out of the blue, the duke arrives. Resigned to another arduous visit, Ella is stunned when it seems he is attempting to court her.

Impossible!

Could her dream of a happy marriage be about to come true?

Everything hangs on a snowstorm, a herd of cows and an uninvited guest!

Rescuing Her Knight

The *de Wiltons* — Book One

A story, invented to keep a little girl distracted, marks the beginning of another tale. One destined to remain unfinished for twenty years.

At thirteen, Adam Marchmain became Kitty de Wilton's 'Knight of the Garden' — a title bestowed following an accident which resulted in six-year-old Kitty having her knee sutured. Kitty never forgot his gallantry, but pledges made as children rarely survive into adulthood.

Their paths separated until Fate decreed, they meet again.

Widowed, badly disfigured and his sight ruined, Adam returns to his family home, a shadow of his former self.

Similarly afflicted, although her scars are invisible, Kitty — against her better judgement — is persuaded to help Adam banish his demons. This requires a subterfuge which, if discovered, might shatter more than the bonds of friendship forged two decades previously.

To Kitty, determined to break through the shield Adam has erected, the risk is worth it.

To see his smile and hear his laughter.

To rescue the knight of her childhood.

Just when a fairy tale ending is within her grasp, Kitty is threatened by the man who murdered her husband. In a cruel twist the tables are turned, and Kitty is the one who needs rescuing.

Elusive Hearts

An Unexpected Romance — Book One

What happens when two people whose elusive hearts fight an indefinable attraction, neither looked for nor desired, dare to dream?

When her fiancé and sister abscond to Gretna Green on her wedding day, Sapphira Beresford longs to escape, to avoid the gossipmongers gloating over her misfortune. Disillusioned, she is determined not to be burnt again, swearing off romance and marriage.

A fortuitous invitation sees her embarking on a journey to Pompeii where she meets Leofwin Colleville, reclusive marquis, amateur antiquarian, and her host for the duration.

Although enamoured of the ruins gradually being unearthed and ecstatic to have the opportunity to assist, Sapphira is troubled by her host's attitude, which blows hot and cold.

A confirmed bachelor, Leofwin Colleville is happiest surrounded by ancient ruins, and would prefer to brave the whole of Napoleon's armies alone, than face a lady on the hunt for a husband. The arrival of an unexpected guest throws his unencumbered existence into turmoil, but the harder he strives to maintain his distance, the more she gets under his skin.

Sparks fly and, as Leofwin's truculence undermines Sapphira's already battered confidence, her adventure of a lifetime seems doomed to disaster.

Until the day she runs afoul of greedy treasure hunters.

In the aftermath what was scorned becomes the one thing they crave above all else, but when it comes to the heart, nothing is ever simple.

His Fiery Hoyden

A Novella

Livvy has no respect for the nobility; they let her down when she most needed them. Why should she accede to their demands now?

Philip, Lord Harrington, is stunned to discover the young heir to the dukedom lives a stone's throw away in a ramshackle cottage, and resolves to restore the child to his birthright.

They meet in a clash of wills, but just when it seems Livvy might surrender, the victory Philip desires, may not taste all that sweet.

A Regency Duet

Luck be a Pirate

Luck wasn't something retired pirate Kennet Alexson believed in — good or bad. However, even he had to concede that landing a job at Trentams shipyard, and meeting Lynette Collins, was more than coincidence.

Fortune it seemed, was smiling on him for once.

As Kennet adjusts to life on dry land, his friendship with Lynette deepens into something far more enduring, and what once seemed elusive now becomes possible.

Unfortunately, fate has other plans, and Kennet's good luck is about to run out.

The Highwayman's Kiss

Surrendered Hearts — Book One

Nothing exciting had ever happened to Juliette St Clair.

Her days were spent assisting her father or calling on friends, wandering art galleries, taking constitutionals or, and more preferably, escaping into her books. Her evenings her evenings — an endless round of balls, where she preferred to remain invisible.

Until the day she was robbed by a highwayman.

A Regency Christmas Double

Heart Rescued

Four years since Jasper lost the woman he was hoping to marry. Four years since he closed his heart and withdrew from Society. He has no idea his reclusive existence is about to be shattered.

Enter his sister's best friend, Harriet, a flame haired beauty, who needs his help.

Reluctantly he agrees and as they spend time together, it is clear their feelings run deep. Although Harriet affects Jasper in a way no woman ever has, he believes her to be out of his league ~ but it's Christmas and she might just be the one to melt his frozen heart

Catch a Snowflake

Romance often blossoms in the most unlikely of places - but in a ward full of wounded soldiers - surely not?

When Lucas Withers comes face to face with Jemima Parsons - a young woman who blames him for her brother's injury - falling in love is the last thing on their minds. What neither of them anticipated, was the magic of snowflakes.

Fate is Curious

A Novella

Happily, ever after? No such thing! Bereft, following her beloved husband's sudden death, Lady Charlotte Sherbrooke has lost her belief in romantic nonsense.

Successful shipping merchant, Zacharie Romain, is no stranger to loss; his business can be hazardous. Moreover, his wife died in childbirth and even though it happened a decade ago, he has no mind to expose himself to such sorrow again.

They meet in less than joyful circumstances but, as the year turns and grief diminishes, the woes of a small boy become the catalyst for something wholly unexpected. Can Charlotte and Zacharie trust what Fate has in store or will past heartbreak prevent them from taking a chance on love?

A Christmas Prayer

with Ashlee Shades

A Short Story

An entreaty from a frightened child.

Orphaned and only nine, Caroline Thorne has to grow up before her time. She is doing everything she can to keep what is left of her family together and out of the workhouse but is terrified her prayers are not being heard. Or maybe they are…

A petition from a woman desperate for a family.

A chance meeting with three orphaned siblings, tugs at Elizabeth Barrington's heart strings. Thus far, she and her husband have not been blessed with children and, as Christmas approaches, a plan begins to form - one which might just be the answer to her prayers.

Two Christmas prayers, as different as they are the same.

Will they hear and, more importantly, heed the answer?

The Lady's Wager

Surrendered Hearts - Book Two

A Novelette

Ged Mowbray will do anything to avoid being married off to the suitable prospects his parents insist on parading in front of him.

Melissa Bouchard is under no illusion her sizeable dowry is the attraction to suitors, not her.

An overheard conversation leads to an offer too good to refuse, but what happens when a lady's wager, becomes a gamble on the happily ever after, you did not even realise you wanted?

Winning Emma

Surrendered Hearts - Book Three

A Novelette

Randolph Craythorpe — earl, covert operative, and occasional highwayman — believed his dalliance with Lady Felicity Hartwich would lead to marriage. It did, but not to him! The arrival of an unwelcome guest, however, provides the perfect opportunity to indulge in a little retaliation.

Emma Newbury accompanies her cousin, Lady Charity Anscombe, to London for the Christmas season. Once there, she comes face to face with the three men who witnessed the humiliating aftermath of her father's disgrace — one of whom, to her irritation, has taken up residence in her dreams.

Their infrequent encounters only serve to confuse but, while winter tightens its grip on the city, what was inconceivable becomes the one thing for which they both yearn, yet bound by Society's rules, cannot admit.

As the snow falls, Randolph begins to understand that to win Emma, he will have to surrender.

Moonbeams and Mistletoe

Surrendered Hearts - Book Four

A Novelette

If we are part of a universe where moonbeams and mistletoe exist, nothing is insurmountable for, otherwise, what is the point?

To Emily Livingston, spinster — this deceptively frivolous phrase was all she had left of her betrothed.

To Henry Bartholomew, widower — the sentiment, while naïve, also serves as a reminder that even in the darkest of hours, light can be found… it was simply a matter of perspective.

When four-year-old twins run into Emily — literally — she has no idea where their unexpected encounter will lead. Determined to ensure his children are *not* being schooled into something nefarious, Henry resolves to meet this mysterious lady who has enthralled the duo with her stories.

One dull and otherwise ordinary autumnal morning, two disparate souls are brought together, and long-forgotten emotions are stirred.

The question is whether Henry and Emily have the courage to follow their hearts or be forever trapped in the sadness of the past. Can moonbeams and mistletoe persuade them, the answer was there all along?

A Love Impossible

A Regency M/M Novelette

Tasked with investigating a heinous crime, Edward Lindsay travels from London to Dublin — a city which holds too many memories — in the guise of guardian to his sister. He knew it could be hazardous, and relished the challenge, but that wasn't what caused his stomach to tighten as they approached landfall.

Dublin held more than just a murderer.

There was also Aidan.

While attending a party, Aidan Griffen is astonished when he comes face to face with a man who fled Dublin two years previously. A man he has desperately tried to forget.

As Edward closes in on his quarry, a fire, deliberately extinguished, is rekindled. But what of it? Edward and Aidan share a love impossible, and to acknowledge their feelings — more dangerous than confronting a killer.

Is there any hope of a happily ever after?

Unravelling Roana

A Regency Novelette

Tired of being ignored by her husband, Roana Dumont, Countess of Brooketon does the one thing guaranteed to get his attention. She runs away… to Venice, leaving behind a set of riddles for him to solve… *if* he feels their marriage is worth saving.

Gideon Dumont, 6th Earl of Brooketon is flabbergasted when he discovers his wife has apparently vanished off the face of the earth. A series of puzzles, the only clue as to her whereabouts.

The question is… will he unravel them?

Love Kindled

A Regency Novelette

Recently widowed, Amelia Ingram - Countess of Gresham, decides to shake off the fetters from her arranged and loveless marriage. Exploiting her new-found independence, Amelia indulges her yearning to explore - incognito.

Her ploy works so well, she receives an offer of employment from the dangerously handsome, Rupert Latimer - Earl of Badlesmere. On impulse, she accepts and finds herself governess to Cate, a delightful scamp of a child. What began as a bit of a game on Amelia's part, evolves into something far more profound, and a flame she presumed impossible to ignite, is kindled.

An unexpected turn of events leads to yet another offer. This time there is far more at stake and, determined history not repeat itself, Amelia confesses her ruse.

Rupert has been burnt once. Will he douse the spark, or take a risk and trust his heart?

FAIRY TALE ROMANCE

Chasing Bluebells

A Fairy Tale Novella

Once upon a time, somewhere in France, there was a man whose reckless obsession led him down a dark path — one which, ultimately, cost him his life.

That ought to have been the end of it.

Regrettably, as is so often the case, those who least deserve it, suffer for the actions of others.

A decade after being sent away, Sebastien Daviau returns to the little village where everything began. Hoping to lay the ghosts of his childhood to rest, he studiously ignores the possibility, he might run into Charlotte de Montbeliard.

As luck would have it, Charlotte is the one who runs into him… well, his horse… and although the brief encounter leaves a lasting impression, neither recognises the other.

A name revealed causes a freak accident, catapulting Sebastien's past into his present, and bringing him face to face with a man whose reputation would intimidate the most ardent of suitors.

Can whatever is blossoming between Charlotte and Sebastien survive the challenge imposed, or is their happily ever after about to fade as quickly as the bluebells they loved to chase?

CONTEMPORARY ROMANCE

Of Ruins and Romance

Kassandra Winters has intrigued Gabriel St Germain since he accidentally knocked her flying outside her university professor's office. Her face haunts his dreams, yet he never expected to see her again. So, he is surprised when she appears, as though destined to do so, in the middle of a ruin, and he concocts a plan to win her heart.

Gabriel's old-fashioned courtship touches something deep inside Kassie and, although struggling to believe someone as handsome as Gabriel could possibly be interested in her, she soon realises she has fallen irrevocably in love with him. However, just as Kassie shares everything of herself with Gabriel, her world comes crashing down.

Can their romance survive, or will it fall in ruins, like the relics of antiquity that brought them together?

All At Once It's You

When Alex arrives in the small village of Rosedale Abbey, to take up a position as a research assistant for a renowned archaeologist, the last thing she is looking for, or expects to find, is love.

Jake was perfectly happy with the status quo. When it came to relationships, he didn't do committed or long term. He called the shots, and if his current flame didn't like it, she knew what to do. A philosophy, which served him well - until he met Alex.

Romance blooms, but even as the untamed wilderness of the North Yorkshire moors weaves its spell, a long-buried secret might yet jeopardise their happily ever after.

Cobweb Dreams

A Novella

A holiday on the Scottish isle of Mull was just the break Chloe Shepherd needed, an escape from her boring office job and her complete lack of anything resembling a social life. Romance, it seems, isn't on the cards and, although Chloe dreams of finding her soulmate she is beginning to believe love is like cobwebs — spun overnight, only to vanish in the early morning breeze.

Under sufferance, Dominic Winters makes a flying visit to Mull to check on a rental property owned by his family. He hasn't got time for this — so indulging in a holiday fling is the last thing on his mind.

A lamb stuck in a bog proves a most unexpected matchmaker and, while Mull weaves its magic, Chloe wonders whether those fragile cobwebs might be far more stubborn than she thought.

Just One Step

A Short Story

In the aftermath of an horrific car accident, Daisy Forrester travels to Italy - hoping, so far from her memories, she might begin to heal.

Archaeologist, and single father, Adam Willoughby is too busy looking after his young daughter to give romance let alone love, a thought.

Neither expects a chance encounter in an ancient ruin to be anything more, but sometimes, that's all it takes.

His Heart's Second Sigh

A Novella

Reuben Faulkner and Paige Latimer are two happily single people, who have no desire to upset the status quo.

Unexpectedly, they are thrown together, only to discover both want far more than a casual friendship.

Just when things take an interesting turn, Reuben's past catches up with them, and threatens to derail their blossoming romance before it has chance to start.

Fast forward twelve years and Bobbi Jo dreams of starting a new life away from the trauma of her past and the antipathy of pitiless relatives.

The nightmare isn't over… but perhaps the tables have turned…

Vindicta - when death isn't retribution enough…

Corrupt Covenant

A pledge of eternal peace and prosperity sounds too good to refuse… unless, of course, the pledge comes from an immortal dragon.

A contract established in exchange for a king's life and the protection of his lineage should have expired when a desperate queen, facing hordes baying for her destruction, loses faith in the oath… but evil has a long memory.

Trapped for a millennium in a sarcophagus at the bottom of the Danube, death lay beyond the queen's grasp until the day nature, fate, and a mysterious archaeologist joined forces to dredge her from her grave.

A life revived. A liegeman doomed to be reborn until he saves his queen. A dragon who has not forgiven an act of betrayal.

Can two souls, separated for a millennium, break the corrupt covenant, or are they fated to dance to the dragon's tune, for eternity?

Echoes & Illusions

The Hunters - Book 1

Twenty years after a global plague, the remnants of civilisation struggle to eke out an existence in a world where humanity is secondary to survival.

On the outskirts of a once vibrant Rome, Gabriel tends his vineyard. From dawn to dusk, he strives to carve out a living, while caring for Bianca, his heavily pregnant wife.

Life might be tough, but at least he had an income, meagre though it was. Trouble seemed a distant memory, until the day he notices their neighbours are not at work in the adjacent fields.

A gruesome discovery sparks a chain of events to rival the conflicts Rome witnessed at the height of its power. Gabriel and Bianca must pit their wits and their lives against a formidable opponent, in an attempt prevent an atrocity none could have predicted.

A bond, forged in a snowy field and strengthened in a city under siege, is put to the ultimate test.

In a world of echoes and illusions, is their love strong enough to surmount the odds, or will it crumble to dust like the empire their enemies are striving to replicate?

The Sela Helsdatter Saga

A Flip of the Coin - Book One

What happens in Helheim *never* stays in Helheim.

Sela Helsdatter wishes it would. Punished for allowing her quest for power to rule her actions, she has endured eons of torment.

The flip of a coin seems to offer some hope of redemption but, tasked with ridding the world of her erstwhile captor and lover, escape does not mean freedom.

No problem for a warrior queen… right?

Wrong!

Sela is no longer in ninth century Norðvegr, but twenty-first century New York with all its challenges, and where slightest misstep could spell her doom.

Aided by the most unlikely hero, Sela scours the city for her adversary, who delights in taunting her, determined to drag her back to Hell.

Will she prevail, or will A Flip of the Coin catapult her back to the abyss?

Conceived Chaos - Book Two

After ridding the world of her tormentor, and finding the love of her life, Sela Helsdatter could be forgiven for thinking she deserves a little peace.

No such luck!

Marriage to the God of Mischief is a walk in the park compared with the terror about to be unleashed from Valhalla. A diabolical edict from Odin himself sees the nine months pregnant, Sela fleeing from the entire Norse pantheon — with no clue why.

A price on her head and a target on her belly, the only person she can trust is her husband, who is keeping her in the dark.

Does her unborn child hold the key to this Conceived Chaos?

Odin's Bane - Book Three

Sela Helsdatter cannot catch a break. Relentless in his jealousy and wrath, Odin is determined that neither Sela nor her infant daughter will survive.

Shattered by loss, and with no time to grieve, Sela has to rely on the one person she believes responsible for her current predicament.

A lost friendship revived, the disparate trio seek refuge in a remote corner of Montana, with the uneasy awareness the child may be the key to their salvation.

Vowing Odin will not harm a hair on her daughter's head, Sela has to use every trick at her disposal to thwart the Norse Deity. At the same time another fiendish subversion threatens the future of humanity.

Will Odin be victorious… or is another power stirring which will prove to be his bane?

Valhalla's Doom - Book Four

The obsidian stone with its strange steak of neon blue, hanging on a gold chain around Anna Helsdatter's neck — forged from the magma surrounding Jörmungandr's cave — serves as a reminder of the last terrible battle against an insidious evil. The day, Anna came into her full power to defeat the All Father when he sought to destroy not only her family, but also every one of the Nine Realms.

A stone which, unbeknownst to Anna — currently contending with an even greater challenge, that of being college student — hides its own secret.

Putting her past behind her and, despite contending with a family composed of the most powerful deities on Earth or in Valhalla, all Anna wants to do, is to enjoy being a normal nineteen-year-old.

Then again, things involving the Helsdatters, are anything but normal, and Anna is catapulted into another life-or-death struggle. The only problem is, this time the stakes are higher… and one wrong move could spell disaster — especially when saving Earth, might herald Valhalla's Doom.

Just your typical rock and hard place!

Arcane Alchemy

Freya's Fate

A Helsdatter Sage Novella

What happens when the goddess of seduction and love finds herself on the losing end of a romance...to a human no less? She packs up, summons her carriage, and sets off to unravel a mystery which has intrigued her for eons.

Where are the deities of this realm? Have they fallen to their doom, never to be revived?

Freya's odyssey takes her to far-flung temples, ancient ruins, and bustling cities, but she is no closer to resolving the riddle, until she arrives in Dublin. In a land where myth and legend are interwoven with everyday life, Freya teeters on the brink of achieving her goal *and* her happily ever after, only to flee to the very couple who triggered her quest.

An unexpected discovery spurs a repeat performance but, this time, Freya no longer cares about the answer. As far as she is concerned, every last god deserves to be consigned to oblivion.

All she wants is to find peace.

Once again, it hovers… tantalisingly close.

Only to be snatched away...

…for Freya's fate is inextricably linked to the one person she is determined to avoid and, to ignore the not-so-subtle summons for help will lead to tragedy.

Some deities have not vanished, some prowl on the periphery preparing to pounce and, as ever when gods interfere in the lives of mortals, chaos ensues.

It will take more than a touch of arcane alchemy to avert the looming catastrophe.

Lesser of Two Evils

If you ask the average American who they intend to vote for in the next election, inevitably, and almost predictably, their reply will be... THE LESSER OF THE TWO EVILS.

Usually, things even out and saner heads prevail… but what happens when the sitting president tries to tip the scales too far in his narcissistic favor simply to get re-elected?

As the world teeters on the brink of a grim fate, it is up to a lone reporter to prevent that from happening…and to stay alive.

Deadly Incision

From the learned halls of the London Hospital to the squalid, bustling streets of Whitechapel surrounding it, life and death walk hand in glove with one another.

This, somewhat fatalistic, status quo was shattered in the autumn of 1888, when Jack the Ripper prowled the darkness, perfecting his 'skills' on unsuspecting women of the night.

Follow us down these same dark and deadly alleyways to hidden corners and stairwells, stained with blood by the legendary Leather Apron's blade to discover a new twist to his story.